GOLIATH'S HEAD

GOLIATH'S HEAD

a novel

Alan Fleishman

BB
B. Bennett Press
San Carlos California

Published by B. Bennett Press
San Carlos, California

This novel is a work of fiction. Although based in historical
fact, references to names, individuals, places, and incidents
either come from the author's imagination or are used ficti-
tiously. Any similarity to actual persons, organizations,
events, or locations is wholly coincidental.

Book design by Burche-Bensson
Cover photos used under license from Shutterstock:
Photo of St. Petersburg churches © mcseem
Photo of Star of David © Jennifer Gottschalk

LIBRARY OF CONGRESS control number: 2009913454

ISBN-10: 1-4499-4653-4
ISBN-13: 978-1-4499-4653-1

PRINTED IN THE UNITED STATES OF AMERICA

First Edition

www.alanfleishman.com

To my darling wife Ann
whose love and devotion
have given meaning to my life.

and

To my grandparents,
Max and Tillie Fleishman,
who brought our family
to America.

RUSSIA

October 21, 1905

When they come, Victor Askinov will be leading them. And tonight I will kill him.

I couldn't drive that thought from my mind, no matter Uncle Yakov's warnings. The *pogrom* had begun. The mob would be coming soon, determined to slaughter the men, rape the women, and burn our village to the ground.

I waited, crouched behind a makeshift barricade of overturned horse carts, scarred work tables, and oak barrels filled with dirt. The full moon cast crisp shadows in front of us. The chilly October night announced the approach of another brutal winter on the Russian plains. Fires from burning buildings lit the sky at the other end of town, the drifting smoke stinging my eyes and churning my stomach. Only the occasional crack of gunfire in the distance and the protest of a barking dog broke the stillness.

Uncle Yakov crept up on me so quietly I jumped when he touched my arm. He peered over our barricade at the empty street in front of us. "They'll hit here first," he whispered without turning his head. "They'll have guns and clubs. Some torches. Banners. Big crosses. Make sure none of your men hurts a priest." I nodded.

Uncle Yakov commanded our small band, the only one among us who knew how to fight. He had been a soldier in the Tsar's army for years until his arm was wounded beyond repair. I was a youngster then, only twenty-three years old. But he picked me to lead the squad defending the key southern approach to the village.

"They'll be full of liquor. They'll beat their big drum, chant to work themselves up." He concentrated on the dancing shadows down the street as though he could smell their presence. "You'll hear them a good way off."

"Maybe they'll go after one of the other barricades first."

"This is where the synagogue is." The strain in his voice matched the tension in his face. "They want to burn it down, first thing." Our decaying synagogue sat across the market square behind us. From here I could see Poppa's tailor shop even in the moonlight.

"How much longer do we have to wait?"

"Not long."

The Tsar's army lost its war with Japan, and now the whole country was coming apart. Peasants, workers, intelligentsia, gentiles, Jews - everyone in Russia - took to the streets protesting against Tsar Nicholas. All demanded political reform, and nothing less than a democratic congress would satisfy them. So the Tsar and his government did what they did whenever they were in trouble: They turned the madness of the masses against the Jews. The gullibility of these Ukrainian peasants baffled me. If Jews were as strong and sinister as the government's propaganda professed, how come we were so poor and powerless?

Till now, the Jews always submitted to these *pogroms,* these anti-Jewish riots, and waited for them to pass. With so few of us in this vast sea of hate, most Jews thought fighting back would only make it worse. Not this time. This time we would fight.

Across the Ukraine Jews were arming. In our neighborhood, Uncle Yakov organized and trained a group of young fighters to defend ourselves. But many more in our town of Uman trembled and prayed behind shuttered windows and locked doors.

"No one has to die here tonight." Uncle Yakov said.

When I grunted, non-committal, he grabbed my lapel with his good hand and fixed his black eyes on me. He knew I itched to settle old scores. "Just follow the plan."

"I'll try," I said. But I had no intention of following this order, not if I had a clear shot at Viktor Askinov.

"Follow the plan, damn it. You want to get everyone killed?" He held his gaze on me a moment longer, then dropped his hand to his side. "I'm going to check on the other strong points." He pushed himself up and marched off toward our eastern barricade.

My friend Simon, crouching next to me, witnessed our exchange. "You'd better listen to Uncle Yakov," he said.

I didn't answer him. Uncle Yakov had more confidence in his plan than I did. He wanted to avoid a fight. Not me. We had to fight tonight, and somebody was going to die. My wife Sara huddled with the other women and children in our house, down the street from the synagogue. I prepared to defend her and our new-born son, never considering the possibility of my own death.

This moment had been coming since I was a little boy. I prayed to God He was on our side and that He would forgive me.

At last I heard the faint sound of their beating drum.

ONE

June 1891

I was only nine years old the day I met the Devil for the first time.

The house was quiet except for the squawking chickens out back. I sat all alone at the crude dining table in the big front room, just starting on my after-school studies. Sweat, burned kerosene, and the stale odor of rendered chicken fat saturated the rough grey wood walls and floor. An angry green fly kept attacking me.

No sooner had I opened my book than a determined banging assaulted our front door. I shuddered, too scared to move. The hammer pounded again, louder and harder. When Momma or Poppa didn't come to answer, I got up, and eased the door open only enough to peek out.

Constable Askinov stood there glaring down at me, the thumb of one hand hooked in his black belt, the other gripping his truncheon. He was a terrifying man with a tangled black beard, greasy hair, and a coarse grey uniform.

His son Viktor stood by his side in the same threatening pose. Viktor Askinov must have been a year or two older than me, and much bigger. I was afraid to look at him. He might have been the

Evil Eye our momma was always warning us about.

"Get your father. I want to talk to him." Constable Askinov beat his truncheon against the palm of his hand. I couldn't move. "Go," he yelled.

Just when I turned to go find Poppa, he hurried into the room, wiping his delicate hands on his threadbare pants.

"Ah, Constable Askinov. How can I help you?" Poppa forced half a smile and nodded his head in a bow. He and the Constable weren't strangers. I had seen him grovel to the Constable before, like all the other Jews in the village.

Viktor Askinov stared at me through grey eyes the color of steel. His lips turned up in a sneer. He enjoyed Poppa's embarrassment and my trembling.

"That dress you made for Madam Korolov. She says you cheated her." He beat his truncheon against his palm a few more times. Every Jew in the village knew he wasn't reluctant to use it, even on children. "You must give her money back."

Poppa was a tailor and Madam Korolov his most disagreeable customer. Her sunken eyes, tightly wound hair, and aristocratic nose revealed the Angel of Death. He hoped she would go elsewhere but she liked his work. Sometimes I helped out in the tailor shop. Whenever she barged into the shop, I looked for someplace to hide, or escaped out the back door.

"But your honor," Poppa said to the Constable. "I only charged her what we agreed to." He clasped his hands in front of his chest, squeezing them together so hard they turned crimson. He looked like he was begging.

"You used cheap cloth and wide stitches." Constable Askinov's voice rose. He didn't like some Jew challenging him. "Fix it or she will take you to court." That meant trouble because whenever there was a dispute between a gentile and a Jew, the judge always ruled in favor of the gentile no matter what the circumstance. Poppa would pay a high price if he offended Madam Korolov and resisted Constable Askinov. He fidgeted with his hands, eyes wide and lips pressed together. His balding head glistened with perspiration. He could not afford to lose any of his scanty earnings.

"I am so sorry for the misunderstanding," he said. "What can I do to satisfy Madam Korolov?"

"It was no misunderstanding. You cheated her."

Poppa bit his lip as though he were going to cry, and that made me want to cry. "Forgive me, your honor. May I suggest a solution? I can make a dress for her daughter from the same material, no extra charge. It will be nice. Mother and daughter can dress alike." He waited, holding his breath as Constable Askinov mulled over his proposal.

"Is this some Jew trick?"

"No, no your honor." Poppa's hand quivered as he raised it to touch his beard. "Anything she wants, but this is a much better offer."

The Constable hesitated, then turned his head and spit out a brown gob from the tobacco he was chewing. "Alright. I will tell her. She gets a new dress for her daughter." He leaned his face forward, close to Poppa's. "No charge."

"Thank you your honor." Poppa relaxed his tense shoulders and let out a sigh.

"But no tricks or I will be back."

All this time I hid behind Poppa, but I could see Viktor Askinov glaring at me. He made contorted faces and pounded his fist into the palm of his hand like his father pounded his truncheon. As he and the Constable were leaving, Viktor kicked over our milk can sitting by the side of the front door. Then, giving me one final Evil Eye, he ran his finger across his throat. My stomach twisted and jerked inside. Why was he being so mean to me?

Maybe because he was the Devil, I imagined in my little-boy mind.

Poppa closed the door slowly and stood there without moving, hand on the latch. His shoulders sagged. He looked like a man who had just escaped a death sentence. Momma rushed into the room. Her frightened face scared me nearly as much as Viktor Askinov's threatening eyes.

"Are you alright Mottel?" she asked, holding her hand to her large bosom.

"Yes. Everything's fine," he answered quietly, without conviction. "We won't lose any money."

They always worried about money. They had many mouths to feed: my older brother Lieb, younger sisters Ester and Zelda, Markus - the baby in the family – and me. We weren't the poorest people in Uman but sometimes food ran out before the Sabbath if there wasn't enough work in the tailor shop or a customer like Madam Korolov was slow in paying.

"May the worst of the ten plagues visit her!" Spittle sprayed from Momma's mouth.

I fumed. Viktor Askinov terrified me and Poppa's cowardice angered me. He had been humiliated and I was ashamed of him. He hadn't even noticed Viktor Askinov threatening me. And I was ashamed I had been so afraid.

"You didn't cheat her," I screamed at him, tears running down my face. "Why did you say you did? You're a coward."

"Avraham, don't talk to your father that way," Momma snapped. I thought she was going to slap me, something she never did.

I had to get away. I rushed out the front door, slamming it behind me, and ran down Potocki Street's well-worn wooden sidewalk. Drizzle from the darkening sky soaked my shirt. I ran past my friend Duv's house, past Simon's, past the old tavern, past storefronts, and past our small tailor shop.

Tears blinded me, my footsteps beating on the planks like horses' hooves. My skull throbbed and my heart pounded. I headed for the person I always went to when life confused me, my teacher Jeremiah Brodsky.

I ran through the synagogue courtyard and into the side vestibule connecting the synagogue to the school. Jewish children in Uman didn't attend public schools. Those were only for the gentile children.

Frantic, I burst through the door searching for Jeremiah. A couple of rats scurried away, escaping into cracks between the uneven planks of the floor. Our classroom was a dark, dismal place with paint peeling from the walls, crowded desks, and the smell of stale body odor. Like the houses in the village, it was an inferno in the summer and freezing in the winter.

Jeremiah sat alone at his desk underneath the map he used to teach us about the world beyond Uman. He was a handsome man in his mid-twenties with thick brown hair, a confident smile, and a determined square jaw. All the young girls fell madly in love with Jeremiah but he paid them no attention. No one knew much about Jeremiah. He just showed up one day a couple of years ago, and quickly won Rabbi Rosenberg's respect. Everyone in the village gossiped about him.

He looked up when he heard me come in. "Avi, what's the matter?" He jumped from his chair when he saw my condition and hurried toward me. He bent down and wrapped his arms around me. I felt safe for the first time since the knock on the door.

I stopped crying and poured out everything: how Poppa had been a coward, and how much this boy, Viktor Askinov, scared me.

"Your father is an honest man," he said, patting my back

while he spoke. "Wise and brave."

"He is not!" I yelled back.

Jeremiah sat down in a chair next to mine so he didn't tower over me like most adults did. Then he described the Jewish plight in Russia, how so many of the gentiles hated the Jews, and how powerless we were to confront them. He talked to me as though I were a grownup. He was always challenging me, sometimes more than a little boy could absorb. Most of the time I liked that, but today I wanted answers, and I wanted comfort.

He stood up and looked over my head as though he were addressing some ethereal throng. "A Jew must live by his wits if he is to survive here. He must have the strength to do what he knows he must do." He turned back to me. "Your father does what he does for you, your momma and your brothers and sisters. He outsmarted the Constable. He got to keep the money and stayed out of trouble with the police."

His explanation made sense, but I wasn't ready to let go of my resentments yet. So I listened. He paused, running his finger along a grooved scar in the desk next to us.

"Remember last year when your friend Simon Frankel's mother had a run-in with her neighbor? She chased the neighbor's pig away when it came rooting in her garden." Jeremiah snorted like a pig. I laughed.

"The neighbor complained to the police because Mother Frankel scared her pig. And who got in trouble with the police? Mother Frankel. The neighbor lied to the police and made up stories. She even had someone give false testimony."

Jeremiah shook his head. "Mother Frankel ended up paying a fine she couldn't afford. If anything goes to court, your poppa's going to lose. He'll have to give back all of Madam Korolov's money and maybe pay a big fine on top of it. So, he was smart to do what he did."

"But why do the gentiles hate us so much?" It was the first of many times in my life I asked this question. But no one ever had a good answer.

"Because we're different. We worship God in very different ways. And their savior is not our messiah. We separate ourselves: Where we live, how we dress, what we eat. We do different kinds of work than they do. We speak Yiddish and they speak Russian."

"I can speak Russian," I said.

"But they can't speak Yiddish."

"But why does Viktor Askinov hate me? I never did anything to him."

"I know his father, the Constable. He's a bad one," Jeremiah said. "He's not much better off than we are. He blames us for his circumstance, though how he does that I don't know. His parents were peasants. People like Madam Korolov treat him like he still is one. So he lords the little power he has over every Jew he meets. It makes him feel like a big man. The son sounds worse. Maybe you should just stay away from him."

I nodded. His answer didn't remove any of my confusion, but the more I talked to him and the more he talked to me the less angry I was at Poppa. Jeremiah seemed old to me then, but in truth he wasn't old enough to have earned so much wisdom. Perhaps being subjugated all of your life makes you grow old faster.

"Everyone knows your momma and poppa are generous," he went on. "If a beggar passes through the village in need of a meal, your mother gives him a little food. Your father always finds a few kopeks for him." Now I was starting to feel guilty about the way I talked to Poppa.

Just then, Lieb tiptoed into the back of the classroom. He looked unsure what to make of the scene in front of him. My skinny brother always looked unsure. He was two years older but I could run faster and beat him whenever we wrestled. But he was never jealous, even when everyone marked me as the smart one in the family.

"Go away," I said when I saw him.

"Momma and Poppa are worried about you. They sent me to find you," he said gently. I got up slowly and went with him. Outside, the rain clouds had passed. We trudged home in silence, his arm around my shoulder all the way. Lieb was kind and gentle like Poppa, but he wasn't brave. He ran away from fights. So I shivered when I thought I saw Viktor Askinov down the street. We kept walking, only faster.

Momma hugged me when we walked in the door. She wiped my tear-stained face. "I'm sorry, Poppa," I said. He forgave me like I knew he would.

Maybe this was when I first began to understand some things about my father. He accepted the miserable condition we were in. Yes, he was smart and clever in how he dealt with it, but he showed no shame, no rage, and no ambition to change our situation. He was a poor tailor who found his comfort in his religion and his traditions, like his father and his father's father. He expected my life to be the same. My mother was different.

Before I fell asleep that night, I heard them arguing in loud whispers from their bedroom. Second cousins, they had loved each other nearly all of their lives. Nonetheless, theirs was an arranged marriage, like all of them in their time. But that custom was dying out.

They never argued, particularly in front of us children. This clash was so unusual it stirred up both uneasiness and curiosity inside of me.

The doorway to their bedroom was covered with nothing more than a curtain, so it was not hard to hear what they were saying. There wasn't much privacy in our little house. The big room, a sleeping alcove and two small bedrooms housed all seven of us.

"We have to get out of this place," Momma whispered. "This is no place for the children."

"Where are we going to go? The tailor shop is here. And our friends. The synagogue. Pop and Mom are buried in the cemetery here, may they rest in peace."

"We could go to Odessa like your sister."

"Odessa? You think Odessa is better? Jews are Jews no matter where they go."

"I hear Jews can go to university there," Momma whispered. "Avi could go to university. He's a very smart boy."

"The Messiah will come, Rukhl. He will come right here."

"So how long have we been waiting? Five thousand years?"

"This is where we belong," Poppa said, his voice rising.

"Ssshhhh. You'll wake the children."

I fell asleep worrying about leaving my friends if we moved to Odessa and worrying how I was going to keep Viktor Askinov from hurting me if we didn't. He scared me, but I didn't tell Momma and Poppa. I was too ashamed.

Many children probably think of their childhood tormentors as the Devil. In the case of Viktor Askinov, it was true. He had singled me out for special treatment and I never knew why. Whatever his reasons, there was nothing I could do about it.

Two

January 1893

One winter passed, another came, and Viktor Askinov faded from my mind.

All night we watched the first heavy snow of the year come down so fast you couldn't see beyond the windowsill. The next morning the sun peaked out, the squalid streets and houses transformed into winter's fantasy.

Uman was a pretty town if you lived on the other side of the river where the gentiles lived, but we hardly ever got to go over there. The houses on their side were painted in colorful blues, yellows and greens. The onion-shaped spires of their churches stood as majestic sentries against the clear Russian sky. Streets were paved and cobble stoned.

On our side, where the Jews lived, everything was grey, the color of rotting wood and raw stucco. We were too poor to afford paint. The streets of hard packed dirt turned into muddy seas of slop when the spring thaw and rains came. It was crowded, everyone packed together like blintzes in a box. Still, even on our side, Uman could be beautiful under the quilt of snowy white.

Lieb and I dashed off to school early so we could play on the way. Our little brother Markus always tagged along. He wanted to be a part of whatever his big brothers were doing.

Clouds puffed from each breath. My thick winter coat, scarf, and hat pulled down over my eyes shielded me from the cold. Only my nose stuck out, glowing red and dripping a stream of phlegm.

Our friends Duvid Eisenberg and Simon Frankel joined us when we passed their houses. Simon was the quiet one, smart and good. He looked like every other kid in the village except for his beaked parrot's nose.

Duv was my best friend. He wore the face of an angel that girls soon wouldn't be able to resist. He did his best to break every one of the Ten Commandments, except for the one about killing. He stole. He took the Lord's name in vain. He cursed his father. He lied. He coveted his neighbor's wife, but was still too young to do anything about it.

Nothing was sacred to Duv. He was the one who first made me wonder whether everything we were taught about God was really true. I liked going to synagogue, but Duv got bored. So he gave me a running commentary under his breath all during the service, making fun of the readings from the Torah, the rabbi, the cantor, and Reb Henkel, the synagogue's rich elder.

"If Adam and Eve were the first people on earth, where did Cain find a wife?" he asked me one day, a sly smile curling his lips. No one else ever heard his remarks, but the whole congregation heard me laugh. Poppa frowned, and gave me a rare tongue lashing when we got home.

I felt sorry for Duv sometimes. His mother died when he was a little boy. His father worked so hard he didn't have time for Duv. He didn't like his new stepmother, but he didn't talk much about it. Today he came out of the house with an ugly welt on the side of his face. He said he fell down, but it was impossible to keep a secret in our village. His stepmother had hit him with a broom handle because he was sarcastic to her.

We slipped and slid along the sidewalk, pushing, shoving, and laughing every time one of us took a tumble. But when we came around the corner into the courtyard of our synagogue and school, a fusillade of icy snowballs bombarded us. Viktor Askinov, his younger brother Olek and two friends were in a line hurling missiles. Each one of them looked big enough to alone squash all five of us.

The first snowball smashed Simon in the back of his head. The second one hit little Markus on the leg. The third blasted my shoulder. It stung even through my layers of clothes. We raced for the school, Markus with his short legs struggling to keep up. I stopped to shield him and was hit in my left ear. Its sting made my head ring. Our tormentors laughed and hurled insults as wounding as their balls of ice.

"You killed Christ! You killed Christ!"

"Run Jew Boy, run."

My heart exploded as we crashed through the door. I shook like I did the first time I looked into Victor Askinov's evil eyes. Markus was sobbing. "Are you okay?" I asked.

He nodded, tears running down his cheeks. He wiped them on the back of his glove. I helped him off with his coat.

For days, Lieb and Markus were as scared to go to school as I was, but none of us wanted to tell Momma and Poppa. I was ashamed of myself. Duv and Simon joined us every morning. We all hung our heads like murderers off to the firing squad, hesitated briefly before rounding the corner into the synagogue courtyard. Then we ran for the door, met with a withering attack and escalating insults about our sisters and mothers.

Viktor Askinov and his pack would be gone for a few days. We'd relax, only to be attacked again. This went on all winter and into the spring. Sometimes it was snowballs, sometimes sticks or rocks.

They chose me for special attention, capturing me alone whenever they could. It could be a punch in the stomach or stealing the hat off my head, leaving me exposed to the frigid winds. Torrents of slander poured out of Viktor Askinov's mouth. He made the word "Jew" sound like sewage. I lived each day as his prey.

Jeremiah never said anything directly, but toward the end of every day he gave us a bible lesson about Joshua, Gideon, or one of the other Jewish warriors in the bible. Throughout his narrations, he looked right at me as though I was the one he wanted to hear his message. I squirmed.

What did he want from me? I was only eleven, and Viktor Askinov was much bigger than me. Those Jews in the bible were brave. God talked to Gideon and Judah Maccabee, and performed miracles for them. Where was my miracle? I wasn't going to fight until God spoke to me, and he hadn't done that yet.

On our way out of class one day, I said to Duv, "If we're His chosen people, how come He lets bad things happen to us all the time?"

Duv stroked his chin as though seriously pondering the question. "I don't know. Maybe he's chosen someone else this time." Maybe he was right, I thought.

A couple of weeks after Viktor Askinov's attacks first started, Madame Shumenko walked into Poppa's tailor shop with her son Sergey. I was there helping out. By the time I was nine, I could work the sewing machine with some skill. I could take it apart and fix it whenever something broke.

Madame Shumenko was Poppa's best customer. It seemed she always arrived about when I began hating all gentiles. "It's freezing," she said, taking off her black fur coat and hat. "I'm keeping these on till I warm up." She held up her leather-gloved hands. Her high cheek bones were rosy from the cold. She wore one of Poppa's creations underneath her coat, a smart long blue skirt and jacket of imported blue worsted. Her frame was as sculpted as the mannequin standing in the corner. She wore a paisley scarf around her neck, not on her head like the Jewish women.

Madame Shumenko brought a cloth bag filled with treats when she visited. She handed it to me. I pulled out a pastry, smelled it and licked it before biting off a chunk. It was filled with a mix of poppy seeds, walnuts, honey and a touch of whiskey, then coated with sugar and cinnamon.

"Save some for your brothers and sisters" she said. Her voice was gentle as a cloud, like her smile and her green eyes.

I never thought of her son Sergey as a gentile, just a friend. I pulled out the Lotto board, a Russian game Poppa kept in the shop for us. I was very good at it and could beat Sergey any time I wanted. But I let him win often enough so he would keep on playing.

While we played, Poppa and Madam Shumenko discussed her dress. She asked his opinion and he gave it, as comfortable as he was around Jews. She laughed at one of his well-worn jokes others moaned at.

Poppa got home a few hours later, pounding his feet at the door to knock off the snow before crossing the threshold. He shut the door behind him quickly but the numbing freeze followed him inside. He was in a good mood.

He went over to Momma, who was cooking on the stove, and gave her a kiss on the cheek. She put down her big wooden spoon and returned his kiss with a hug. He glanced around to see if any of us kids was watching. He thought he was safe so he gave Momma a pinch on her behind. She yelped and poked him back with her soup spoon, turning her head to hide a smile. I looked over at them and grinned.

Lieb finished school that summer and had his bar mitzvah. He didn't like working in Poppa's tailor shop and didn't want to grow up to be a tailor. Poppa was disappointed but he got him an apprenticeship with a baker who owned a shop on the other side of the market square.

Lieb was now a man they said, but at thirteen he was no more a man than I was. Only Lieb wasn't confused like me. He didn't think so much, and didn't ask so many questions no one could answer. I wanted to know why gentiles like Viktor Askinov hated me, and what I was supposed to do about it.

Perhaps those snowballs Viktor Askinov threw at me were only snowballs, but they were supposed to teach me my place. The reading from the haftorah on Lieb's bar mitzvah day said "The lessons of youth are not easily forgotten." The lessons I learned were that Jews stayed put, took their beatings in stride, and found comfort in God. But sometimes I heard Momma and Jeremiah whispering in my head: "It doesn't have to be this way."

THREE

July 1894

Tsar Alexander III died in March. His son Nicholas took his place, but it made little difference to us. One tsar was just as hard on the Jews as the next. That's why we needed the Sabbath, so we could forget our troubles. Sabbath dinner was like celebrating an important festival every seven days. The one that July shouldn't have been any different.

We ate a lot of potatoes and beets during the week so we could have a feast on the Sabbath. Sometimes Momma roasted a whole chicken in the oven, or made a chicken stew to stretch the food a little further. The chicken came from our coop out back. She took it to the butcher on the market square whose job it was to slaughter it the kosher way.

These kosher dietary laws didn't make sense to me even when I was little. I asked Momma to explain it, but she never could. I asked "why" until she got frustrated with me. "Because it's the way God wants it." She failed to convince me. Did God really care how we killed our chickens? A dead chicken, after all, is a dead chicken.

On Sabbath eve, we men and boys gathered our clothes and towels and trooped to the community bath house behind the synagogue. It was only used this one time a week. A Jew couldn't face the Sabbath without a clean body. On the way home, we passed Momma, Ester, Zelda and the other women parading to the bath house. I wonder if they even changed the water for the women.

In the evening when the sun set, Momma lit Sabbath candles, covered her eyes with her hands, and chanted a prayer. Ester and Zelda did what Momma did. Poppa, Lieb, Markus and I said "Amen" when Momma finished.

On Sabbath morning the Shamash, the rabbi's aged helper, knocked on our window to call us to prayer. We spent all morning in the stifling synagogue. This one particular Sabbath was so wet-hot even the big green flies were too lethargic to attack.

Even this blazing furnace from hell couldn't stop us from gorging on the leftovers from the night before as soon as we got home. "Take a nap after lunch," Momma said to Poppa as we finished. He nodded. This was his one day to indulge himself and put his troubles aside.

A slight breeze came through the open windows. "Poppa, can we go outside and play?" I asked as soon as we were done eating. This was also the one day we kids had to indulge ourselves.

He didn't hear me. He raised his hand to his mouth, lips pressed together, and gazed out the window from the corners of his eyes. Then his eyes opened wide. His body tensed. "Wait!" His voice didn't sound like my poppa's. "What's that noise?" He stood up.

"What is it, Mottel?" Momma said. She puckered her brow and held her hand to her breast.

"I thought I heard something." He went over to the window and peered out. I held my breath and heard some muffled sounds that might have been shouts.

Poppa rushed outside leaving the door open behind him. We followed him. Down the street people scurried every which way like a herd of mice. Some fled inside their houses, closing the shutters over the windows. Some yelled out something but I couldn't make out what they were saying. The muffled banging of a bass drum thumped from the direction of the synagogue. I ran toward the sound to find out what was going on.

"Come back here," Poppa called after me. I kept running until I got close enough to hear what people were saying. I stopped so abruptly I stumbled.

"*Pogrom*! *Pogrom*!" they hollered. I turned and ran back toward Momma and Poppa as fast I could. Poppa shouted for Momma and the kids to get back in the house.

"Hurry, hurry," Poppa yelled to me. I dashed through the front door. Poppa slammed it shut behind me.

Everyone but Poppa froze. He barked orders with a command I never heard from him before. "Momma, take Ester and Zelda and lock all the shutters in the back rooms. Markus, you go too. Lieb. Avi. You lock the shutters here in the front room. Then help me move the table to block the door." The sound of the drums was growing louder and my heart was beating faster. I knew about *pogroms*. They were coming to kill us.

Before we moved the table, Poppa ran outside and grabbed the axe he used to cut firewood. On the way back in he picked up the empty milk can from near the front door and handed it to Lieb. "Use this if they come through the door," he said. "Momma, if they break in, take Ester and Zelda out the back window. Hide behind the chicken coop." Momma nodded.

I needed a weapon too, so I went into the kitchen and found the big knife Momma used to cut meat. I still felt helpless. I tried to be brave, but our makeshift defense couldn't stop a mob from breaking in.

We waited in the muted light. The house grew hotter and hotter from the searing July sun. Sweat rolled off my back in a river, soaking my good Sabbath shirt and pants. My face, hair and the palms of my hands were as wet and slippery as a fresh fish.

Poppa crouched behind one window, Lieb behind another, and me behind the last one. No one said a word. I strained to hear what was going on outside. Then I saw the lock on my window's shutter was broken and beginning to give out. It hung open enough for me to see outside, which meant they could see inside.

And now the beating drum was very loud, almost on top of us. Men were yelling and chanting. I thought they were attacking Jewish homes. In my mind's eye I could see blood flowing down the street.

I kept peeking out of the partially opened shutters but didn't see anyone. Now the noise was clear. A large group of men chanted "Haidamack! Haidamack! Haidamack!" They drew closer and closer. At last I could see the front of the column. There in the lead was Constable Askinov, his son Viktor on his left side. Their priest was on his right, ominous in the black garb that covered him from head to toe.

Some men carried crimson banners. Some held huge wooden crosses over their heads. One giant carried an effigy of a man hung on a pole with a sign around its neck that said "Jew." Another carried one with a sign that read "Pole." And one carried a dead dog, a real one, hung from a pole. Behind the three, another man carried a big sign that read "A Pole, a Jew, and a dog – all of one faith."

I quivered, sure I was going to die. I knew about the Haidamacks. A couple hundred years ago the Polish king conquered the Ukraine and brought Jews into the country to administer his new lands. The Christians in Western Europe persecuted the Jews unmercifully so they were happy to come east. Of course the

Ukrainians didn't much like being conquered by Poland, so a horde of enraged peasants and Cossacks, calling themselves Haidamacks, rebelled. They rampaged across the countryside, killing all of the Jews they could catch, and some Poles too.

Uman was a fortified Polish garrison town back then, so Jews fled there seeking protection. About 8,000 of them made it inside the stout town walls. But the Polish commander in Uman turned on them, opening the gates to the Haidamacks to save his own life. Over the next few days, the Haidamacks slaughtered every one of the Jews. They thrust some through with spears, threw some from rooftops, ran down others with horses, and shot the rest. In the end, the Haidamacks turned on the Poles and killed many of them too.

Now they were back, ready to do it to us again. I watched as the throng reached our house. "Don't stop. Don't stop. Keep going," I begged.

"Avi, keep quiet," Poppa whispered. I didn't realize I was actually saying the words out loud.

Twenty men passed by, then thirty, then fifty, and a hundred. Maybe there were two hundred in all. They kicked up a cloud of dust from the hard packed dirt street. Some toward the back of the column had kerchiefs pulled over their noses. The drums beat in my ears. Boom! Boom! Boom! Every muscle in my body tightened into a bundle of fear.

They kept marching, except for one, Viktor Askinov. He stood by the side of the street, his steely eyes fixed on our house. He stared right at me through my partially opened shutter, a sneer on his curled lips. He grew since I saw him last winter, and now stood as tall as many of the grown men.

He turned his back to the house and for a moment I couldn't make out what he was doing. When he turned around, his pants were open in front and he relieved himself on our doorstep, his yellow stream wetting the stoop. When he finished, he roared in triumph, closed his pants, and ran to catch up with his father at the front of the column.

I held my breath until the last man passed down the street and the pounding of the bass drum began to fade. Poppa let out a big sigh. I started shaking and couldn't stop. My stomach felt like it had been stuck with porcupine quills. I'm not going to die, I thought. I opened the shutter to get a better look outside and gulp in some air.

I hadn't noticed my little brother Markus huddled beside me. He must have been there the whole time. He whimpered, his body heaving. He had vomited all over himself. I picked him up and hugged him closely to me. His smelled putrid. "It's alright, Markus. They're gone."

The sound of the drums disappeared and everyone began coming out of their shuttered houses. The air outside which had seemed so burning hot an hour ago now felt like a welcome relief from the inferno of our closed and shuttered house. People gathered in the street, abuzz with talk about the confusing events of the *pogrom* that didn't happen, this parade of intimidation.

That day the Uman orthodox Christians launched a new holiday to celebrate the Haidamack slaughter of the Jews and Poles here 126 years ago. And Jews prayed in thanks to the Lord for delivering us. Poppa had been determined to protect us. But Viktor Askinov had won again.

I rarely felt safe as a little boy, but this day a new terror took root. I saw what a *pogrom* would be like. The flow of Jewish blood was all that was missing. From then on, the crosses they carried over their heads sent a chill up my spine whenever I saw one.

Jews were debris in a sea of more powerful people possessed by irrational hatred of us. I felt trapped and hopeless. Momma and Poppa couldn't protect me, and offered nothing more than platitudes about finding comfort in God. I had no where to go and no one to turn to. I was trapped.

FOUR

September 1896

Every fall when the leaves start to turn I think of the sunny September morning I met Uncle Yakov for the first time.

I was sweeping Poppa's tailor shop when I saw through the front window a man in an earth colored army uniform marching ramrod-straight down the street toward us. He carried a big duffle bag over his shoulder as easily as if it were a feather pillow. We never saw soldiers in our part of town so I was curious. He marched with his head high and his shoulders back, unlike the slump-shouldered Jews. He looked as squat and ferocious as a bulldog.

"Look, Poppa," I said, pointing out the window.

Poppa glanced up from the dress he was sewing. "My god. Is that Yakov?" He sprang from his seat and ran out the door. The soldier quickened his pace when he saw Poppa, his teeth bared in a grin that covered his face. He stopped and dropped his duffle bag to the ground. They embraced in a bear hug, thumping each other on the back. Poppa pulled away to give him a big kiss on the cheek.

"Come, come, Avi. Say hello to your Uncle Yakov," Poppa

shouted as they came into the shop, arms around each other, laughing. This larger-than-life man intimidated me. Poppa often told us tales of Uncle Yakov's fabled adventures and legendary valor in battle.

"Avi. Look at you. You're a man." Uncle Yakov said, clapping me on both shoulders with his open hands. "Last time I saw you was your *bris*. Still a baby."

I held out my hand to shake his, trying to stand as tall as I could. His firm grip felt rough, his hairy fingers enveloping mine. "Hello, Uncle Yakov," I said. "Pleased to meet you."

"Poppa wrote me what a smart boy you are. What a good worker."

I caught Poppa out of the corner of my eye trying to hold himself as erect as Uncle Yakov. He puffed out his chest with pride. You would think I had done something exceptional just because I was able to shake hands and speak a complete sentence.

Actually, I only mumbled an awkward "thank you," my eyes fixed downward on Uncle Yakov's shiny brown riding boots. Somehow none of the dirt from the hard-packed street clung to them like it did to the ripened work boots the rest of us wore.

Uncle Yakov and Poppa hadn't seen each other for fourteen years. He didn't write Poppa often, but when he did, he wrote long, detailed letters. Poppa savored each one. He read us tales of China and Turkey, strange lands so different from anything I knew. His letters excited my yearning to see the world beyond Uman.

Uncle Yakov ended up in the army the way most Jews did. They shanghaied him. The Russian government forced many Jewish boys into the Tsar's army, often when they were as young as eight years old, and then kept them for twenty-five years. They thought they could convert them to Orthodox Christianity. The army promised big rewards, both in this life and the next one. But the conversion didn't work on Uncle Yakov and it didn't work on most of the other Jewish boys.

When the promise of rewards didn't work, soldiers dragged Uncle Yakov into church in the dead of winter and ordered him to accept Christ. When he wouldn't, he was forced to kneel on the hard, cold stone floor, hour after hour until he passed out. He got no food and no chance to relieve himself in the proper way. He only got enough water to keep himself alive.

But the army was as determined as Uncle Yakov was obstinate. They shoved him outside on a frigid night and chained him to a pillar of ice. Snow and wind lashed him until he was near death. Uncle Yakov wouldn't surrender.

Who knows where it would have ended if a new commanding officer, Captain Aleksandri Petrov, hadn't arrived. He rescued Uncle Yakov from further punishment. Petrov must have seen in his resistance his potential as a ferocious fighter and leader. The captain learned Uncle Yakov was also a natural horseman. Uncle Yakov repaid him by becoming a soldier without equal, and a devoted disciple.

He stayed with Petrov as Petrov moved up to Colonel and commander of a light cavalry regiment. Uncle Yakov rose with him to the rank of a senior non-commissioned officer. From his letters home, there was no missing his affection and admiration for Colonel Petrov, and Colonel Petrov's for him. They waged war side by side in many battles. Uncle Yakov must have fought particularly well against the Turks at Mangidia because he was awarded the Tsar's Own Heroes medal, the second highest citation the army could give. Uncle Yakov never talked about it, but my thought is he probably saved Colonel Petrov's life. The colonel became his lifelong benefactor, without limits.

By the time I met Uncle Yakov, he was an agnostic, but still considered the possibility of God. Whatever his faith in God, even after many years in the army, he still defiantly proclaimed himself a Jew - a warrior Jew.

When we were a few houses from home, Uncle Yakov stopped in the middle of the street, threw back his head, closed his eyes and inhaled deeply. "God be praised." He held out his arms to the heavens. "Is that Rukhl's borscht I smell?"

As soon as we walked in the door, Momma screamed and came running. Lieb, Markus, Ester and Zelda were as shy at first as I had been, but no one resisted Uncle Yakov for long.

He threw his duffle bag in a corner, loosened his tunic and took off his handsome leather riding boots. When no one was looking, I held the boots to my nose and inhaled. For an instant, images of courageous cavalry charges and splendid military pomp flashed by.

Momma broke into the store of food she was hoarding for the Sabbath. The smells of potato pancakes frying in rendered chicken fat soon mixed with simmering beet soup and roasting chicken. Momma set the table with her Sabbath china and lace tablecloth.

Uncle Yakov attacked the food like a soldier on the march. He slurped his soup, a spoon in one hand, a chunk of black bread in the other. "Momma says we're not supposed to make noise when we eat soup," Zelda scolded. The corners of Uncle Yakov's mouth turned up. He gazed at the little brat out of the corner of his eye and went on eating.

"Zelda, stop already," Momma chided. Uncle Yakov finished his soup. Momma refilled his bowl.

He grabbed a chicken leg in his burly hand and ripped it with the teeth of a ravenous wolf. "Momma says we're not supposed to eat with our hands," Zelda said. I nudged her under the table with my foot. She whacked me on the shins with the toe of her shoe. That little sister of mine tormented me constantly Uncle Yakov patted my forearm before I could retaliate.

Between bites, Uncle Yakov told of deeds on horseback, strange foreign people with slanted eyes, and travels to the ends of Russia, Turkey and China. He waved his chicken bone in the air as though it were a cavalry saber. Momma and Poppa interrupted with questions as wide-eyed as the kids. He stopped occasionally to take a gulp of vodka and stuff a piece of potato pancake or herring in his mouth. Then he refilled his glass from the bottle sitting between him and Poppa. When dinner was over, Momma, Ester and Zelda cleared the plates.

"That was a meal made in heaven." Uncle Yakov patted his stomach and belched. Zelda started to say something but stopped, her mouth locked open. She looked at Momma out of the corner of her eye. Momma shook her head. Zelda closed her mouth slowly and resumed clearing the table.

Every so often Uncle Yakov caught me staring at him and smiled or winked. I was searching for anything in their looks that said he and Poppa were brothers. But Poppa's face was long, with big ears and a big nose. Uncle Yakov's face was square with a chiseled chin. His nose was straight; his ears close to his head. He had the bushiest black eyebrows I'd ever seen.

Poppa's lips were full, his hair balding, and his body lanky and fragile. Glasses made him look vulnerable. Uncle Yakov's military haircut was like a full brush, sandy brown compared to Poppa's greying black. His square shoulders looked like a boxer's, ready for a fight. Poppa's beard hid a lot of his face. Uncle Yakov wore a small scar on his clean cheek below his left eye.

The scar pointed me to his eyes. That was it. Poppa and Uncle Yakov had the same dark, kind eyes that sparkled at those they loved.

Uncle Yakov's eyes twinkled whenever he spoke to us children. Years later, I saw those same eyes switch from a twinkle to the deadliness of a man who had killed and was ready to kill again.

One thing Uncle Yakov didn't talk about was the fighting. Toward the end of the evening, Lieb blurted out, "Did you ever kill anyone?" Uncle Yakov's smile vanished.

"Lieb. Such a question," Momma scolded.

"It's alright, Rukhl," Uncle Yakov replied quietly. "But that's for another day."

"Off to bed with you," Poppa said getting up from his chair.

Uncle Yakov's eyes sparkled again. He hugged each of us one by one. He gave Lieb, Ester and me a kiss on the cheek. The little ones, Zelda and Markus, he kissed on the top of their heads.

"This one's going to break a lot of men's hearts," he said after he kissed Zelda. She was only eleven but everyone was already saying how pretty she was. Ester was kind like Momma, and as unattractive. Momma and Poppa worried about her finding a husband. But they worried about Zelda for different reasons. Even at her young age, she challenged every Jewish custom and tradition.

When he went to bed, he took off his uniform and hung it on a hook in the front room. He didn't put it on again until he was ready to leave three weeks later. But he never took off one medal, the red, white and blue one he earned at the Battle of Mangidia. He wore this one on his collar all the time. He said it was his passport into any tavern in Russia. And Uncle Yakov did like to visit the taverns, sometimes tiptoeing out after we were all in bed.

On the Sabbath we took Uncle Yakov to synagogue with us. We all wanted to show him off to our friends. Uncle Yakov looked like a soldier even with a *tallis*, a prayer shawl, wrapped around him. I sat between Poppa and Uncle Yakov. It felt like everyone was looking at us.

Our synagogue was a simple place. It was one long, low-ceilinged room with an elevated altar at the end. The Torah scrolls rested in a cupboard behind a blood-red curtain where the eternal light burned above it day and night. The wooden floor sagged in spots, and in one corner you could see through to the ground below. The small windows gave off little light on dark days. A picture of the Tsar hung next to the front door, as it did in every church and synagogue in Russia. Only the bright colors of Hebrew prayers painted on one wall relieved the drabness.

Toward the end of the service, Poppa and Uncle Yakov rose to say the Mourner's *Kaddish* for Grandma and Grandpa Schneider. I'd heard this prayer many times, but tonight their mournful voices penetrated my bones. I thought of the time some day when Lieb and I would do the same for Momma and Poppa. I put one hand in Uncle Yakov's and the other in Poppa's. "Never forget who you are," Uncle Yakov whispered.

At the end of the service, Rabbi Rosenberg said a short prayer "to the good health of the Tsar." If he didn't, the police would close down the synagogue.

On the way out, I introduced Uncle Yakov to Jeremiah, Duv and Simon. The next day Duv and Simon came over to our house to see the medals on Uncle Yakov's tunic. I showed them off as though they were mine. Duv extended his hand to touch one of them. "No," I barked. He pulled his hand back. I was the self-appointed curator of Uncle Yakov's medals, with important duties to fulfill.

Poppa and Uncle Yakov spent a lot of time talking, whether it was at the tailor shop, around the dinner table, or on long walks. Sometimes Momma joined them. Mostly they reminisced.

They talked about how much they missed Grandpa and Grandma Schneider. Grandpa was a tailor just like his father before him, and like Poppa after him. That's how we got the name Schneider. It means tailor in Yiddish. The Russian gov-

ernment made the Jews pick permanent surnames, but in synagogue we still used our old Hebrew names. Mine was Avraham ben
Mottel - Avraham, son of Mottel.

As soon as the kids were in bed, Momma, Poppa and Uncle
Yakov sat around the hearth and continued talking quietly. Lieb
fell asleep right away. I wanted to hear what they were saying.
One night, soon after Uncle Yakov got there, I heard them raising
their voices.

They were talking about how the family got into the mess we
were in. It started a hundred years ago when the Russians won the
Ukraine in a war with Poland. They strangled the Jews right from
the start. To the Russian Orthodox Church, Jews were enemies of
Christ who had to be punished. The Tsarina, Catherine, was eager
to do her part in the punishing.

She passed new laws restricting Jews to this one section of
the country called the Pale of Settlement, where we lived now.
Jews could only work in the worst jobs, couldn't own property
except their houses, and couldn't go to most of the public schools
or universities. Anyone caught where he shouldn't be or earning
money in ways he shouldn't was treated like a criminal. The Tsar
had special taxes for Jews on things like our Sabbath candles,
prayer books, and prayer shawls. Places like Uman got more and
more crowded and the Jews got poorer and poorer.

Sometimes Lieb's snoring got so loud I couldn't hear what
they were saying. I gave him a kick to shut him up. He moaned
and rolled over, deep in dreams. I heard a chair scrape on the
wooden floor. Someone had gotten up from the table. I imagined
Uncle Yakov standing in front of the fireplace.

"Remember when the second Tsar Alexander was killed?"
Uncle Yakov asked.

"May his bones rot in hell," Momma said.

"So they blamed the Jews. What's new?" Poppa answered.

"Then the *pogroms*," Momma said. "Everywhere."

"The government instigated them," Uncle Yakov said. "They were scared stiff of a revolution." There were attacks in over 200 towns. Jewish homes and businesses were ransacked, synagogues burned down. Many Jews were killed and injured. Many Jewish women were raped.

"Not here in Uman, heaven be praised." Poppa said. He sounded so exhausted.

But they rioted in Elizavetgrad, only a hundred miles away. And they rioted in Kiev, even closer. The instigators brought in trainloads of Russians from all over. Police and soldiers joined the rioters. No one helped the Jews.

"Lieb was only a baby." I could hear a disturbing tremor in Momma's voice.

"Please stop already. You think I don't remember?" I smelled the smoke from Poppa's pipe and pictured him puffing on it, sending up a cloud. "So why weren't there *pogroms* in Uman? Because the mayor and the police chief – *the goyem* - stopped it before it started."

"Avi, go to sleep!" Momma yelled to me. How could she possibly know I was listening? I didn't answer.

I didn't hear anything for a few moments and thought maybe they had gone outside. Then Uncle Yakov spoke, as though he was apologizing. "I was in the army by then. On the other side of the world."

"Such craziness," Momma said. "So what happens next? They blame the *pogroms* on us. More laws. More punishment. More places Jews can't live."

"I must admit, Uman got very crowded after that," Poppa said. "Such troubles."

That's also when the Church pressed a new policy on the government to solve the Jewish problem. One-third of the Jews would be converted, one-third would die, and one-third would flee the country. Such a policy seems preposterous even now.

"It's not getting any better," Uncle Yakov said. "Maybe you should think about going to America."

"Enough! We will think about it later," Poppa said. "But not tonight." When Poppa said he would think about something later, it meant the subject was closed. He wasn't going to discuss it any more.

I lay awake long after they went to sleep. I couldn't imagine these things they talked about. And what was this place called America? I asked Duv the next morning. He told me in America the streets were paved with gold and kids could have all the sweets they wanted. Jews could live and work anywhere. I didn't believe him at first.

The next night, after the kids were in bed, Momma, Poppa and Uncle Yakov sat around the hearth again and talked quietly. Lieb fell asleep. I didn't.

"What I'm trying to tell you, Mottel, is you should leave Uman," Uncle Yakov said.

"Leave Uman? Where are we going to go?" Poppa asked. I heard the strike of a match and then smelled the smoke from Poppa's pipe.

"Mom, may she rest in peace, wanted to leave Uman," Uncle Yakov said. "Pop wouldn't budge."

"Why budge? The tailor shop fed us, God be praised."

"If it fed us any better we'd have starved to death." Uncle Yakov laughed at his own joke.

"We haven't had a *pogrom* in years, knock on wood." Poppa didn't mention the one we almost had the day the gentiles celebrated the Haidamack uprising.

"This Tsar is going to get us in trouble." Uncle Yakov said.

"This Tsar should croak like a dead fish, may he forgive me,"

Poppa said. It sounded like he spit.

"What are you waiting for Mottel?" Uncle Yakov asked.

"What am I waiting for? You can see what I'm waiting for. The Messiah."

"The Messiah isn't coming anytime soon."

"Please stop already. Such craziness." I could see Poppa shaking his head. Momma probably sat there knitting.

"Yakov, don't bang your head against the wall," Momma said. "He won't listen."

"Take Rukhl and the children. Go to America. It's possible," Uncle Yakov said.

"From your mouth to God's ear," Momma interjected.

"Don't get me wrong," Poppa said. "America's probably a very nice place. But it's no place for a Jew."

"It's going to get worse here, believe me." Uncle Yakov's words were starting to scare me, and I didn't like to hear them arguing.

"America. What do we know about America?" Poppa responded.

"Enough for tonight," Momma said with the tone that ended all debates in our house. "Let's go to bed. We'll solve the problems of the world in the morning."

I heard Poppa and Uncle Yakov laugh about something. Chairs scraped on the wooden floor. A short while later the oil lamp went off in the front room.

I lay awake listening to Lieb snore, wondering again about this place, America, they talked about. Uncle Yakov said "go." Poppa said "don't go." I'd do anything to get away from Viktor Askinov, but I wondered how far away it was. Would I be able to come back to see Duv and Simon? My teacher, Jeremiah, mentioned America a few times. I'd ask him about it tomorrow.

From the moment he arrived, I wanted to talk to my uncle about Viktor Askinov. He was fearless, not like most of the other Jewish men in Uman. He would know how to handle my tormentor. But I rarely had Uncle Yakov to myself, and when I did I was too ashamed to tell him how helpless I was. When he returned to his regiment in another week, I might never get a chance to ask him about it. Then I got lucky.

"So, boys," Uncle Yakov said to Lieb and me. "How would you like to go hunting?"

Poppa looked up from the fish he was gutting. "No," he barked. "No. You want my boys to learn to kill for entertainment?"

"Please, Poppa, please," I begged, jumping up and down. Shooting a gun sounded too exciting to let it pass.

"I don't want to go," Lieb said, shaking his head. "I don't want to kill anybody."

Poppa studied the insides of the dead fish.

"But Mottel. It's just rabbits," Uncle Yakov said. "It's food."

"It's *trafe!* It's not kosher. Jews don't eat rabbits."

"Maybe they should learn."

"No means no." Poppa slammed the big knife down on the counter. His face turned red.

Uncle Yakov walked outside into the yard without saying a word. I was disappointed, as surprised by Poppa's prickly reaction as Uncle Yakov was.

Poppa followed him outside, slamming the door behind him. They argued loudly enough for the neighbors to hear, and then quieted down after a few minutes. I couldn't make out what they were saying. Poppa came in the door by himself.

"Alright, Avi. You can go with Uncle Yakov." I didn't care how Uncle Yakov had convinced Poppa. I was just glad he had.

I didn't see Uncle Yakov for the rest of the day but after everyone else was asleep, I heard him tiptoe into the front room. He smelled of alcohol and cigar smoke. On an earlier night, I heard Momma and Poppa whispering about Uncle Yakov "drinking and whoring with his *goyish* army friends at their tavern." I didn't know what whoring meant until Duv explained it to me. Maybe that's what a real man like Uncle Yakov should be doing, but I knew it was a sin.

Now I'd get to shoot a gun, and it might be my last chance to find out from Uncle Yakov how to protect myself against Viktor Askinov. The next day it rained hard so we couldn't go. The day after that it rained even harder. Only five days now remained until Uncle Yakov had to return to the army.

But the day after that, the sun broke through and we set out across the wet field for the nearby ravine at Sukhi Yar. It was my favorite place in the whole world. Fall's blanket of orange and yellow draped the rolling hills. Random chestnut trees surrounded the ravine.

Sometimes I roamed Sukhi Yar all alone, exploring the long-dry gulch, climbing trees, running after butterflies, or picking wild apples. Baby deer, muskrats, woodchucks, possums, and skunk cabbage owned it. In the fall, wild grapevines wrapped themselves around the trees. I harvested them, hoping I could convince Momma to make some jam.

Sukhi Yar was the place where I played war with my friends, chased squirrels, and then found love for the first time with a pretty young lady. My heart rejects the notion that unspeakable things could happen in this beautiful place full of such tender memories.

From a rise, the Ukraine plain stretched in all directions as far as the eye could see. Peasants gathered in the honey colored ripened wheat, stacking it in grand mounds for wagons to collect.

A thick strand of trees ran up to one side of the ravine, with a clearing in the middle where Lieb, Duv, Simon and I hid from the world. Uncle Yakov made a straight line for it. "You think you're the first ones to discover this place?" He laughed. "Your poppa and I played here when we were kids."

Not many Jewish boys knew how to shoot. The government didn't allow Jews to own guns. But Uncle Yakov used his army comrades to get whatever he wanted. He cradled the rifle in the crook of his arm as comfortably as I held a pen. He looked like a soldier.

I wanted to start shooting as soon as we reached the clearing, but that's not what Uncle Yakov had in mind. First, he made me learn how to hold the rifle steady and how to aim it when I was standing up and when I was flat on my stomach. "Squeeze the trigger. Don't pull it," he said. He made me practice over and over. Then he made me take the rifle apart, clean it, and put it back together again time and again.

I did it very well, but I was getting annoyed. It was getting dark and I wasn't going to get a chance to shoot today. I sulked all the way home, losing the chance to talk to Uncle Yakov about Viktor Askinov.

The next day we marched out again for Sukhi Yar, Uncle Yakov striding purposefully across the still-soggy field, with me struggling to keep up. He pulled a box of bullets out of his pocket as soon as we entered the clearing in the woods.

He fixed a target to a stout oak tree thirty or forty meters away. Then he lay on his stomach in a bed of pine needles, motioning me to stand behind him. He took a breath and pulled the trigger.

The rifled thundered, followed by a puff of smoke from the barrel. I yelped. Splinters flew from the tree. The smell of the gunpowder went up my nostrils and into my memory.

Before I could register a thought, he slid the bolt and pulled the trigger two more times. Each round hit the middle of the target. The echo faded, the woods silent again. He took the rifle from his shoulder, supporting himself on his one elbow, and turned to me with a smile. We walked up to the target together. All three rounds had gone right through the center, embedding themselves in the tree. I put my finger in the holes.

Uncle Yakov spent the rest of the day teaching me how to fire. Soon the kick against my shoulder and the noise became familiar. All the time, he talked to me about everything having to do with gunfire. Stay calm. "Shut out everything going on around you," he said. Sometimes he yelled or threw a small branch at me just when I was ready to squeeze the trigger. After awhile I could ignore everything but the target in front of me. We practiced and practiced. I hit any target Uncle Yakov put out there.

"You're a natural," he said. He praised me over and over. I was proud of myself.

"Can we shoot a rabbit before we go?" I begged.

Uncle Yakov took the rifle from me and got up from the ground, brushing off the pine needles and the dirt. He emptied the chamber, and then bent over to pick up the empty shell casings. I helped him.

"Tomorrow a rabbit."

It had been a fine day. I felt very close to Uncle Yakov, and wished Poppa was more like him. He watched me take the rifle apart and clean it. I wanted to talk to him about Viktor Askinov, but I didn't know how to start the conversation.

"What's it like to be in a battle?" I asked.

Uncle Yakov cleared his throat, then touched the medal on his lapel. He turned to me, expressionless, and began speaking slowly and quietly.

"It's mayhem. Nothing you won't do to stay alive. You're an animal. No thinking."

"Did you ever kill anyone?"

He nodded with his whole body, his mouth shut tight, his eyes half closed. He didn't say anything for what seemed like forever. The quiet unsettled me. "When you kill you kill part of your own soul." He heaved a sigh.

"Did God protect you?"

"There's only your comrades."

"Don't you fight for the Tsar and for Russia?"

"No," he answered in a monotone. "Only my comrades."

"Were you ever wounded?"

He reached up and grabbed his left shoulder. "Once in the shoulder and another time in the rear end." There was the hint of a smile as he patted his right cheek.

"Was that when they gave you a medal?"

"Colonel Petrov seemed to think I stopped the Turks all by myself." He chuckled. Then he picked up a stone and threw it, hitting the tree that held the target. "Truth is, I was just too scared to stop shooting."

"But you were brave."

"I was scared to death. There was no glory. Only fear. Anger." His eyes were vacant, unblinking. I don't think he was even conscious any more he was talking to a fourteen year old boy who couldn't absorb what he was saying.

When he finished, his shoulders slumped and his eye lids drooped. I thought maybe war wasn't such a fun game after all. My problem with Viktor Askinov seemed too trivial to talk about right now. But he had to leave in only three more days.

The next day Uncle Yakov was cheerful, as though yesterday's conversation never happened. It was time for me to kill a rabbit.

We lay on the hard ground in the clearing, cushioned by the pine needles. The crystal air was quiet except for crows yelling so loud I thought they would scare off the hares. Rays of afternoon sun filtered through the trees creating shadows that danced when the limbs of the evergreens stirred in the breeze.

Before long, two rabbits paused forty meters to our right. Uncle Yakov nudged me, pointing in their direction. He held his finger to his lips. He fired, knocking one of them to the ground, and lightning-fast fired again killing the second one.

"Let's go." He leaped up from his prone position.

Moments earlier the rabbits had been so furry and cute. Now they lay motionless, their eyes staring off, unmoving. Blood spilled everywhere, their mushy insides oozing out. It smelled.

"That's what a dead animal looks like. Take a good look."

But I didn't want to take a good look. I wanted to vomit. Shooting rabbits wasn't as much fun as I thought. Uncle Yakov dug a shallow hole, put the rabbits in, and covered the hole with dirt and leaves.

"Your turn. Remember what I showed you," he said. "Sight down the barrel. Hold the rifle tight against your shoulder. Take a breath. Hold it, and squeeze the trigger. Don't pull it."

We lay down again and waited for a rabbit. A big brown beauty moved into view, looking around, sniffing for danger. I had the rabbit in my sight. I took aim, drew a deep breath, and squeezed the trigger. But I lowered the sight a tiny bit, missing the rabbit and hitting the ground in front of him. He scampered off. The recoil of the rifle punched my shoulder. Smoke and smell of gunpowder hung in the air. I looked over at Uncle Yakov, afraid I had disappointed him.

"It's not a bad thing you can't kill." He placed a hand on my shoulder. "But if the time comes when you have to, remember this. You can do it."

I nodded, but I had failed him. At least Poppa would be relieved I didn't kill anything.

"Let's go by the stream," he said. "Might not get another chance." We followed the overgrown path through the woods. Uncle Yakov carried the rifle casually by his side. Still embarrassed, I didn't look him in the eye.

When we got to the stream, we sat down on the huge trunk of a fallen moss-covered tree. Uncle Yakov propped the gun against the trunk. Then he got out his tobacco and rolled a neat, perfectly round cigarette with his burly fingers. He lit it, puffed, and exhaled a fog of smoke. "There's something you want to talk to me about?" he said. I stammered, not knowing where to begin. But once I started, everything poured out.

I told him about Viktor Askinov. I described the first time I met him at our front door, his evil eyes, how he, his brother Olek, and his friends terrorized us all the time. I told him how afraid I was whenever I saw him.

When I wound down, Uncle Yakov patted me on the back. "He sounds like the Devil himself."

I hoped Uncle Yakov had some secrets he would share to help me fight back. He didn't. Instead he talked about how, when he first went into the army, he was beaten up many times for being a Jew.

"But getting beaten up isn't the worst thing," he said. "When you stop fighting back, then they know they can do anything they want to you. I could show you how to box or how to use a club. But courage is your real weapon."

"But I don't have any courage." I struggled to keep from crying. Uncle Yakov put his hand on my arm.

"Courage is when you do something even though you're afraid to do it. That's how Duvid beat Goliath."

"But Jews aren't fighters any more." I forgot for a moment

who I was talking to.

"The heart of a warrior's still there. It's in you."

I felt brave for an instant, but fear returned immediately. I wanted Uncle Yakov to solve my problem for me. Instead he made it worse. Now not only was I afraid of Viktor Askinov, I was also afraid Uncle Yakov would think I was a coward. I had no idea where I was going to find the courage he talked about. We walked home in silence, but he kept his hand on my shoulder all the way.

The night before Uncle Yakov left, Momma broke into her store of food again to fix a special dinner. "You look like ate a sour tomato," he teased me, but I didn't feel like laughing. "Don't be so sad. I'll be back."

But who knew when I would see him again? Soldiers fight wars, and sometimes they die.

After dinner I asked him to let me touch his medals one more time. He had taken his most prized medal, the Tsar's Own Heroes, from his lapel and put it back on his uniform tunic. I touched each medal with a careful hand. He watched me for a few minutes. "Courage doesn't come from medals," he said. "It comes from inside us. When you need to do something important no matter what. You can do it, Avi."

I didn't fall asleep that night until the first light came in the window. In the morning Uncle Yakov had a big smile on his face, and I resented it. How could he be so happy when I was so miserable? When he put on his uniform, he was a soldier again.

Poppa borrowed a horse and wagon to take Uncle Yakov to the train station. The wagon was a small old derelict in danger of falling apart. The horse was no better. Momma and Poppa decided it was best if we kids said good-bye at the house. When it was time, we all went outside. Rain clouds were gathering and the wind began to blow. The dust from the streets covered our boots and clung to our clothes.

Uncle Yakov threw his big duffle bag into the back of the wagon as though it were a small satchel. He gave Momma a big hug and a kiss on her cheek. Then he went to each of the children and did the same. First came little Markus, then Zelda, then Ester, then Lieb, and finally me. "You can be like Gideon and King Duvid," he whispered in my ear. "But whatever you do, I will love you."

Uncle Yakov climbed up in the wagon beside Poppa. I watched their backs until they disappeared around the corner, emptiness pouring through my heart.

Every fourteen year old boy should have an Uncle Yakov come and visit him. A lot of what he said was too much for me to understand back then. But he disrupted many of my notions about what a Jew was supposed to be like, and what my life would be like. I wonder if he meant to do that.

FIVE

July 1897

N
ine months passed since Uncle Yakov returned to his regiment. We didn't go to school in the unbearable July heat and humidity, so I worked with Poppa in the tailor shop all morning. Markus, now eleven years old, learned the family trade too. The temperature inside the shop was dreadful, sweat rolling down my back, soaking my shirt.

Outside, waves of heat shimmered off the hard-packed street and buildings. The large square in front of the synagogue was packed with market day crowds. Once every week, farmers from the countryside brought their produce, meats and cheeses into town. Artisans brought their wares, bakers their special breads and pastries, and peddlers their pots, pans and used clothes. They set up open-air stalls and pushcarts, crowding the square. This was the one time Jews and gentiles mixed freely.

Every market day was like a carnival. Poppa's shop was near the corner of the square and I could watch from the front window. Peasants dressed in billowing pantaloons and colorful peasant blouses contrasted with the Hassidic men in their long black coats and black felt hats, no matter the heat of the day.

The Hassidics were Jews too, but so odd with their long curly sideburns they embarrassed me. You couldn't pick out the Hassidic women so easily except for their drab dresses and scarves covering their heads. Some of them shaved their heads on their wedding day and never grew hair again.

Everyone I knew growing up was Haskalah - modern, open-minded Jews. Unlike Hassidics, we dressed like the gentiles. Haskalah wanted to become a part of Russian society. Jeremiah said this was the way to overcome anti-Jewish sentiments, not by living in a mental ghetto like the Hassidics. In their schools, Hassidic boys only studied the Torah. Rabbi Rosenberg insisted our school also teach us Russian subjects like literature, science, geography, languages, mathematics, and history.

Though all the Jews in Uman were one big tribe, many Hassidics thought us impious and had little to do with us. Their rabbi argued with our rabbi all the time about whose was the right course to God and to heaven. I hoped our rabbi was right.

"Avi, take Markus and go swimming," Poppa said. "Cool off. Maybe Lieb is done too."

Lieb worked as an apprentice to the baker in the shop across the square. His schooldays were over and he was glad of it. Not me. I wanted to go on to one of Uman's two universities, but few Jews were ever admitted.

We picked Lieb up; Simon joined us. Then we pushed through the mayhem looking for Duv. Some of the men, and more of the women, gave us an elbow or a kick in the shins and a dirty look.

Children scampered between the stalls. Buyers shouted back and forth with sellers, bargaining for every kopek. The smell of cooking onions, sausage and smoke from an open grill drifted about. Men and women bunched with their friends to catch up on the latest gossip, islands in the eddying stream of the crowd. Boys and girls flirted, but mothers kept vigilant watch, protecting their daughters or restraining their sons.

Of course that's where we found Duv, entertaining three girls, their mothers nearby, alert and disapproving. He already had a reputation. I envied him his confidence with girls, while I stumbled and bumbled.

Every now and then Duv turned serious. "We can't all be as good as you, Avi," he once said, without a trace of resentment. "I wish I could be." Those were the times when I knew he wasn't having as much fun as he wanted everyone to think he was.

Duv tore himself away from the girls and joined us. We meandered down Nevsky Street toward the river, kicking dust up with our shoes. Duv pulled a stolen apple from under his shirt and took a big bite.

When we got to Saint Vladimir's Orthodox Church, we crossed the street and ran past it as fast as we could. The crosses out front and on top of the onion-shaped steeples sent a shiver up my spine every time. They said inside the church a Jewish man was nailed to a cross, on display for everyone to see. I didn't believe it but Moishe Stepaner insisted his father had been inside and actually saw it. He swore an oath it was true.

At the bridge, we climbed down to the river's edge and trooped along the well-worn path.

Patches of wild grass and bushes dotted the rock-strewn river bank. In July the river was so shallow in many places you could walk across from our side to the gentile side, but we didn't dare do that. We pushed through the thick brambles that covered the entrance to our secret spot, a large clearing by the water's edge. Here there was a deep pool of clear cool water.

Then a rock dropped into the water behind us making a splash. I didn't take much notice until another splashed, then another in quick succession. I turned around. Viktor Askinov and his two friends stood astride the path we had just walked. Ahead of us and to our side were high banks we couldn't scale. I looked around for an escape. We had none.

Askinov glared, his upper lip curled in a smirk. "Today you're going to die, Jew boys," he snarled.

He held a large rock in each hand. So did his friends, and his brother Olek on top of the river bank above us. I was breathing hard, unable to move. Markus tried to hide behind me. Viktor Askinov took his time.

He let one rock fly, striking near my feet. One from Olek up above landed at Duv's feet. Others landed near Lieb and Simon. They were toying with us, like a cat teasing a wounded bird. Viktor Askinov's grey eyes bored into me, his teeth bared like a growling dog. A gigantic raven called out to its friends to gather for a feast.

They took one step forward, then another. We backed up toward the high bank at the end of the clearing. Olek threw a big rock down, landing behind us. And another. A warm gust of wind blew sand in my face.

There was no place to run. I thought about climbing up the riverbank or jumping in the water but those routes wouldn't work. I turned around in circles, sure we were going to die, helpless prey. I was too scared to pray to God or cry out for my mother.

"Do something," Markus yelled when another barrage of rocks landed near us. One hit Duv in the leg; he yelped. Viktor Askinov cackled, and inched forward.

One hit Simon on the shoulder. One hit Lieb, and another struck Duv. We tried to protect our heads with our arms. Two hit me, one in the shoulder and one in the back. Maybe someone would see our situation and rescue us. But no one could see this concealed place.

More and more rocks found their targets as they advanced.

Three of them in a row hit Markus. They were targeting him. He hollered like a lamb being slaughtered. I tried to shield him but had to protect myself from the next hailstorm.

Viktor Askinov bellowed at the same time he heaved the next one at Markus. His rock struck Markus in the temple, above his left ear. My little brother crumbled to the ground, blood pooling by his head. They cheered. Markus lay still. The rocks flying, they kept closing in, preparing to kills us all.

When I saw Markus on the ground, I felt nothing but fury. I didn't think; flashes of red and yellow stormed through me. I picked up a big grey rock in each hand and charged at Viktor Askinov. Simon told me later I roared like a wild boar, but I don't remember.

Viktor Askinov's eyes opened wide. His jaw dropped when I attacked. He froze. When I was almost on top of him, I threw. The rock struck him square on the forehead. He crumbled to the ground. Blood gushed out, staining his shirt and the earth around him. He looked up at me, dazed. I stood over him and howled.

His friends and Olek stopped their assault, bewildered by what they saw. Duv hurried to Markus, took off his shirt, and used it to stop the flow of blood.

I brought Goliath to his knees, and now it was time to take his head. I raised the biggest boulder I could find in both hands, taking aim. He raised his arm to protect his face, whimpering.

"Avi, that's enough!" Lieb screamed. He grasped my arm, yanking the boulder from my hands. It crashed to the ground in front of me.

Olek and their two friends rushed over to Viktor Askinov, helping him to his feet. Olek stuck something on his gooey wound. They half-carried him back along the path toward the bridge, one arm around each of his friends.

He turned to me as they left. The evil had returned to those cruel grey eyes. But this time he didn't scare me. I was too numb, in a stupor.

"Is Markus alright?" I asked, staring at Viktor Askinov's back until they disappeared into the brush and trees.

"He's fine," Simon answered.

"You did it! You did it." Markus jumped up and down, showing no pain.

Lieb led me home, never letting go of my arm. Simon nearly carried Markus all the way. We took a detour to avoid the marketplace.

I nearly killed the Constable's son. I would have killed him if Lieb hadn't grabbed my arm. I wasn't sorry for what I did. But I was afraid I was in big trouble. Momma and Poppa would figure out what to do, I hoped.

This was one time Momma didn't know what had happened before we got home to tell her. She did a quick examination of Markus' wound and announced there was no cause for alarm. She peppered us with questions while she washed his blood-encrusted head. Markus was giddy, like he had too much wine. "Avi beat up Viktor Askinov," he kept saying.

Lieb, Markus and I all started talking at the same time, jabbering like a bunch of crazed monkeys. The more we told her, the more she frowned and shriveled her brow. Her questions came one after another, all the time clutching and twisting her hands. Where on his head did I hit him? How much blood was there? Were his eyes open? Did he say anything? Could he walk home or was he carried? What did his friends say? Did anyone else see the fight?

Poppa barged in a few minutes later. He still had on the eyeshade he wore when he was sewing. He rushed over to Markus and examined his head closely.

"God help us. The word is all over the village," he said.

"Believe me, every gentile in town will know soon enough."
Poppa looked as worried as the first time Constable Askinov
showed up at our door.

He stroked Markus' hair. Ester and Zelda listened to every
word from the kitchen. Zelda sniffled like she was going to cry.
Ester put her arm around her. Momma and Poppa had no doubt
Constable Askinov would retaliate, but the question was how. He
could take it out on me, or on the whole family. Maybe he would
take it out on the whole village.

I wanted to lie down and go to sleep. Poppa paced back and
forth, his hands behind his back. Momma checked Markus' head
again. He pulled away and went into the kitchen with Ester and
Zelda. Lieb and I sat at the table.

"What if Avi went to my sister's in Odessa for awhile?"
There was little emotion in Poppa's voice. "Just until this blows
over."

Momma nodded. "It's a long way. Isn't there anyplace closer he could go?"

"I don't want to go," I pleaded. Lieb frowned. Zelda sniffled
some more. Markus and Ester watched quietly.

"This is serious, a Jewish boy hitting a gentile." Poppa
walked over to examine Markus's wound yet again.

"Who knows what the *goyim* will do?" Momma said.

"We'll see what happens, pray God," Poppa said.

"He's not dead, knock on wood," Momma answered.

My victory over Viktor Askinov hadn't solved anything. I
was glad Poppa wasn't making me go to Odessa yet, but what
were the authorities going to do to me? There was nothing to do
but wait.

The next day we tried to act as though nothing happened, but
the whole village was buzzing. At the Sabbath communal bath
that afternoon, the men talked of nothing else.

"What's going to happen if they punish the whole village?" a fat, hairy man asked.

"I suppose I could take my family to my cousin's in Tefka," the hairless, toothless one answered.

"Let me tell you something," Reb Moskowitz said. "It's not such a bad thing, a Jewish boy beating up one of those gentiles." He made a spitting sound.

Markus had a headache for a few days but was proud of the bandage on his head. His version of the fight got better every time he told it, exaggerating my heroics more and more. He started what quickly grew into a legend.

On Sabbath eve, the July heat turned the synagogue into the fires of hell. Rabbi Rosenberg read the passage from the bible of Duvid's triumph over Goliath, his voice loud and emotional, punctuated with theatrical gestures I'd never seen from him before. He said a few prayers asking for God's mercy.

The next morning, word of reprieve flew about the synagogue. A dependable gentile source confided in Jeremiah that there would be no reprisals for what I had done. Rabbi Rosenberg cut the service short so everyone could get on with their gossiping.

"Constable Askinov was so embarrassed by his son losing to a Jew," Jeremiah said. "All he wanted to do was hide."

"Believe me, that's a fine boy you have there," the fat, hairy man said to Poppa.

"To tell you the truth, I'm as proud of him as if he were my own son," the hairless, toothless one said.

Reb Moskowitz shook his head, and patted me on the back.

Poppa strutted, Momma beamed, and I felt like a fraud. The scene at the river bank replayed in my mind like a movie. There were the rocks flying, Viktor Askinov closing in, my fear, and the shock when one of those rocks hit me. I couldn't find inside me the rage I felt when Markus crumbled to the ground. But I saw

Viktor Askinov's fright when I stood over him, the boulder raised above my head.

I was no hero. Uncle Yakov said courage is doing something even though you're afraid. So I couldn't have been courageous; not if I wasn't even thinking about what I was doing when I went after Viktor Askinov. I didn't want anyone to know I was only a little less scared of Viktor Askinov now than I was before.

The next day Madam Shumenko came into Poppa's tailor shop while I was there. Her son Sergey was with her. I hadn't seen him for months and I missed him. We were young men now, too old and too busy to follow our mothers around on their errands. But the real reason could be it was no longer acceptable for Sergey to be friends with a Jewish boy.

We huddled together in a corner of the shop while Poppa and Madam Shumenko tended to the fitting of a new cape. Sergey had heard about my encounter with Viktor Askinov.

"I saw him," he said. "He has a big gash on his forehead, a broken nose, and bruises on his jaw. His face is all reddish and purple."

"But I only hit him on the forehead."

"His father did the rest, they say. He thrashes him all of the time, ever since he was a little boy."

"Why?" I asked. I couldn't imagine Poppa doing that to me.

"He drinks all the time. And when he's drunk, he beats up Viktor, his brothers and his mother." Sergey let out a sigh and shook his head. "He's poor and he blames the Jews for it. He hates Jews, like the church tells us to. Now his son loses a fight to a Jew."

"Why don't you feel that way toward Jews," I asked.

"Maybe I do, a little. But it's all so stupid. I like you." He took a bite of one of the cookies his mother had brought us. "The priest teaches us Jews must pay for killing Christ. But Mother says you're God's children too."

"I think it's hard for you to be friends with me," I said.

"I may not see you for awhile. These aren't good times." I nodded, fingering a cookie. I didn't even want a bite.

If anything good came from my fight with Viktor Askinov, it was that maybe he would think twice before attacking me again. He couldn't be sure I would run away next time. But I didn't feel like the hero everyone said I was. Maybe if I wrote to Uncle Yakov he could help me figure it out, I thought. That night I began a long letter to him. I never finished it.

The very next day Poppa received a letter from General Aleksandri Petrov, Uncle Yakov's commanding officer. He examined it, turning it over and back again before he opened it. His hand trembled. He glanced down the first page, and then read it out loud to us.

My Dear Mottel Schneider,

I take liberty in addressing you with the familiar, to which I trust you will take no offense. Your brother Yakov speaks of you so often and with such affection I feel I know you like a brother also.

I would not be writing you had I not the gravest news to report. I have waited until now because I have wanted to be able to assure you that your brother is not in danger from his wounds, and will survive. He is not yet able to write you himself.

Yakov was struck in his right leg, abdomen and left arm. The worst of the wounds is to his arm. He should recover completely from the ones in his stomach and leg but, to his great misfortune, his left arm will be forever damaged.

I have made certain he is receiving the best medical treatment from the best doctors and nurses we have. I will watch over him until he is fully recovered.   Because of the permanent nature of the terrible wound to his arm, he will be discharged from the Tsar's army.   Once again I assure you I will take care he is well provided for in his pension.   He will have enough money to live on, if modestly, for the remainder of his life, may it be a long one.   I can do no less.   He has saved my life too many times in the past, and received these latest wounds in once again protecting me.

I write this to you from our position in Siberia near the border with Mongolia.   This is a difficult land, inhospitable to man or animal.   We are defending the Russian workers as they build the Trans-Siberian Railroad of which you may have read.   It will be a monumental achievement for the Tsar and our motherland.   Mongolia is filled with bandits who believe wrongly that this land belongs to them but who are in truth no more than thieves who raid us without end.

Sergeant Yakov Schneider was wounded in such a raid, defending my headquarters to the death against a much larger force while so many of our soldiers ran away in fear, to their eternal disgrace.   May they land in hell.   Your good brother and my good friend Yakov would not run even if his own life depended on it.   Badly wounded as he was, he kept fighting until all the bandits were killed or driven away.   I am forever in his debt.

I have served the Tsar and fought with Yakov beside me for the past twenty-four years.   I will not again know the pleasure of soldiering with him at my side.   May God protect him and his majesty Tsar Nicholas II for all of their days.

In the service of his majesty, I remain your servant.

Alexandri Petrov

Brigadier General

15ᵗʰ Lifeguard Cavalry, Commanding

Momma let out a wail like a dying goat, closing her eyes and beating her chest with a closed fist. Poppa took her in his arms, a tear dripping down his cheek. "He's alive, the Lord be praised," he said. "He'll come home."

It took nearly a month for General Petrov's letter to reach us. Who knew Uncle Yakov's current condition or where he would go when he was discharged from the army? I prayed he would come back to Uman. Poppa wrote him a letter immediately.

Months went by with no reply. I asked Poppa every day if a letter had come. He shook his head. I imagined every possible tragedy. Maybe Uncle Yakov hadn't recovered from his wounds. Maybe he didn't want to come back to Uman. Or maybe he was even dead. I was so lost in my own misery, I didn't see Poppa's.

I didn't notice he wasn't eating much, not even during Sabbath meals. He lost weight. Shortly after each letter Poppa wrote, I began pestering him to write another. After seven or eight months with no reply from Uncle Yakov, I begged Poppa to write to General Petrov. He did.

Six weeks later, in April of 1898, a long white envelope from General Petrov arrived. It was the last day of Passover. Poppa tore the letter open and read over it quickly. "He's alive," was the first thing he said. The muscles in his face relaxed, then his brow wrinkled again.

The army discharged Uncle Yakov a couple of months after General Petrov wrote Poppa the first time. Though his body mended, his heart did not. His other wounds healed but his withered arm would never be fully functional.

For awhile after his discharge, he stayed near the army camp, but he was detached from everyone. He even lost interest in horseback riding, which he loved. The general's letter continued:

The Mongolian devils he killed in his final battle, and the wounds they inflicted, haunted him. One moment he was withdrawn into himself. The next moment he exploded. He drank too much and got into fights in taverns. Even with only one good arm, Yakov is a match for any man.

General Petrov got him out of trouble often. Then his army unit, the 15th Lifeguard Cavalry, deployed to a new location as the construction of the Trans-Siberian Railroad moved on. From that time, Uncle Yakov roamed from place to place all over Siberia. The general tried to keep track of him through his military network, but Uncle Yakov was illusive, like a ghost. There were reports he lived with a young woman for awhile in the town of Szavyanka, near where his old army post was located. He returned there from time to time.

Whenever he is seen again, I am told about it. Then I make sure he is being provided for. I promise you his physical needs are being taken care of, but unfortunately I can do nothing to repair his troubled mind. It pains me to be so helpless to care for my old and dear friend, your brother Yakov. I have from time to time seen such trouble in wounded comrades who have been in horrible battles. Often they heal themselves in time. Yakov is a strong man and if any man can heal himself, it will be Yakov. I will pray for him and continue to do everything in my power to protect him.

When Poppa finished reading, I wandered off by myself to the creek at Sukhi Yar where I had first told Uncle Yakov about Viktor Askinov. I sat on the same log we sat on, threw stones into the water, and brooded about what Uncle Yakov would have thought of me now.

After that, I stopped pestering Poppa to write to Uncle Yakov or General Petrov. I prayed to God every night before I fell asleep, and every Sabbath in synagogue, that Uncle Yakov would heal himself and come home to Uman.

Viktor Askinov did not go away. I beat him, but I did not conquer him. He avoided me whenever he could, so I rarely saw him up close. Instead, he now harassed the Schneider family in ways we could never prove.

Lieb found one of our chickens strangled, its guts cut open. Then someone stole our milk can from in front of our door. A rock smashed Poppa's shop window. Another day we had to work for hours removing the words "Christ killer" painted on the shop's door. After that, a crude wooden cross was planted in front of our house. Finally, there was the dead cat.

Every time one of these happened, I ranted about the revenge I wanted to take on Viktor Askinov. And each time Poppa counseled me to let it pass. "You beat him. It is enough," he said. I welcomed Poppa's counsel because, in truth, my fear of Viktor Askinov had only diminished a little. I didn't want to fight him again.

Once I heard Poppa talking to Madame Shumenko about Viktor Askinov. "He's like a pet dog that has been beaten so often by his master until he turns into a savage beast," Poppa said. "So maybe it's not the animal's fault it's so vicious."

"Maybe not," Madame Shumenko replied. "But the animal still needs to be disposed of before it kills someone."

Was Viktor Askinov as evil as I say he was? Yes, of that I have no doubt. I don't know if there is a God and a Devil, but if there is, Viktor Askinov was surely the Devil's disciple. Time would prove me right. I could have killed him that day, then and there. I didn't, but I would get another chance.

SIX

August 1898

Duv taught me everything a sixteen year old boy needed to know about fornication.

My awakening happened by itself, but if it wasn't for Duv I still may not know what purpose it served. Lieb's ignorance rivaled mine, and Poppa was too embarrassed to talk about it. Duv finally got tired of my unyielding arguments about how babies came about and decided to educate me.

He took his mentoring role as seriously as he took anything. I feared whatever felt that good must surely be a sin. But Duv showed me passage after passage in the bible about fornication. He pointed out dogs and goats in the procreation act and provided appropriate commentary. If you're a sixteen year old boy, even dogs and goats are arousing.

Only the good Lord knows how Duv got a hold of dirty pictures in Uman. He said they were French but France was a whole different country, far from Russia. He had post cards of women with no clothes on, standing in front of the camera. You could see everything, from their big breasts down to their hairy places.

I had seen Ester and Zelda with no clothes on, but I was only six or seven years old, and they were littler. They didn't have a hairy place then, and I didn't want to even think about whether they had one now. Once I caught a glimpse of Momma. She was changing her clothes when I barged into her bedroom. I was old enough to be mortified.

The pen and ink drawings Duv showed me looked like he had drawn them himself. Some of his drawings actually showed men and women doing things. I was embarrassed just looking at them, afraid God was going to punish me any minute.

I couldn't look Momma and Poppa in the eye for a year, afraid they could see every naughty thought. My face glowed red with embarrassment all the time. I overheard Momma urging Poppa to have a talk with me, and prayed he wouldn't.

Then Duv led me on a daring deed sure to send me straight to hell. On Sabbath eve, we had our usual weekly community bath. "Meet me out back after you dry off," Duv whispered. "I'm gonna' show you something unbelievable. Don't let anyone see you." I made up a story for Poppa why I wouldn't be home right away.

When we left the synagogue, Duv checked to be sure no one was watching us. Then he snuck off behind the bath house and hid in the bushes. I followed right behind him. Soon we heard the women and girls coming down the street laughing and babbling on. They disappeared inside the bath house.

"Don't make a sound," Duv whispered. He scanned carefully in all directions. Then he crept up to the back of the bath house. He motioned for me to join him. I was afraid to breath. He crouched on his knees and pushed one of the boards of the bath house to the side, opening a small crack. He put his eye up to it and peered in. After a moment, he pulled away and signaled for me to take a look.

I could see right inside. Some of the women were still undressing, revealing themselves a piece at a time. There were plump ones, skinny ones, young ones and old ones. Nearly all were appealing. The girls already undressed stood by the side of the bath or lowered themselves into the water. I could see everything they had. I saw my sister Ester and her friends. I peeked at Golde Skolnick, Bayleh Zuckman and others. And I rose, quivered and groaned. Duv pulled me away. I didn't want to go. He yanked me so hard I almost fell over, saving me from an embarrassing accident.

We snuck away. As soon as we were in front of the synagogue, we started to run. We were puffing hard when we stopped to catch our breath.

Duv laughed hard, grabbing his side. "So how did you like that?"

I moaned. I ached down below, ready to explode. I sweated. "Let's do it again," I said.

"Next Sabbath eve. I promise." He was pleased with himself.

I had never even seen a girl's naked ankles before. Now this. But what I had done was a sin. I was ashamed of myself. What if Momma and Poppa found out?

I didn't pray at that night's services, afraid He couldn't forgive me. I didn't say much at dinner and didn't eat much. I kept my eyes glued to the food on my plate. Momma asked if I was okay. I told her I had an upset stomach, which wasn't entirely a lie.

"Why don't you help me feed the chickens," Poppa said to me the next day when he woke from his Sabbath afternoon nap. He rarely paid any attention to the chickens. That was Momma's job. And he didn't work on the Sabbath. I followed him outside, afraid of what was coming. The chickens squawked when they saw us.

It was another of those hot, muggy August days you don't forget. Poppa sat down on the edge of the well and motioned for

me to join him. The smell of the privy and the chicken coop
enshrouded us.

Simon's father already talked to him about how babies were
made. It would be too embarrassing if Poppa got into that now.
Poppa was as awkward as I was. We both studied our shoes and
kicked at the dirt.

"So, do you already know about making babies?"

"Yes."

"Any questions? Anything you don't understand?"

"No."

I had lots of questions but I would rather die of the plague
than ask Poppa. If I had questions, I would go to Duv.

Poppa looked up in the sky as though seeking divine intervention. "As the bible says, Jewish girls must be virgins when
they marry. Their virginity must be respected and protected by
everyone." I didn't move an eyelash or make a sound, begging for
my torture to end.

"Let me tell you something," Poppa continued. "It's a sin to
steal an innocent girl's virginity. You and Lieb have two sisters,
God bless them. So I ask you, do you want them to be virgins
when they're married?"

"Yes."

There wasn't much more than that. Poppa was as thankful as
I was when our conversation ended. He smiled and slapped me on
the back, satisfied he had done his job.

But some of Duv's questioning infected me. What if the girl
wasn't an innocent girl? Then was it okay? And how could anything so gratifying be a sin? Why would God do that? Just to
tease us?

On the other hand, Poppa's admonitions weren't wasted on
me. I did think about Ester and Zelda. And it was important any
woman I married be a virgin. So maybe it wasn't right to take any

girl's virginity before marriage. Poppa's lesson was one of those that never goes away entirely, even when we learn the world isn't so simple. Growing up could be so confusing.

In spite of Poppa's lecture, I thought all week long of the next chance to peak at the naked girls. Sabbath eve Duv and I snuck out behind the bath house again.

Catastrophe! Someone had boarded over the crack between the slats, and trimmed the bushes to the ground. There was no where to hide. When I saw the Shamash in synagogue that night, the rabbi's antiquated helper gave me a severe look and shook his head. I was embarrassed, afraid he would tell Poppa.

If Poppa's job was to constrain his sons, Momma protected her daughters' chastity and reputation with the ferocity of a mother bear. How else were they to find suitable husbands? She kept Ester and Zelda by her side, and when she couldn't, she made sure they were chaperoned. Sometimes this duty fell to Lieb or me.

Ester and Zelda were taught to be pure and religious, fearful of making a mistake, with an exaggerated caution toward young men. I found out soon enough all mothers in the village were like Momma and the girls like Ester.

As I got older, other mothers watched me as if I were a fox after their baby chicks. These village mothers presented formidable barriers. With chaperones around all the time, there weren't many opportunities for any of us to lose our virginity before our wedding night.

Duv never lost hope and never stopped trying. I did. But he would not have me accept this fate. So he took my education to a new level.

"Have you ever kissed a girl?" he asked.

"Well... maybe... maybe not."

"It's time we fixed that." He slapped me on the back. "I have the perfect girl for it. Bayleh Zuckman."

I got hot all over. "I can't do that. Leave me alone." I was excited, but a little scared. I didn't know how to kiss a girl.

"It'll be great. She's an expert kisser, and she won't tell anyone. She knows lots of things."

Bayleh Zuckman was nice enough looking, even if she was a little bit stout. But I couldn't be choosy. When I looked through the slats in the bath house and saw Bayleh Zuckman without any clothes on, I was aroused. But I didn't want to make a fool of myself.

Duv read my mind. "Go home and practice on a tomato." I didn't realize he was teasing me, so I did what he told me. I wondered if Lieb or Simon had kissed a girl yet. I doubted it.

The very next day Duv told me Bayleh was glad to help. "But kissing only," he said. I only expected a kiss. What else could she be thinking of besides kissing? Duv arranged for me to meet her down an alley by an abandoned barn behind the blacksmith's shop. No one went back there.

I couldn't concentrate on my schoolwork all day. My teacher, Jeremiah, called on me several times and I didn't even hear him. "Avi, are you with us today?" he asked late in the day.

When school was over, I lingered outside the front door long enough for everyone to leave. "Don't keep the young lady waiting," Duv teased. He patted me on the back offering needed encouragement. I checked to be sure no one was watching, and then snuck down the passageway separating the school and the blacksmith shop.

There she was, leaning against the side of the rundown barn. Her skirt was pulled up so I could see her stockings well above her ankles. Bayleh gave me an inviting smile, wetting her lips with her tongue.

"Hello Avi." Her voice was husky, like her dark eyes. "I've been looking forward to this."

I mumbled, embarrassed.

"Don't be shy. We all have a first time." She ran a hand through her dark, ruffled hair. "And I've wanted to kiss you."

I couldn't believe Bayleh Zuckman even knew I existed, no less wanted to kiss me.

"So aren't you going to say anything?"

"Thank you," was all I could think of. She laughed. Then she took my hand and guided it around to her back. I was aroused. With the other hand she reached up and took hold of the back of my head . Then she gently kissed me on the lips. I kissed her back. She pulled away slightly, my one arm behind her back and the other dangling by my side.

"Did you like that?" she asked.

I nodded, "Very much."

"That wasn't so hard, was it? Let's try it again, only this time put both arms around me."

I did, and she wound her arms around me. We kissed again, this time a long one. We kissed a few more times. I got warmer and warmer all over. I could feel the softness of her breasts pushing against my chest. I wanted to touch her, to explore other parts of her but I was afraid to move my hands. Maybe she would get mad and stop. I didn't want that.

At the worst possible moment, she abruptly pulled herself away from my puckered lips. "That's all for today," she said, a pleasant smile on her face. She took my hands from behind her back and deposited them by my side. "You're a good student."

"Did you like it?" I begged.

"Yes I did. You're a good kisser." She touched me lightly on the cheek.

"I'll see you tomorrow. Same time." She sashayed down the passageway toward the synagogue, hips swaying. She looked in both directions to be sure no one saw her, and then disappeared around the corner.

I was madly in love with Bayleh Zuckman. I couldn't wait to tell Duv about it, and I couldn't wait until tomorrow to see Bayleh again. But Poppa's admonitions intruded on my imagination. I shoved them away.

The next day was interminable. Jeremiah scolded me again for my inattention. As soon as school ended I bolted for the door and up the passageway, disregarding who might see me.

Bayleh leaned against the side of the barn, tantalizing me with her smile as I got closer. I threw my arms around her and began kissing her. She pulled her head back.

"Aren't you even going to say hello," she said, her hands resting on my hips.

"Hello, Bayleh."

"My, we're eager today, aren't we Avi."

"I've thought about you every minute." I was panting.

"Aren't you cute." Her words crushed me. Your brother's cute. Your dog is cute. But not your lover.

She put her arms around me and started kissing me. I kissed her back and rubbed my hand up and down her back. She pulled away again. "You're a much better kisser today."

Then she stuck her tongue in my mouth. I nearly gagged. She rolled it in and out. I liked it. My lust rose and I was in a dangerous state. She stopped abruptly like she did yesterday.

"That was a French kiss," she said.

"Mmmm," I slobbered.

"Those French do interesting things," she said. I tried to kiss her again but she pulled her head away and pushed my arms to my sides. "That's all for today."

"Will I see you tomorrow?"

"Same time." She smiled and ran her tongue across her wet lips. Then she vanished down the passageway, leaving me breathless and frustrated. I wanted it to go further but I thought about what Poppa said about virgins. I hoped Bayleh was a virgin. I wanted to marry her.

The next day Duv and I walked to school alone. I told him everything about my encounters with Bayleh.

"Do you think she's a virgin?" I asked.

"Avi, this is just for fun. That's all." He looked like a Cheshire cat.

"I think she's a virgin."

"I promise you she's no virgin," he said emphatically, more serious than usual.

I stuck my hands in my pockets and didn't say anything the rest of the way to school. I was jealous and angry with Duv. How would he know whether or not she was a virgin? Was there no limit to his indecencies?

The first day Bayleh Zuckman offered surprises, and the second day even more. Maybe today she would give me the biggest surprise of all. By the end of the day I was on the verge of an embarrassing explosion. I raced to the barn.

She waited in the shadows, pacing. If lust was in my groin, it was painted all over her brooding face. She held out her arms when she saw me coming. We wrapped our arms around each other without saying a word, our lips locking and tongues probing. She rubbed against me in rhythm, and I responded. I slid one hand down her back to her *tokhes* – her ass. I squeezed. It was so soft and cushy. She took my other hand and moved it to her breast. She yelped when I squeezed too hard. I lightened my touch. She moaned and that almost did it to me.

Bayleh pulled back abruptly and shoved me away. "No more. Lessons are over."

"I'm sorry, Bayleh. What did I do?"

"I'm not seeing you again. That's it. No more." Sweat glistened on her forehead, her face contorted. She straightened her hair and her dress, and stormed off. She didn't look back and didn't even check to see if anyone was watching when she reached the end of the passageway.

I watched the passageway well after she disappeared around the corner, confused by what happened in these three days. I was sorry to see the last of Bayleh Zuckman. She was a good teacher and I never forgot her. But she wasn't a virgin, so there was no future with such a girl.

Duv was relieved when I told him I wouldn't be seeing Bayleh again. "I hope you had a good time," he said without his usual enthusiasm.

A few days later Rabbi Rosenberg came into our class to deliver a lecture directed at the awakening of young men. He told the biblical story of Sodom and Gomorrah, and how God destroyed these towns by "brimstone and fire from the Lord out of heaven" because of the wickedness of the people. They committed every imaginable sin of the flesh. He didn't tell us what those sins were but I imagined he was referring to looking at dirty post cards, peeking at girls through a crack in the bath house wall, and French kissing. The rabbi scared me, but he didn't deter me from trying. Nothing could.

I didn't expect to meet Bayleh Zuckman again behind the barn. I wasn't even sure I wanted to. But when school ended the next day, I walked up the passageway to the decaying barn. She wasn't there. I waited for awhile, then drifted home. I told myself she was an immoral girl and I didn't want anything more to do with such girls. But finding the right virgin took awhile.

About three months later, Duv knocked on our door one quiet Sabbath afternoon. He wasn't wearing his usual mischievous smile. "Someone told me Bayleh Zuckman had to leave Uman," he said.

I took a hold of his forearm and led him around back by the well. The chickens let out a holler. I sensed this wasn't going to be a good story and I didn't want anyone to hear us.

"What happened?" I asked.

"She's going to have a baby."

"Lord help me. Did I do it?" Pins poked at the inside of my stomach. I didn't want to be a father, not with Bayleh Zuckman.

Duv forced a smile. "You didn't even take your clothes off, did you?"

"No, but we French kissed."

"Haven't I taught you anything?" He frowned, creasing his forehead. His shoulders sagged. "You can't be the father. But I could be." I never saw Duv truly troubled until now. "I don't know what I'll do if she's pregnant. Her father and my father would make me marry her. I don't want to marry her. I don't want to marry anyone." He brushed the corner of his eye with a finger.

I put my arm around his shoulder. "It's going to be alright," I said, not certain it would be. What else could I say?

Duv was only sixteen years old, like me. We were only kids having fun. Bad things like this weren't supposed to happen when you're a kid. I didn't want to lose my best friend. But Duv violated one of God's commandments. At least I think it's one of His commandments. It's a sin, anyway.

He learned a couple of weeks later he wasn't responsible for what happened to Bayleh. The father was an older man, a cousin, from the town of Yurkivka, fifteen miles from Uman. Bayleh moved there with him. Fortunately for Duv, the baby looked just like Bayleh's husband, the proclaimed father.

Soon enough Duv was his old self again, pursuing new sins. I thought more than he did about how his life would have changed if he was the father, and how Bayleh's life had changed. She was only a year or so older than I was. Now she was married with a child on the way.

Bayleh and her husband moved back to Uman several years later but I never saw her again. Still, one never forgets his first kiss. She deserved a better ending than the one she got.

Poppa's admonishments became a part of me, often struggling with the enticements of the Bayleh Zuckmans and encouragements from Duv. Poppa won out most of the time.

SEVEN

May 1900

On New Year's Eve a new century began, but to the Jews of Uman it looked very much like the old century. The new tsar, Nicholas II, was no more a friend to us than his father had been.

As my eighteenth birthday approached, my years in school ended. By the time I finished, I knew the Torah. I read Tolstoy, Dostoyevsky, Pushkin and Shalom Aleichem. I spoke and read five languages: Hebrew, Yiddish, Russian, French and a little bit of English. Jeremiah told me I was the best student he ever had.

I wanted to go to the university, but they didn't admit any Jews that year. My boyhood Christian friend, Sergey Shumenko, got admitted and I knew I was much smarter than he was. I was angry for awhile, left without a direction. So I went to work with Poppa in his tailor shop. Tailoring satisfied me, but I didn't want to live out my days like him in the monotony and misery of Uman.

Duv, Simon and Lieb were all working too. We were now old enough to visit the tavern and have a whiskey with the other men of the village. Most of them were Jews, but some were poorer gentiles who lived on our side of the river. We tolerated each other but they sat at pockmarked tables in their end of the room and we sat at ones in our end.

Beams and cross-beams supported the tavern's low ceiling, its old wooden walls sagging in places. It reeked of beer, onions and men's stale sweat. The tavern was where we learned the latest gossip, heard about the news of the world, and witnessed debates about problems of the Uman Jews.

Ester's girlfriends visited our house more often. When they did, they looked at me, giggled, and flirted. Ester told me they thought I was handsome. Momma and Poppa encouraged me to take a look at these girls but I didn't want everyone in the family knowing my business. I was still looking for another willing girl like Bayleh Zuckman.

Momma and Poppa worried that Ester hadn't found a husband yet. She was nearly seventeen years old. Lieb hadn't found anyone either, though there was no hurry for him. He was even more awkward than me, skinny and funny looking.   He wore glasses now which accented his big nose and ears.

The myth of my Duvid and Goliath encounter with Viktor Askinov grew larger every year, just like the biblical myth. But it was only one lucky shot delivered on fear and impulse. I prayed I wouldn't need to face a challenge from Viktor Askinov ever again. He continued to harass our family, getting bolder and bolder: Dead fish, a torn up vegetable garden, a wood pile set on fire. On occasion he stalked Markus, Ester, Zelda and their friends. He was a vulture, waiting for me to be wounded so he could swoop down.

He grew into a muscular young man, bigger and more powerful than me. He and his best friend, Igor Czajkowsko, were in training to join the police force. That prospect frightened me.

One sunny springtime morning I worked at the sewing machine by the window like I often did. Poppa was fitting a dress on the mannequin. Every once in a while I looked out the window to break the tedium.

Legions of scruffy beggars were becoming a more frequent sight. This one beggar moving down the dusty street toward us didn't look much different from the others. His greying hair was long and unkempt, like his bushy beard. I wouldn't have recognized him except for the army duffle bag and riding boots.

"My god, its Uncle Yakov," I screamed, shooting from my chair. I exploded out the door toward him. "Uncle Yakov." I waved and ran toward him. He opened one arm to me, the other hanging limply at his side. A sad smile crossed his lips. When I reached him I threw my arms around him, buried my head in his shoulder, and cried.

"Avi. Avi," he said softly. He patted the back of my head. Poppa ran up behind me and spread his arms around both of us.

"The Lord be praised," Poppa said. "We thought you were dead."

"I was," he said quietly.

I picked up his duffle bag and carried it home. Poppa locked up the shop and followed us. I laughed and chattered all the way. Uncle Yakov said little. He plodded along, struggling to keep up with me. I slowed my pace.

The bags under his eyes were black, his eyes glazed and ringed with red. He was so thin I felt his bones when I hugged him. I couldn't take my eyes off his left arm hanging by his side.

Momma screamed when she saw him. Ester and Zelda threw themselves at him. A few minutes later Markus and Lieb burst through the door. Everyone in the village heard about it when Uncle Yakov was lost, and everyone heard when he returned.

I helped him take off his riding boots. He threw them in a corner of the front room, and put on some peasant shoes. Those once-shiny boots now looked like any beggar's, scarred and dull. The only sign he was a soldier was the red, white and blue medal, the Tsar's Own Heroes, in his lapel. For dinner that night, Momma broke into her Sabbath reserve. But this dinner wasn't like the first time. The rest of us jabbered away. Uncle Yakov said little, eating mechanically. I told him about my encounter with Viktor Askinov. Lieb and Markus embellished the story. "Good," he said in a monotone, like he hadn't been listening. Soon we all ran out of things to say.

We asked him to go to synagogue with us on the Sabbath but he declined. I prayed hard to God, thanked him for returning Uncle Yakov to us, and begged Him to help Uncle Yakov get well.

I was feeling sorry for myself, and angry. I had waited three and a half years for his return. Now this stranger shows up. But my Uncle Yakov was hiding inside of this man, and I was going to get him back.

In the days that followed, Uncle Yakov spent most of the time staring into space, lost in his own thoughts. Sometimes he went out back and sat by the well. It was quiet and secluded there, shaded by an oak tree. He talked little, he talked quietly, and forced empty smiles.

Sometimes I sat down beside him at the well and talked about nothing much. He occasionally said something trivial or touched me with his good right arm. He tried to hide his feeble one. I asked him now and then if he would like to take a walk by the stream near Sukhi Yar. "Not today," he always replied.

"You're helping him," Poppa said one afternoon when I came into the house with a long face. "Don't give up. He needs you." If it hadn't been for Poppa, I would have given up. I was afraid for Uncle Yakov, but didn't know what to do.

Poppa wrote to General Petrov as soon as Uncle Yakov arrived to tell him he was with us and the condition he was in. The general's long letter to Uncle Yakov arrived six weeks later. When Poppa gave it to him, he stuffed it in his pocket. He never told us what was in the letter, but from the moment the letter arrived Uncle Yakov began pulling himself together. It happened so gradually I didn't notice for awhile.

One afternoon soon after General Petrov's letter arrived, I asked Uncle Yakov if he wanted to play chess. I didn't even know if he could play. Jeremiah taught me when I was about thirteen or fourteen, and soon I was beating him regularly. I beat everyone.

"Let's play." His voice was a little stronger. We sat at the kitchen table, neither of us saying much, concentrating on our game. He wouldn't yield and I wouldn't yield. We played all afternoon until shadows began to lengthen. Then he raised his eyes from the board and trained them on me.

"You're very good. But I will beat you!" His voice rose, strong and threatening. He eyes looked deranged, his teeth bared. He unsettled me and threw me off my game. A few moves later and he had me in check mate.

"Intimidation. It's part of the game." He smiled, satisfied, the first genuine smile since he returned. This was the one time I didn't mind losing. We played almost every day after that. Sometimes he won. Sometimes I won. He didn't intimidate me again.

He still didn't talk much but he didn't spend all day staring into space any more either. He trimmed his beard and hair. He didn't look like a solder, but he no longer looked like a beggar. I made a new shirt and pants for him at the shop. He wore them all the time.

Uncle Yakov made friends with other army veterans at a tavern in the poor gentile part of Uman, on our side of the river. He found companionship with other Jewish men at our tavern. He spent a lot of time in these two taverns. Word got back to us he was also visiting with a gentile woman named Leitz. She was a pleasant, plump, childless widow.

Every now and then he wrote to General Petrov and the General wrote to him. Uncle Yakov's mood improved whenever a letter arrived. He read me some of the interesting parts.

His smile and good humor emerged. He visited the tailor shop from time to time for no other reason than to be with us. He tried to help out in small ways but his withered arm annoyed him. He took to smoking a pipe because he couldn't roll cigarettes with only one good hand. Watching him load a pipe frustrated me. I wanted to take it from him and do it myself, but Poppa cautioned me not to.

Uncle Yakov made no secret he had not come to terms with God. He doubted there was a God, but if there was one, he was mad at Him. Nonetheless, our Jewish traditions made him feel he belonged somewhere. He rarely went to Sabbath services at the synagogue, but he never missed a Sabbath meal at our house.

Until now, I didn't talk much about Viktor Askinov to Uncle Yakov. But Viktor Askinov's threats were growing. So I asked him again to take a walk by the stream at Sukhi Yar.

"Not today." He paused. Then he smiled like my old Uncle Yakov. "Ask me again tomorrow. I'll say yes." He laughed at his little joke.

The next afternoon was clear and blue but the ground approaching Sukhi Yar squished under our feet from the recent rain. He struggled like an old man when we came to a slope, not the powerful strides of the soldier he was the last time we came here. His arms no longer swung freely at his sides. His left one was tucked into his left pants pocket, useless.

"I'm not the youngster I was." He paused at the top of one

small rise to catch his breath.

We labored past the ravine to the stream, and sat down on the same moss-covered tree stump we sat on years before. The morning sun warmed me, but an occasional dark cloud promised afternoon showers. The air smelled fresh as a cucumber just picked. Two crows screamed. Occasionally I threw a stone in the creek. He threw one at a tree, and missed. He grunted, maybe in mild frustration.

I told him about my fight with Viktor Askinov, and that he wouldn't stop harassing us. "Duvid never had this problem when he defeated Goliath," I said.

"Duvid cut off Goliath's head. You didn't. Someday you may have to." He rubbed the shoulder of his bad arm with the hand of his good one.

"Everyone thinks I'm brave, but I'm not. I just got mad. I didn't know what I was doing. If I'd thought about it, I wouldn't have done it"

"No one's brave. We do brave things to protect ourselves sometimes. Or someone we love. If we thought about it, nobody would do it."

"So what do I do?"

"Are you still afraid of Viktor Askinov/"

"Not like I used to be."

"You have courage. But courage isn't what you thought it was. You'll have it when you need it."

I nodded. I wasn't going to get any more from him, so I rose to leave. He sat a moment longer.

"I'm proud of you... what you did," he said. A rush ran through me.

He reached out his good hand for me to help him up. He moaned as I pulled.

He hadn't told me what to do about Viktor Askinov. But he

did something better. He told me he was proud of me. I'd get him to tell me what to do about Viktor Askinov some other day.

We went to Sukhi Yar nearly every day that summer. We wandered the fields, sat by the stream, hid in the clearing, or examined the big ravine. Each visit he got a little stronger until he was marching like he did before, leaving me scampering to keep up.

We talked about many things, much of it of no consequence. But every now and then he shared some little bit about himself he probably didn't share with anyone else.

When he talked about General Petrov, he spoke of loyalty. "There's nothing more important. Friends, family, and some day a wife. Once you've earned it, don't squander it. The currency is too high." This became my eleventh commandment.

He was still angry with God, the Tsar and the Mongolians who shot him. "I can forgive those bastards for trying to kill me," he said, a quiver in his voice. "But I can't forgive them for making me kill them." I doubted I could ever feel that way about Viktor Askinov.

He even told me about a special woman he met wandering Siberia after he was wounded. He lived with her for awhile, and she nursed him back to health. I think he loved her, but he said he was too full of mean spirit to be with a good woman like her. "So I moved on," he said. He was quiet the rest of the day.

I don't know what moved Uncle Yakov to share such intimacies with his eighteen year old nephew. It was a lot for a young man like me to comprehend. But by the end of the summer I understood my love for Uncle Yakov carried responsibilities as well as privileges. And I understood if there was one person I could rely on for anything, it was Uncle Yakov.

When the new year arrived, he was again a man, but never again the man he was before. He still relished good food, plump women, and a warm, clean bed. He moved out of our house and went to live as a boarder with the gentile woman, Leitz. He never talked about her or acknowledged their arrangement as anything more than a boarder paying rent. Everyone knew better. Thanks to General Petrov, his army pension provided enough for him to live modestly.

Though he moved out of our house, his riding boots remained in the corner of our front room, waiting.

EIGHT

May 1901

Lieb surprised everyone when he announced he and Golde Skolnick were getting married. He was only twenty-one years old. Golde was a pleasant girl, though a bit hefty, with plain brown hair and dull brown eyes. She would rule their household, but she would take good care of Lieb.

Their wedding day was one of the first good days of spring. Lieb and Golde stood under the canopy to say their vows and prayers. They loved each other and for one of the few times in my life I envied my big brother. I wondered if I would ever find someone to love and to love me. A couple of attractive young ladies were possibilities but they intimidated me.

Our whole village was there, in their finest Sabbath clothes. Jeremiah came by himself. Though still in his early thirties, a few strands of grey dotted his dark hair, and a few wrinkles creased his flawless face. All the young women still fell madly in love with him, but he still paid no attention. By now everyone knew about the *shiksa* girlfriend he lived with. In a different time and place, he might have married her. Here it was forbidden by both Jews and Christians. Jewish parents disowned their children if they married outside the faith, mourning them as if they were dead.

Poppa and Momma would never do that.

We celebrated all day long. The tables sagged under the mountains of food and drink. The village band played and people danced, sometimes men with men and women with women. Sometimes men and women together. Things were changing.

I never let Zelda out of my sight all day. Rumors floated which could embarrass the family and make it impossible for her to attract a good husband. So while I was trying to consume the wedding, I was also keeping Zelda caged.

My little seventeen year old sister worried Momma and Poppa with her independent ways. Where Ester was gentle and warm, Zelda was feisty and independent. And where Ester was ordinary looking, with protruding teeth and coarse hair, Zelda caught men's attention. Who knows where her curly red locks, dark green eyes, and sculpted body came from?

When the sun went down, we lifted Golde and Lieb onto chairs and paraded them through the crowd until I felt my arms would break.

After the wedding, Lieb moved in with Golde's parents like all newlyweds in the village. I still saw him often, and sometimes he and Golde came for our Sabbath meal. But it wasn't the same as having him there all the time. Our house seemed so empty.

Starting that summer of 1901, every time I picked up a newspaper it announced a protest, strike or riot somewhere in Russia. Everyone had a complaint with the Tsar: intelligentsia, peasants, workers, Poles, and Finns. On the opposite side were those ready to attack anyone who disagreed with the Tsar about anything. With secret support from the authorities, gangs clubbed and intimidated the opposition.

The more the disturbances went on, the more the government clamped down. Some of the unrest seeped into Uman. Viktor

Askinov was always ready for any opportunity to wield a club, particularly now that he had the cover of a police cadet.

Uncle Yakov paid attention again to the world outside Uman. He knew what was happening in other parts of Russia even before it appeared in the newspapers. He had his network of army veterans and his contact with General Petrov. They exchanged letters frequently. Once Uncle Yakov went to Kiev to see him on one of the General's official trips. He had received another promotion and now commanded a cavalry division near Tsaritsyn.

Uncle Yakov saw me reading a book one day about America. "Soon we'll have to make some hard choices," he said.

"Poppa ignores all the bad news." I was getting frustrated with Poppa. He acted like he had given up.

"Making no decision is a decision."

"What should we do?"

"I don't know yet. Maybe America." He pointed a finger on his good hand toward my book. "Or join the Bund. Maybe go to Palestine."

"Pray the Tsar treats us better?" I said sarcastically.

"That's what most Jews in Uman will do." I wondered if he was talking about Poppa.

Only a few people I knew had gone to *Eretz Ysrael*, though the Zionists were recruiting vigorously. The Bund was a different story. Jeremiah told me at Lieb's wedding he had joined. "There aren't many members yet in Uman, but it's growing," he said.

The Bund was a political party and a labor union, determined to earn acceptance for Jews in Russia. It tried to increase support by uniting with the larger Social Democratic Labor Party, the first Marxist party in Russia. Most of the Bund members were workers and artisans, like carpenters and craftsmen, but some were intelligentsia and idealists like Jeremiah. I didn't know where I would fit in but I craved anything that offered hope for something better. These people were fighters, not meek like most Jews. If Jeremiah belonged, I needed to consider it. I thought about getting Duv and Simon to join with me.

Several people I knew went to America or had relatives who had gone. Having a relative in America made you a celebrity. The men read the letters their relatives wrote home to everyone in the tavern. They described a place where Jews weren't persecuted. There were no Cossacks and no *pogroms*. Everyone was free to live anywhere they wanted and to earn a living any way they chose. They could vote. It was a land of milk, honey, and streets paved with gold. Of course to a Jew in Uman, a street paved with anything was a wonder.

Every time I heard one of these letters I felt the tug of adventure and destiny. I started paying attention to the handbills the steamship lines posted all over the village. The advertisements said their ships sailed to a life of riches and freedom. When they dropped their fares substantially, I figured we might be able to afford it.

One market day in late September I saw a well-dressed man setting up a table on the square near the tailor shop. I had heard about these agents from the steamship lines visiting other towns, but never Uman. Soon a crowd gathered around him. I noticed Duv standing near the back. Poppa was off tending to something. "Watch the shop," I said to Markus and ran to join Duv.

The agent from the steamship line was well-spoken and formal. His black pinstriped suit was immaculate, of the latest style, with a vest and a gold pocket watch on a chain. He spoke fluent Yiddish, but also English.

The agent swept his hand through the air. "The mountains are golden. Everyone can vote in America. Jobs and abundance await you if you have the courage to go."

"Even for Jews," someone yelled from the crowd.

"Yes, of course. Especially Jews," he said. "President Roosevelt has asked me to come here to Uman and personally welcome you to the United States."

There was a murmur throughout the crowd. It was unbelievable that the President of the United States would actually send someone to our town to invite Jews to come to America. It never occurred to me the agent might be making it up.

"Um…. What if speak you only not good English," I asked in English, trying to impress him. Everyone turned their heads toward me.

"Ah, you speak English. And what is your name?"

"Avi Schneider, your Excellency."

"Mr. Avi Schneider. You speak such good English you will have no problem in America."

I puffed out my chest, and strutted like a rooster. This man from the steamship company impressed me. I would have left immediately if I had the money, and if I could convince Momma and Poppa. I grabbed a brochure from his outstretched hand.

Duv and I walked toward the tavern. "America must be a very rich country if it can send a man all the way to Uman just to ask us to come there," I said.

Duv laughed. "Avi, he's a salesman. He wants to sell tickets on his ship. President Roosevelt didn't send him any more than the Tsar sent him."

"You mean none of it was true?" Duv was ruining my fantasy and I wasn't happy about it.

"It's true about America. But maybe not exactly what he said. My cousin's in America. He said it's quite a place. But it is hard work and not everything is so different from Uman." Duv saw the frown on my face. "Let's have a drink."

"I want to go to America," I said.

"I'm going. Soon."

"No." I stopped abruptly at the door of the tavern.

"My father has a nephew who went to America last year, to New York City. He asked Father to join him."

I was jealous. How could he go to America without me, his best friend. I'd be stuck in this awful place by myself. "When do you leave?" I asked.

"We have a long time," he said. "Enough for us to make a lot more mischief." He flashed that smile that promised adventure. "Father will leave in a couple of months. The rest of us will come after he finds work and a place to live. Probably in a year."

"Let me come with you."

"Of course." He punched me lightly on the shoulder. "We'll make some trouble together in America."

I didn't know how I was going to convince Momma and Poppa. I ran all the way home, and burst in the front door gasping for breath. Poppa sat in his comfortable chair by the hearth reading his prayer book and drinking tea from a glass. Momma kneaded and rolled out dough on the kitchen counter. They both startled. "You look like you just spotted the Messiah coming down the street," Momma said, putting down her rolling pin.

I should have thought more about what I was going to say, but I was in too big a hurry. I told them about the agent from the steamship company, Duv going to America and asking me to go with him. I thrust the brochure into Poppa's hand. He didn't even glance down at it.

"Such craziness, " Poppa said, pursing his lips. "Nobody's going to America."

"Why not?" I snapped. "There's nothing here in Uman for a Jew."

Poppa shook his head slowly. "We've been born and buried here for hundreds of years."

"But Poppa, there's nothing here for me except the tailor

shop, a pharaoh's slave to the likes of Madam Korolov." I paced back and forth, gesturing wildly. "Someone like Viktor Askinov or the Constable will always be there to make life miserable."

"Stop already. You are obsessed with this Viktor Askinov. Make your peace with him."

I looked over at Momma, hoping she would intervene for me. But she kept her head down, and kept rolling out the dough and cutting it into little squares.

I didn't know what to say; Poppa filled the silence. "You think America is so wonderful? The streets aren't paved with gold like you think. They hate Jews there too." He slammed his glass on the little table so hard I thought it would break.

"But you don't know anything about America."

"The devil you know is better than the one you don't. This is where we'll wait for the Messiah."

"Next year in Jerusalem," I mocked. "For how many centuries have we been saying that? It's not going to happen, Poppa."

"Don't say that!" Poppa waved his prayer book at me. "In America it's all about money, not God. There they've forgotten the Torah."

"Poppa, please. I don't want to live my life afraid of a knock on the door or another *pogrom*. I want a chance."

"We're not going to America and that's the end of it." He threw the brochure from the steamship line on the floor. Then he picked up the prayer book and began reading again.

I sighed dramatically. Neither Momma nor Poppa looked at me. "I'm going to feed the chickens," I said.

The laundry Momma had done this morning was flapping on the clothes line near the now-barren vegetable garden. I seethed. Poppa was so stubborn. He wouldn't fight and he wouldn't move. He just submitted to whatever the gentiles did to him.

I threw some grain to the chickens, and then heard the door

close. Momma came around the side of the house carrying an empty wicker basket. She started taking the laundry down from the clothes line. I went over to help her.

"We're getting older," she said, wadding up a bed sheet and putting it in the basket. "Change scares us. There's comfort in the familiar. The synagogue, our friends, the tailor shop. Poppa's father worked there, and this house is where Poppa grew up."

"But Momma, I want the chance to see the world outside Uman. I want a chance for something better than this."

"You have to understand your poppa. Tradition is how we get through the day." She concentrated on taking down the laundry and putting it in the basket, never looking directly at me. "His momma and poppa are buried in our cemetery. He visits their graves. He says Kaddish for them. He wants you to do the same for him. That's the way it's always been for him."

"Momma, what do I do?"

She stopped taking the laundry down. She put her arms around me, hugging me close to her like she did when I was a little boy with a hurt.

"You must go, and he must stay," she said softly into my ear.

I had never fought with Poppa like this. It was disrespectful and I knew it. My insides churned. When I went into the house to apologize, he was still sitting in his chair. He smiled. "You're a good boy, Avi," he said, patting my hand. I put my arms around him and kissed the top of his head.

I wish I understood then that Poppa had his own kind of courage. He survived the way Jews survived for two thousand years, engulfed by hatred. How hard it must have been for him to see his wife and children lashed by intolerance. There were so many of the oppressors and so few of us. We were powerless, and there was no where to hide.

But Jews like Poppa were obstinate. He and the others could

have given in and accepted Christianity. It would have made life a lot easier. He refused.

I probably would have left for America with Duv when the time came. But sometimes there is a larger plan than our own.

NINE

April 1902

I saw her for the first time in the early sun of an April morning.

The first good weather brought out crowds of peddlers and shoppers on market day. Stalls overflowed with food, house wares, clothes, books, stuffed dolls and every imaginable treat. The tree in front of the synagogue blossomed, the air smelled like violets.

Simon and I snuck away from work for a few hours. We wandered through the stalls, looked over the merchandise for sale, and inspected every young woman we passed. Most girls were either not attractive enough for my taste, or too attractive. The former repelled me and the later intimidated me. The few I met at weddings and synagogue that fell between the two extremes bored me in no time.

The rugalah in one stall attracted Simon. I waited for him to pick out just the right one. He could ponder such choices forever. I scanned the crowd for something more interesting. There by a vegetable cart across the way, this gorgeous young lady fixed her eyes on me.

Her hair shined like gold in the morning light, her eyes as

soft as clouds in a blue sky. Her innocent smile captured me. Our eyes locked. I smiled back. Every nerve in my body quivered. I had to get to her before Simon or anyone else could get to her, but a wall of shoppers blocked me.

I started toward her without thinking, set to force my way through. But, thanks be to Moses, the crowd parted like the Red Sea. Her blue eyes grew wider and wider the closer I got; her smile invited me to come and get her.

"Hello, I'm Avi Schneider." I said.

"I'm Sara Kravetz."

I'd never talked so effortlessly to an attractive young woman before. We began a long conversation though I can't remember a thing we talked about. I tried not to stare, but her drab grey dress couldn't hide her ample breasts and hips. Instead I examined her perfect ivory teeth and full lips. A few freckles punctuated her fair skin. A grey headscarf pulled her golden hair behind her ears.

I hardly noticed she had a girlfriend standing next to her. When Simon caught up, he and Sara's friend talked politely to each other. Sara and I didn't pay any attention to them. Simon later told me the girlfriend was boring, but he said all girls were boring.

We walked around the market, chatting aimlessly. I don't know whether we walked and talked for fifteen minutes or two hours. Occasionally our shoulders bumped when the crowd pushed us into each other. The touch sent a shiver all through me. She was totally unaware of the lustful looks men gave her, and the envious looks they gave me.

"This was nice, but I've got to go now."

"Will I see you at market next week?" I asked. The fear she might say no turned my throat into a desert. I stuck my hands in my pockets trying not to look too eager.

"I'll try." There was that inviting smile. I knew she meant it.

"But Father doesn't always allow it."

"You must come. I'll meet you right here, at this stall at the same time." I pointed at the rows of assorted eggplant, tomatoes, potatoes and green beans. She smiled again and nodded, but I didn't know what the nod meant.

Simon and I watched Sara and her friend walk away. I couldn't hear what they were saying but they had their heads together, giggling. I knew nothing about her except her name. Sara Kravetz.

"What happened to you?" Simon said. "You look like a man who's just found a gold ruble."

All week long I could think of nothing but Sara Kravetz. She seemed to like me a lot. But she wouldn't commit to seeing me. Why not? Maybe she didn't like me as much as I thought. I had to see her again, no matter what.

The night before market day I lay awake most of the night. I worried Sara wouldn't come. Why should she come when a beautiful girl like that could have any young man in Uman?

The next morning I put on my best work-day shirt, cleaned my boots of the week's accumulation of dirt, scrubbed my face and hands raw, and combed my hair three times until it was perfect. I checked myself in the mirror over and over again.

It was so early farmers and peddlers were only now setting up their wooden stalls and wheeling in their aged carts. I worried she may not come. Then I worried I would look too eager if I got there before she did. So I wandered over to the bakery where Lieb worked and chatted with him for awhile. If Lieb noticed my strange behavior, he didn't say anything.

When it was time, I hurried to the vegetable stall where we were to meet. She wasn't there. It felt like I had swallowed a rock. I waited a few minutes, then turned to leave, shivering with disappointment. What made me ever think a beautiful girl like her would be interested in someone as ordinary as me.

"Avi. Over here," she called from in front of the general store. I turned and saw her pushing through the crowd toward me. When she got to me, I wanted to grab her and kiss her right there, but that would cause a catastrophe. So I smiled as broad a smile as I could.

"I was afraid you wouldn't come." I said, trying not to show my feelings. Her soft blue eyes fixed on me. She's as glad to see me as I am to see her, I thought. The copper in her golden hair glistened in the morning sun. The same plain headscarf pulled her hair back behind her ears.

"Momma needed candles," she said, holding up a bag. "I didn't have no better excuse to come than that."

"Let me carry it for you." She handed the bag to me, holding on long enough for our hands to brush against each other. The look in her eyes and her wet lips set me on fire again from the top of my head to the bottom of my toes.

"This is my brother Josef." He was there to chaperone, even if he wasn't any older than Markus. Josef was a pleasant looking boy, pudgy like with baby fat. I saw some family resemblance to Sara even though his hair and eyes were brown. He had the long Hassidic sideburns and the down on his face anticipated a coming beard. A tailor's son like me would notice his patched black coat, pants above his ankles and beaten up black hat. He was trying to look grown up but instead he looked like a little boy wearing his father's clothes.

Josef was as unpretentious and friendly as Sara. The three of us drifted toward the outer rows of stalls where it was less crowded. I bought a handful of roasted chestnuts from an old lady and gave them to him. He stayed right by us but immersed himself in eating the chestnuts and eyeing other treats in the stalls. Sara made me feel comfortable talking to her, not like with other girls my age.

We hardly noticed Josef, but I wanted to talk to Sara without big ears listening. I had planned all week what I would say to impress her and make her like me. "Here's five kopeks," I said, placing the coins in Josef's hand. "Why don't you buy yourself some sweets."

Sara looked amused as he bounded off. "I think you made a friend," she said.

"I like him." I meant it but I also wanted to gain her favor. Sara's affection for Josef was obvious.

"He doesn't cause no trouble." She laughed.

As we walked, people in the crowd occasionally pushed us into each other. We lingered for a moment, our shoulders or hands touching. She looked at me with eyes that twinkled.

"Poppa owns the tailor shop right over there." I pointed. "I'm a tailor too. Even some gentile men come over from the other side of the river to have me make them suits."

"I live with Mother and Father. My sister Havol's a year younger than me."

I told her about my parents, my brothers and sisters, where I lived, and boasted about all the books I read. I bragged that Poppa owned our house, and mentioned all of the chickens we owned.

"We don't own anything," she said without envy. "Father's a day laborer. Sometimes he does carpenter work, digs ditches or helps the blacksmith." I noticed the hole in Sara's stockings and the worn sweater.

"It's hard work," I said.

"He's not getting any younger." I loved the sound of her voice. As she talked, she described herself without intending to. She was an obedient daughter, her parents depended on her, and she wanted to please them. She worked hard.

Josef wandered back licking his lips, finishing a bun he was eating "Want some?" he asked, holding it out. "I already had one." He looked at me like he wanted to say something but was hesitant. "You're the Avi Schneider who beat up that gentile kid, aren't ya'."

"I am." I tried to sound modest but I wanted to impress Sara too. "It wasn't such a big thing."

"Was so," Josef said.

"Now you're his hero," Sara said. She grabbed his hat and messed up his hair. Josef snatched it back.

We strolled to the well near the synagogue and talked some more. "I'll try to come next week," she said when it was time to go.

"I don't even know where you live." I couldn't wait a week to see her again.

"Not far. On Pushkin Street, around the corner from that synagogue." She pointed toward my synagogue with her long, slender finger. "Our house is on the right side, two doors past the tavern."

"I know where it is. I walk by there almost every day," I lied. "I pick up and deliver things for the shop. Maybe I'll see you."

Her eyes opened wide and her lips curled in a perfect smile. "That would be nice. I'll watch for you. When do you usually go by?" I couldn't believe she was so eager.

"Early afternoon most of the time." I tried to act casual.

She glided away as though she was skating on ice. When she got to the end of the square, she looked back and waved goodbye. I couldn't believe this was happening to me.

When I passed the beggar who usually occupied the best spot in the corner of the market, I dropped five kopeks into his outstretched hand. Usually I only gave him two. "Ah, maybe you are in love with that beautiful young lady," he said, baring his rotten teeth and the spaces where others had once been.

I had never given much thought to love, what it was or where it might lead. But I had never felt like this before, even with Bayleh Zuckman. And no girl ever responded to me like Sara had. Then self-doubt invaded.

I needed to see her and I needed a way to mark her as mine. So I decided to walk by her house every day until I saw her again. And I would make her a beautiful headscarf to replace her drab ones.

I wanted to take that walk right away, but the Sabbath was coming on, so I had to wait. At synagogue services, I felt all eyes staring at me, just like the beggar did. The whole congregation must have known I was in love.

Duv sat next to me and made his usual remarks about the rabbi, but I was lost in my own thoughts. "What's the matter with you?" he asked. "Are you feeling okay?" I nodded without answering. He must have known. I was embarrassed.

Simon joined us for Sabbath dinner. He had been coming over to our house a lot more lately. Maybe it was because Duv was getting ready to go to America and Simon was taking his place in my life.

Duv was exciting to be around. Simon was comfortable. With Duv, I always felt there was more going on beneath the surface than he allowed anyone to see. With Simon, there was nothing going on beneath the surface. He was a good person who didn't much like Duv's morals, but he rarely let it hamper our friendships. Though probably as smart as me, he never competed. Simon was the only person I knew who was as impatient to learn as I was. His ambitions were quiet ones, unlike mine. Maybe what I liked most about Simon was his loyalty to me and my family.

Before we sat down for dinner, Simon whispered the same

question Duv had asked. "Are you feeling okay?" He must have known too, but I hadn't seen Simon since my first meeting with Sara at the marketplace. "The girl you met was beautiful," he said. "I think she likes you."

At dinner, Simon sat between Ester and me; Marcus and Zelda sat next to each other across the table. They kept looking at me out of the corners of their eyes, whispering and giggling. Did they know too? It was as though everyone could look into my mind and see my silly thoughts and childish feelings. If Sara decided she didn't like me after all, it would be humiliating.

First I tried to ignore Marcus and Zelda. Then I got cross at them, but they kept on with the whispering and giggling.

"Stop it," I shouted.

"Avi, no such talk on the Sabbath," Momma scolded. "Zelda and Markus, that's enough."

They covered their mouths to suppress their laughs but they didn't really stop. Simon and Ester exchanged looks and smiled. Momma and Poppa pretended not to notice my condition. I finished supper and got up from the table as quickly as I could. I was all out of kilter. My whole life was out of kilter. I thought of little else but Sara.

The day after the Sabbath I went to the tailor shop early and picked out the prettiest material I could find. The cheery green and blue paisley would look wonderful as a scarf. I made a pattern from one of Ester's and was at the sewing machine when Poppa walked in.

"For that girl?" He stood over me while I worked at the sewing machine.

"It's just a scarf."

"Don't get ahead of yourself," he warned, a trace of reproach in his voice. "You have responsibilities here."

I didn't think my behavior had been so noticeable. People

probably saw us at the market together. And the old ladies had nothing to do but gossip. I felt as embarrassed as if I had been discovered behind the barn with Bayleh Zuckman.

When I finished the scarf, I wanted to rush over to Sara's house and give it to her. But I told her I passed by in the early afternoon and it was still only mid-morning. I busied myself around the shop, finishing a skirt I had been working on. When the time came, I folded the scarf and placed it carefully in my coat pocket. I mumbled a quick "I'll be back shortly" and left the shop.

All the houses on Pushkin Street sagged so badly they looked like they might fall over in a good wind. Wooden shingles had come off nearly every roof. Chickens wandered freely through the missing slats in the picket fences.

Pity for these poor people mixed inside me with a few grains of superiority. We were much better off than them. It didn't seem like the kind of place someone as lovely as Sara would be living.

I tried to walk slowly and casually, but I was eager and anxious. A lot of shouting came from the tavern two doors down from Sara's. It was only early afternoon but some men already had drunk their fill. A couple of cats screamed at each other around the side of the tavern, the skinny black one trying to mount an unwilling calico. The female ran off. The male sat down, nonchalant, as if embarrassed but pretending to the world that it didn't care.

Sara's house looked no better than the others. I slowed my pace to a crawl as I got closer. No one was outside.

Then Josef came from behind the house carrying a bucket of water. He smiled and waved. "Sara's been waiting on you. I'll get her." He disappeared in the front door. I leaned against the fence; it swayed like it was going to fall down. I let go. Sheets hanging on their clothesline had holes in them.

The door opened and Sara bounded down the steps. Her feet barely touched the ground. She stopped with the picket fence between us. If she wasn't perfectly proper, the whole village would start talking.

"I was hoping you'd come," she said. "I've been looking out the window, afraid maybe I missed you... on your delivery." She winked.

"Oh, yes, the delivery. There was no delivery." I fumbled in my pocket. "Except this." I pulled out the scarf with a flourish and handed it to her.

She took it, examined it carefully and rubbed the fine cloth between her fingers. She raised a hand and touched the rough grey headscarf she was wearing.

Her gorgeous blue eyes sparkled. "It's nice. You made it, didn't you?" she asked.

I nodded. "In the shop."

"Then I love it even more." My hand rested on one of the posts in the picket fence. She placed her hand on top of mine. I pushed the top of my hand against the bottom of hers. I wanted to grab her in my arms and kiss her, but of course I couldn't.

"I love it.... But I can't wear it."

"Why not?" My heart dropped. My face must have shown my dejection.

"This is the Hassidic part of town." She looked serious for the first time since I met her. "We're Hassidic. We don't wear bright colors." She moved her hand off mine and caressed the scarf. "But I'll keep it close to me."

This was a calamity. The Hassidics hated us almost as much as the gentiles did. They thought we Haskalah were heretics, unworthy Jews who could never earn God's good graces. And we ridiculed them as ignorant, their beliefs nothing more than superstitions. The gulf couldn't be bigger.

"Did you know I'm Haskalah?" I asked. My hands went into my pockets and her hands went into hers.

"I guess so."

"Does it make a difference?"

She examined the scarf. I waited. "No it don't. Does it to you?"

"Not at all," I said, but the vinegar in my voice caused a shadow of grey to cross her face. It did in fact make a difference, to her and to me. Nonetheless, I wasn't about to end it there.

The front door to her house flew open and a girl a little younger than Sara stomped down the steps. "That's my sister Havol," Sara said.

Havol was pretty like Sara, but taller with darker hair. She had none of Sara's appeal. They looked much alike except where Sara always wore a smile, Havol scowled, as sour as vinegar.

"Havol, this is Avi Schneider," Sara said.

Havol glanced at me and fixed back on Sara. "Mother says you come in the house right now." Josef told me later Havol was always jealous because everyone liked Sara and no one liked Havol.

"I'll be right in," Sara said. Havol stomped back up the steps. "Will I see you on market day?" she asked.

"I must see you." Our hands touched again. She turned to go into the house and I walked back toward the tailor shop. As I neared the tavern, I turned around and saw Sara on her front steps waving goodbye, awash in sunshine. I waved back and walked on, a little less bounce in my step.

I should have known as soon as I met her that she was Hassidic, but she blinded me. What difference did it make? None to me, I told myself. But maybe a lot to her and her mother and father. And maybe it would test Momma and Poppa's generous attitudes more than I expected. Poppa seemed more ready to

understand Christians' thinking than to tolerate the Hassidic inter-
pretation of God's law.

I believed I was open minded and enlightened, accepting everyone. It took many years for me to see my own intolerances as
part of the religious zeal that divides people from each other,
whether Christians from Jews or Jews from other Jews. Right
now my own religious zealotry prepared itself to scorch me.

TEN

June 1902

We met again the next week on market day. It rained hard in the early morning, but stopped by the time the peddlers and farmers started setting up their stalls and pushcarts. The sun reflected off the puddles of water. I stepped in every one of them, oblivious to everything but Sara. She avoided every one without even looking down.

Neither of us talked any more about religion. Her mother, Rivka Kravetz, chaperoned this day. She gave me a pleasant greeting when we met, but no smile. She sounded so tired. Sara's simple clothes accented her beauty, but on her mother they punctuated her poverty. She wore a scarf over her head like Sara's with a little of the same golden hair showing in front and back. Many Hasidic women shaved their heads on their wedding day and kept it that way for the rest of their lives. Thank goodness Rivka Kravetz wasn't like that.

Sara looked much like her. Mother Kravetz at one time surely had been as pretty as Sara, but if she ever had Sara's cheerfulness, it died. Her shoulders and face were weary. The deep etches crossing her brow and around her eyes made her look much older than she was.

Mother Kravetz stayed close as we strolled among the stalls. She stopped now and then to examine the fruit carefully before buying a few pieces. She chose the damaged ones, then haggled aggressively with the farmer until he gave up. She made little conversation with me, and I was too afraid of doing something clumsy to say anything. Sara and I never stopped talking.

When her mother stopped at a stall, Sara motioned for me to follow her around a corner. She pulled part of the scarf I made from her pocket to show me she had it with her. "I love it." Her eyes sparkled and her smile flashed. She stuffed the scarf back in her pocket when she saw her mother coming.

For the next three weeks, I stopped by her house briefly every few days. It wasn't much but it carried me over till market day when we could be together longer. One week Havol chaperoned, then her friend Ida, and Mother Kravetz again. With those three hovering, Sara and I didn't have many private moments. She didn't seem to mind. I was frustrated.

Loneliness invaded when I wasn't with her. I imagined what life with Sara might be like. Our religious differences snuck in now and then, but every time Sara and I met I fell a little more in love with her. I suspected she shared the feelings. She carried my scarf in her pocket or tucked under her blouse all the time. We both talked as though we assumed we would keep on seeing each other.

By now the whole village knew Sara and I were involved. Each week at the market square, she met someone else important in my life: Ester, Markus, Zelda, Jeremiah, Duv and Simon. Sara was so friendly and comfortable with them you would have thought she knew them all her life. They all teased me after, wondering how a girl like that could be interested in a *shmo* like me. I wondered the same thing.

Duv of course admired Sara's ample breasts and behind.

"Wow, she's big," he said, cupping both hands in front of him like he was grasping two melons.

She took to Uncle Yakov and him to her. I never imagined Uncle Yakov could be so shy, or Sara could be so flirtatious.

Six weeks after I met Sara, on my twentieth birthday I took her to the tailor shop to introduce her to Momma and Poppa. I told them before hand she was a Hassidic girl. They hadn't said much about it. Momma welcomed Sara graciously. Poppa explained to her how his sewing machine worked. He had her sit down and showed her how to operate it. "Look Avi. Look what I did." She held up a piece of scrap material with a ragged stitch across it.

A couple of days later Lieb and I had a drink during the day. The tavern was empty except for the two of us and two men sitting at a table across the room.

"So do you like Sara?" I asked.

"What's there not to like? She's very nice. And she's very pretty."

"What did Momma and Poppa think?"

Lieb took a swallow of his beer from his tin cup. "They like her. Everyone does. But they're worried."

"About what?"

"First of all, they don't want to see you hurt."

"Because she is Hassidic?"

"Don't get me wrong. You know in the end Momma and Poppa will love whoever you love."

"But they wish she was Haskalah. Don't they?" I was getting upset, with Lieb and with Momma and Poppa.

"In the end they only want you to be happy. And how can you argue with that?"

"I am happy!" I smacked my hand down on the table. The men at the other table turned and looked at us.

Lieb kept his composure. "How about her father? What does he say?" He drained the rest of his beer and wiped his sleeve across his mouth. "Those Hassidic fathers rule like the Tsar. No one in the family has anything to say but the poppa. I don't know any who let their daughters marry a Haskalah. And they raise their oldest daughter to take care of them in their old age. They demand it."

"So who's talking about marriage?" I wonder if this was the first time I really thought seriously about that possibility.

After we left the tavern, we stopped by the well at the far end of the market square before going our separate ways. "She's the nicest person I ever met," I said. "She's kind and gentle. She works hard to make everyone happy. And she doesn't even notice how beautiful she is. I think she really likes me."

"Everyone can see the way she looks at you." He laughed and patted me on the back. "Just be sure you aren't getting into something you can't get out of."

Everything had been going so well and Lieb had to ruin it. Sara didn't seem worried about her father so I pushed it out of my mind.

I had to get Sara alone and tell her how I felt, and touch her without fear someone would see us. I had to kiss her. So I told her about Sukhi Yar. "It is the most beautiful place in Uman. I want to show it to you."

"That sounds nice." She touched my hand. I thought I saw a twinkle in her blue eyes. "I'll get Josef to come with me next market day." A few kopeks was all it would take to bribe him to disappear for awhile.

The next market day, I found her waiting by the general store with Josef and one of his friends. "Let's go see Sukhi Yar," she said. "Mother and Father had to visit Mother's aunt in Pedorafski. She's sick. Havol went with them." She poked me discreetly in the ribs with her elbow.

I bought Josef and his friend a big bag of roasted chestnuts. On the way out of the market square I dropped a few kopeks in the beggar's hand. He nodded his head in thanks, and smirked.

A bunch of white geese scattered in front of us, squawking. The freshness of this morning would fade into muggy heat by afternoon. Josef and his friend ran ahead of us. As we left the edge of the village, our hands touched. I grasped her hand in mine. She turned her head, smiled and squeezed my hand back. She hummed as we walked across the field.

Sukhi Yar would never again be more perfect than it was that morning. The larks sang. Butterflies danced. Flowers perfumed the air like sugar. I wanted Sara to love Sukhi Yar like I did.

Josef came back briefly to tell us he and his friend were going down by the stream. He gave me a theatrical wink and ran off.

When we came to the top of a small rise, the vast Ukraine plain stretched in front of us, broken only by a few scattered trees, random peasants' houses, and train tracks. I stooped down and picked a bouquet of purple, yellow and white wildflowers. When I handed them to her, Sara embraced my outstretched hand with both of hers, raising the bouquet to her nose.

"They're beautiful."

"Do you like Sukhi Yar?"

"It's very nice."

"I love you," I said. It just spilled out by accident. I held my breath for an eternity.

"Oh, Avi… I love you too."

I put my arms around her and pulled her to me, never taking my eyes off hers. Then I kissed her, and she kissed me back. It was a gentle kiss, short and shy. I didn't want to ruin everything. We pulled apart, but our lips were so close together I could smell the sweetness of her breath.

"You're my first kiss," she said.

"And you're mine," I lied, hoping she had never heard about Bayleh Zuckman.

"Did I do it right?" she asked. It was the first insecurity I had seen in Sara.

"Wonderful." I kissed her again, a longer one this time. We hugged each other.

"Come," I said. "I'll show you my secret place." I pulled her by the hand toward the strand of trees. It felt like we were dancing. The delicious smell of the birch filtered the sunlight into lace. A pair of doves cooed, I swear. Or is it only in my memory.

In the clearing, I showed her the oak tree with the holes where Uncle Yakov shot at the target. She ran her finger over it. I bragged to her about my skill with the rifle, but not about my hesitancy to kill the rabbit.

We embraced again and kissed, our heat rising, and me rising. The kiss went on and on. My left hand moved down to her firm, round buttocks. She pressed closer to me. Bayleh Zuckman flitted through my mind. My right hand crept up to her breast and squeezed.

Sara pulled away, fire in her eyes. "Don't do that!" She raised her hand as though she was going to slap me, paused, and then stalked off down the path. I ran after her, desperate, afraid I'd ruined everything.

"Sara, I am so sorry. I shouldn't have done it. I won't do it again." She kept on walking. "I love you Sara. I'm sorry. I'm sorry."

She stopped but kept her back to me. "I didn't think you could do something like that," she said. "You scared me."

"I'm so sorry, Sara."

"It mustn't happen again." She wrapped her arms across her

chest.

"It won't. I promise."

She turned around and smiled tentatively. "But … you can still kiss me."

We held hands as we walked back to town from the ravine. She clutched the flowers I gave her all the way home.

Josef and his friend raced ahead of us. Sara and I talked away as though a damn had broken. We told each other intimacies about our families, our dreams and our feelings. I still guarded some of my secrets, trying hard to impress Sara with my ambitions and how smart I was. I wasn't ready yet to tell her I wanted to go to America. I didn't want to make another mistake.

We crossed an important line when we said we loved each other. I will hold that magical day in my heart till the end of my time. I didn't grasp then how fragile love can sometimes be.

ELEVEN

August 1902

I don't remember exactly when or how it started, but by August we talked as though one day we would be married.

It had been only four months since Sara and I met. We snuck away to Sukhi Yar on market day every chance we got, even when it meant bringing Havol with us. I still stopped by Sara's house at least twice a week. August mornings were fresh but by noon they were hot and muggy, often punctuated with thunder and lighting storms. This time, Josef came out to tell me Sara was at their synagogue down the street and wanted me to meet her there.

When I went in, Sara stood in the rear talking to her friend Ida and an older woman she later told me was the rabbi's wife. Sara introduced me, touching my arm possessively. I couldn't have felt more uncomfortable if I were in a church on Easter Sunday. Sara was proud of her synagogue and wanted me to take a good look. Hassidic women weren't allowed by the altar. They had a section for women in the back, cut off from view by a screen, or upstairs in a balcony.

I was surprised at how nice it was, given most Hassidics were so poor. It was in better condition than my synagogue. Some Hassidic men were praying silently in their severe black pants, jackets and hat. They didn't sweat even on such a muggy August day. The rabbi came over and tried to start a conversation with me but I cut him off. His friendliness made me uncomfortable.

Sara didn't seem to notice my rudeness toward her rabbi. She beamed when we left. "Rabbi Nachman, the famous Hassidic rabbi, taught here a hundred years ago. He's buried in our cemetery along with the people the Haidamacks killed. It's further down Pushkin Street." She pointed. "Every *Rosh Hashanah*, lots of Hassidic Jews from all over still come to visit his grave and to pray."

"I've heard." We walked slowly back toward her house. A threatening rain cloud passed over.

"If you was to go to our synagogue, you'd sit by the Eastern wall because you're so learned in the Torah." These were the most prestigious seats and went to the most important men in the congregation.

"The husband decides such matters. I will worship in my synagogue and I expect you to do the same." I locked my teeth together and thrust my hands in my pockets.

She stopped, her arms wrapped around herself, face solemn.

"I can't do that." Her voice was little more than a whisper. Tears glistened in her eyes. "Poppa won't allow it."

The sky grew darker, the breeze rustling her skirt. She held it down with her hands. I walked on toward her house. She followed.

"It can't be any other way," I said.

I was angry. It wasn't really about the religion. That didn't matter so much. But how dare she challenge me.

When we reached her house I said a curt goodbye and walked on, not turning to look back like I usually did. I didn't stop by her house the rest of the week. I missed her but I was mad. I couldn't let it go by. This tested how much she really loved me. Yet I didn't like hurting her. On market day she waited in front of the general store. I hoped she was ready to concede. No one was with her. She waved and made an effort to smile when she saw me, but her face held no joy.

"I thought you wasn't coming." Her voice strained.

"Well I came," I said, sullen enough to be sure she recognized my mood.

Josef was nearby, occupied with one of his friends. We walked to the edge of the square where it was quieter and less congested. Her blue eyes were grey. "I love you," she said softly. Sadness covered her face. "I want to make you happy. I'll do what you say."

My tight body relaxed. "I love you." I wanted to grab her but couldn't, so I touched her hand. "Thank you. I can't tell you how much this means to me."

"I hoped when you went to my synagogue you'd like it there. But I knew right away it wasn't going to be." She looked so fragile she made me feel I was being cruel.

"It must have been awful for you. I'm so grateful," I said. Her smile was more like a grimace. I should have been more concerned about Sara's feelings. Her faith was vital to her. But my position of authority was more important. I touched her lightly again. "I love you more than ever."

"And I love you." She no longer needed to prove it.

"How are you going to tell your father?"

"I'm going to need to figure it out." She put her hands in her dress pockets.

Now I worried about her father. Sara was too gentle to stand up to someone like him, or anyone.

Then I put another weight on her shoulders. I told her we would be going to America once we were married. That frightened her. I could see it all over her. Maybe it was fear of the unknown, or maybe reluctance to leave her family. Though I couldn't understand it, she loved them as much as I loved my family. But I demanded she love me more. At first she said she couldn't go to America. I insisted. There would be no discussion. She gave in to this demand as painfully as she had to my other demands.

I felt triumphant, but not satisfied. In the following days I was discontented and didn't know why. Maybe something was missing in Sara. I saw new flaws in her, but was blind to my own. In spite of my doubts, I got excited every time I saw her, and missed her every day we weren't together. I talked about her endlessly, boring everyone.

I shared everything with Duv. "So how far did you get?" was always his first question. At first I wanted to impress him with my successes with Sara, like our first kiss, but I no longer cared about that.

Sara asked so little of me or anyone. I made her a new blouse and skirt of fine material but in plain grey and brown with a simple, elegant style. Madame Shumenko helped me pick out the material and the style.

As I led her across the market square toward the tailor shop, I told her I had a surprise for her. Havol tagged along, brooding, hands shoved in her skirt pockets. Poppa welcomed both sisters warmly when we walked in. I made Sara close her eyes. When she opened them they ignited.

"Avi, they're so nice. You made them for me?"

I nodded.

Sara held it up to her front for me to examine. "I love it." She grabbed me by the arm and whispered in my ear, "I want to kiss you but it will have to wait for later." So she hugged my arm. "Havol, do you like it?"

"Yes." Havol folded her arms across her chest, lips locked.

I wrapped the skirt and blouse in coarse brown paper and tied it with some thick cord.

As soon as we closed the door to the shop behind us, Sara stopped abruptly. "Oh, I forgot something," she said. "A young man handed me this just before you got to the square." She pulled a folded note from her pocket and gave it to me.

"What does it say?"

"I don't know. I can't read," she said.

I read it and my hand began to tremble. "AVI'S WHORE" was written on the note in big block letters .

"What does it say?" My reaction must have confused her.

"It says: *Avi's Woman*," I lied.

"Oh, that's not so bad," she said, relaxing. A smile crept in. Her soft blue eyes twinkled again. "I like everybody knowing I'm Avi's woman." She grabbed my arm and hugged it to her chest. She no longer seemed concerned about who in the crowd would see her, but Havol gave her a disapproving look.

"What did the person look like who gave it to you," I asked, but I had already guessed who it was. My stomach churned.

Sara described his steely grey eyes and the sneer. She said he handed her the note and stared, his wild eyes not blinking. He let out a growl and walked away. She hadn't been frightened until I told her it was Viktor Askinov. She had heard of him.

"Keep away from him and tell me right away if you see him again." I hid my anger and fear, afraid it would scare her.

Havol listened, and for the first time I saw some emotion toward me other than contempt. Her dark eyes showed fright. "Didn't you hit him once with a rock and knock him down?" she asked. I assured her I had.

Viktor Askinov was back. I prayed I wouldn't need to do anything about it because I had no confidence I would succeed. But I had to protect Sara. He was bigger and stronger now than he was five years ago, and a cadet in training to be a policeman. He would turn out to be a policeman just like his father, the Constable. Only worse. I had to be smart about how I was going to take care of him. Maybe Uncle Yakov would know what to do.

When we said goodbye, I went looking for Uncle Yakov and found him in the tavern. It was still early in the day but he had already consumed a fair amount. A bottle of vodka sat on the table in front of him.

"You're still afraid of him?" He filled a glass and pushed it toward me.

"What do I do?"

"Nothing."

"Nothing? I'm supposed to do nothing?" I took a sip of my vodka.

"Someday. Not now."

"I don't understand."

"This is bigger than you." He twirled his empty glass on the table. "For now we avoid a fight. That includes you. Tell me if he bothers Sara again."

I hoped he meant he would help me take care of Viktor Askinov. "Sometimes she is so innocent, like a child." I said. He nodded, a small smile crossing his face.

All week, when I wasn't worrying about Viktor Askinov, I was thinking about what Sara said about not being able to read. Everyone I knew could read. Momma could read. Ester could read. Zelda could read. So why didn't Sara read? Maybe she wasn't smart enough. I couldn't imagine going through life with a woman who wasn't interested enough to read. Even then, at twenty years old, I knew I was going to keep on learning. How could she go to America if she couldn't read?

I confronted her with my worries the next time I stopped by her house. "Sara, you must learn to read."

"I can't," she whispered, not looking up.

I pressed on, repeating my arguments. She didn't argue back. She never did.

She looked up at me, misery in her eyes and on her lips. "I can't stand it any more. I am what I am and can't change it!" She sounded forlorn, defeated.

I wondered if this was how it would end. Maybe knowing how to read shouldn't be so important, but it was to me. I felt awful about hurting her but frustrated she wouldn't confront her handicap.

"Will you try?" I asked.

"I've been afraid this'd happen."

"But can you try?" I pleaded.

"I'll try."

"Thank you." I grabbed her hand and squeezed it hard, chancing someone would see us. She squeezed back.

"I can't live without you," she said.

"And I don't want to live without you." We smiled, the tension drained. I wanted desperately to kiss her.

I really couldn't imagine life without her, but her flaws were mounting.

TWELVE

October 1902

Workers in Uman held more rallies and carried out a widespread strike. The Jewish Bund joined, along with students and peasants. At the larger rallies, police moved in quickly, dispersing the crowd and clubbing whoever they caught. Newspapers reported similar things happening in many parts of Russia. Yet most Christians still had faith in the kindness of the Tsar. He would listen and change things if only he knew how badly his people were suffering. Tsar Nicholas and his faithful followers believed the Jews were the real source of the misery.

In our tavern, the men talked about little other than these tensions. A few said we needed to arm ourselves because trouble was coming, but most argued it would provoke the authorities to take action against us. Squabbles grew more heated.

Gersh Leibowitz, a friend of Jeremiah's from the Bund, argued with anyone who challenged his call to arms. "We have to be ready to fight," he protested nearly every day from a raised platform in the rear of the tavern. His muscular biceps, straining against his rolled up shirt sleeves, suggested he would back up his words with deeds.

Gersh was a low-paid laborer in Uman's biggest steel foundry. His father worked there too until he was killed a few years ago in an accident when a big crane dropped a load on him.

Sometimes he railed about capitalism's exploitation of the workers, his face red as a tomato, his dark eyes on fire. His answer was a socialist government. He aroused everyone with his passionate oratory and booming voice.

If Uncle Yakov was there, Gersh looked in his direction, seeking his approval. But Uncle Yakov sat in the corner, said nothing, and chatted with whoever was at his table as though unaware of Gersh. Undaunted by Uncle Yakov's indifference, Gersh kept trying.

While my mind was more and more on the possibility of *pogroms*, Sara's was more and more on marriage. I loved her enough to marry her. But I thought I should go to America first, get set up, then send for her and get married there. I was only twenty years old and ready for adventure.

Sara loved me, but maybe she was also eager to escape her father's household. Sara and Josef described Reb Kravetz as a tyrant who ruled with a heavy hand. Sara submitted to his will, and probably loved him in a way I couldn't understand. His enforcement of Hassidic tradition was ferocious, taking the bible as literally as his rabbi. He was so poor and life so hard he could only pray his rewards would come in heaven.

Reb Kravetz could barely read and write. He had squeezed all joy from Sara's mother, Rivka, long ago. She looked dead inside. It was impossible to see where Sara and Joseph got their warmth and acceptance of people who were different from them.

By the last week in October, I still had not met Reb Kravetz though Sara and I had now been involved for six months. I only saw him once. Some weeks before, Sara and I were talking in front of her house. The curtains in their front window pulled back and these deranged eyes stared at me from amidst a bush of wild grey-black hair and beard.

"Who is that?" I motioned toward the window. Sara waved to him. The faintest hint of a smile crossed his squeezed lips. He lowered the curtain and moved away. Asking him for permission to marry Sara would take more courage than facing Viktor Askinov.

One sunny autumn morning, Sara and I strolled by the side of the stream at Sukhi Yar. Josef read a book under a tree in the shade some distance away. "He reads more since he met you," Sara said. "I think he wants you to think well of him." I had lent Josef some of my precious few books.

The clear water in the stream trickled around the rocks like the sound of gentle bells. The sunshine gleamed off the water. The tree leaves had turned deep orange, releasing the perfume of nostalgia. One tree clung tenaciously to its sparse green leaves.

We held hands, hers rougher than mine. We were the only two people in the world. I looked down at our reflection in a pool of water imprisoned at the edge of the stream. We belong together, I thought.

"Will you marry me?" Who knows what made me ask her this particular morning? I hadn't been planning it. The moment I said it, a feeling mushroomed inside me I had never known until now: protective, unselfish, joyful, embracing only Sara.

"You want to marry me?" She sparkled like the sun reflecting off the water. "You want to marry me?" she asked again as though she didn't believe me.

"Yes, right now!" I grabbed both of her hands. "Will you marry me?"

"Yes, yes, yes." She threw her arms around me. We kissed and kissed - her lips, her nose, her forehead, her cheeks. I didn't want to let go. I pulled her scarf off her head and ran my hands through her golden hair. This time she did not pull back. She pressed herself against me until I hardened.

She eased away and fumbled in her pocket. She pulled out the scarf I had made for her months before. Never taking her eyes off of mine, she tied the scarf around her head.

"You look so beautiful." Why had I ever doubted I wanted to marry this woman? I took her face in my hands and kissed her gently. We meandered alongside the stream, hand in hand. Every so many steps we stopped to kiss again.

"I must get back," she finally said. "Mother will be wondering what happened to me." She took off the scarf and put it in her pocket. She kissed my hand and lifted it to run my fingers through her hair. It felt like fine silk under my fingers. Then she put her plain grey scarf back on.

"I have to talk to your father right away. Ask for his permission." Tomorrow was the Sabbath so I would have to wait until the following day. The thought of speaking to Reb Kravetz terrified me, but I was ready and eager.

"I need to talk to him first," she said. The sunshine disappeared from her face.

"Will he object?" That possibility flittered through my mind before but never lingered long. Now I fixed on it.

Sara stopped walking and turned to me, our hands still clasped. "Avi, this is the most wonderful day in my life and I'll never forget it."

"But will he say yes."

"I don't know. I'll talk to him tomorrow. Sabbath is a good time." I didn't like the darkness in her eyes.

"How will I know his answer?"

"Josef will bring a message."

Parting from Sara had never been as hard as that day. I wanted to shout to the world that I was getting married to the most wonderful woman in the world. But Sara's father made me hesitate.

When I burst into the tailor shop, Poppa was sitting at the sewing machine. Momma sat in the other chair basting the sleeves on a blouse. Both looked up and knew immediately this was a special day.

"*Mozel tov*," Poppa said before I even told him. He pounded me on the back, kissed my cheek and shook my hand. "Mozel tov, mozel tov a thousand times."

"God be praised. Another daughter." Momma kissed my cheek and squeezed my head so hard I thought she would break it like an eggshell.

But the threat of Reb Kravetz must have shown. Momma's laughter stopped. "So, what's the matter?" I told them about Reb Kravetz. Now they were anxious too.

I couldn't sleep all night. When we went to synagogue the next evening to welcome in the Sabbath, I begged God to hear my prayer. I pleaded for Him to intervene on my behalf with Reb Kravetz. I made Him more promises than I could ever keep.

Sabbath day dragged. I only nibbled at the meal Momma fixed, staring into my dish or into space. Uncle Yakov, Ester and Markus tried to start conversations. Zelda teased me. I didn't respond. When Poppa laid down for his Sabbath nap, I went outside and sat on the doorstep, shivering in the chilly air even in my warm coat. Clouds blocked out the sun. I tried to read a book but couldn't. I thought about nothing but Sara and the life before us. I forced myself to dream of the days to come, but dark thoughts intruded. A life without Sara would be a horror. I argued that it was impossible Reb Kravetz would say no, then argued it was more likely he would say no. I looked up from my book every minute or two to see if Josef was coming.

At last I saw him, walking too slowly. Come on, Josef, hurry, I thought. I stood up. When I could see his face clearly, my heart dropped. He was not smiling. He kept looking down at his feet as he walked up the sidewalk, as if he were an old man afraid he would trip on the uneven wooden planks.

I hurried out to meet him. He looked like someone who had peered into a grave and seen his own death. Josef didn't say a word. Instead, he reached into his frayed coat pocket and pulled out a folded piece of paper. He shook his head as he handed it to me.

"Sara asked me to write this for her." His tone was flat.

I unfolded the note, my hand shaking so badly I could hardly read it.

Poppa says no. Never. I must marry the rabbi's son. I can't ever see you again. I will love you all of my life. I will never forget. Goodbye my love.

Sara

My stomach swirled. I tasted bile. "This can't be!" I grabbed Josef by the shoulders. "What happened?"

"Father hollered like I never heard before. Knocked over a lamp. Broke it. Said he'd never let no daughter of his marry a Haskalah." Josef stood motionless, arms at his side.

"Is there any hope?" I pleaded.

He shook his head. "Sara got down on her knees and begged. She cried so hard. Father just stood there with his arms folded. Like a rock. I pray to god he falls and breaks his neck."

"What do I do, Josef?" I choked out the words, tears wetting my cheeks.

"She asked him over and over why he let it go on so long. All he said was he didn't know you two was so serious about each other." Josef clenched his fists and curled his lip. "I hate him!

I'll leave his house as soon as I can."

Momma and Poppa were waiting when I walked back into the house. I shook my head. Momma grabbed me in her arms and nestled my head in her bosom like she did when I was a little boy. My whole body shook. Poppa patted me on the back. There was nothing either could say. My life had been destroyed.

THIRTEEN

November 1902

Aweek went by. Momma and Poppa left me to mend in my own way. I stayed in the house most of the time, thinking and aching. I went to the tailor shop now and then, and struggled with a few pieces. I wanted sympathy but snarled at Ester and Lieb when they tried to give me some. I talked to Duv and to Simon but they didn't understand. Nobody could help but Momma; I wasn't ready to hear her yet.

The November winds and grey skies suited my mood. I took a couple of walks by myself to Sukhi Yar. I felt sorry for myself, angry at her father, angry at Haskalah and Hassidics, angry with the rabbis. And I was angry at Sara for rejecting me. I attempted to negotiate with God but the words wouldn't come. I was angry at Him too.

Recounting Sara's flaws didn't lessen the pain: her religion, she couldn't read, she didn't want to go to America, and she was too eager to please everyone. She didn't love me enough to stand up to her father. I didn't think of what this must be doing to Sara.

But no matter how critical I was, it didn't work. There were too many beautiful things about Sara. So in the end I hurt more, not less.

I imagined her marrying a tyrant just like her father, and in twenty years she would die inside like her mother. Maybe I would go to America with Duv in the spring. Anything was better than staying around Uman knowing she was here.

On market day I went to the square hoping to have a chance to talk to her. I waited by the general store, and then by the fountain. I wandered through the stalls but didn't see her, Josef, Havol or her mother. Then I saw her friend Ida by one of the pushcarts. She said she hadn't seen Sara for more than a week, not even at synagogue on the Sabbath. She didn't seem to know anything was wrong between Sara and me, and I didn't tell her.

When I got home, Momma was there alone, sweeping the floor and cleaning, preparing for the Sabbath. She stopped when I walked in the door. "You didn't see her?" she asked.

I shook my head.

"Sit down." She motioned to the big table, then sat down next to me. "Your eyes look so sad." She reached out and touched the side of my face.

"There's nothing I can do about it," I snapped.

"Do you love her enough to give up everything?"

Something burst inside me. I buried my head in my arms on the table and cried like I hadn't since the day Josef told me I had lost her. Momma put her arm around me and stroked my hair like she had when I was a little boy. I raised my head and wiped away the tears.

"Momma, what can I do?" I begged, my voice hoarse.

"Go to Reb Kravetz and plead for her. Give him everything he wants."

"He already said no."

"What do you have to lose? And whatever happens, Sara will always know you did everything you could." She kissed me on the top of my head.

But how could I yield my dignity to that son-of-pig? And I didn't want to hurt my own father to satisfy hers. "What will Poppa say?" Momma patted my hand and looked at me with soft eyes.

"I will talk to Poppa. You talk to Reb Kravetz."

For the first time in a week I felt something besides hope-lessness. Changing her father's mind was impossible, but I liked the idea of making the noble gesture to lessen the pain of my lost love. Prince Andrei in *War and Peace* would have done something like this.

Momma got up from the table and went into her bedroom while I sat there working out what I was going to say to Reb Kravetz. One moment I was going to attack him and the next it was complete submission. Momma returned from the bedroom and sat down opposite me.

"This was Grandma Schneider's." In her outstretched hand she held the etched silver locket she wore on the Sabbath and holidays, her most prized possession. "Grandma was a special woman. I loved her like my own mother, and she loved me like a daughter."

I took it from her and examined it carefully, the long black ribbon drooping from my hand. I saw it every week but never paid any attention to it.

"She gave it to me the day we told her and Grandpa Schneider we wanted to be married. It had been her mother's." She grasped my hand in both of hers. "I want you to give this to Sara when that day comes for you." I put the locket and ribbon in my pants pocket.

I made up my mind to confront Reb Kravetz on Sabbath af-ternoon. It was my best chance. For the next two days I rehearsed what I would say and how I could persuade him. Most of the time I thought it was hopeless but now and then Uncle

Yakov's words about courage crept in. At Sabbath services I prayed for God to help me find courage and words to change Reb Kravetz's mind. I wondered what Sara was thinking. Maybe she accepted her father's decision as it was. Maybe she even welcomed it, a relief from my demands and dissatisfactions.

After lunch on Sabbath day, I whispered to Momma as she cleaned up, "Have you talked to Poppa?"

"I'll talk to him later. Don't worry. Go do what you have to do." She grabbed me by the arm, her jaw set. She kissed me on the cheek.

I put on my heavy jacket and cap against the brisk November wind. I don't remember the walk to the Kravetz home. The boards creaked when I walked up the steps. I knocked firmly on the weathered door, and held my breath. What if Sara answered the door? I hadn't thought of that. I hoped it would be Josef.

The door opened slowly. It was Havol. "Sara can't see no one." She snarled. "I can't imagine what possessed you to come here." She kept one hand on the door handle, preparing to slam it in my face.

"I'm here to see Reb Kravetz," I answered as evenly as I could.

She looked puzzled. "Wait." She closed the door with a boom.

So I waited, sweating through the chilling wind, fingering Momma's locket in my pocket. I closed my eyes and recited the Psalm of Duvid, hoping he would help me: *Yea, though I walk through the valley of the shadow of death, I will fear no evil, for thou art with me.*

But I did fear Reb Kravitz, even more than I feared Viktor Askinov. They were evil by different names.

The door opened. "Follow me," Havol ordered. She closed the door behind me and disappeared into another room.

The cold wind seeped through the crude slats of unadorned grey walls. The sagging floor creaked underneath me. It was smaller than our house. I looked around for Sara. Maybe she was in the bedroom, or up in the loft. I stood in a barren room with little more in it than a stove, counter and a few cabinets. Reb Kravetz's long black coat and high black hat hung on a hook by the door like the guardian of death.

He sat alone at the scarred plank table, a vodka bottle and empty glass at his elbow. His large pouting lips protruded through his coarse, bushy black and grey beard. A yarmulke perched on top of his head. Fringes of his *tallit katan*, the Hassidics' sacred undergarment, hung out of the bottom of his shirt. His powerful arms locked across his chest. He glowered at the pocked wall across from him, his almond eyes peering through red streaked rivers. He scared me like the ghost of Haman.

Not even the tiniest piece of Sara showed through in him. He didn't say a word or move a muscle when I came into the room. His eyes didn't move or blink.

"Good Sabbath, Reb Kravetz," I left my hat on to show my respect. "Thank you for seeing me."

He didn't respond.

The table stood between us, me holding one hand in the other, unsure how to begin. He stared at me, eyes glassy from too much vodka.

"I have come to speak with you because I love your daughter Sara more than I love my own life." I swallowed, my throat dry as dessert sand. "I know you have strong objections to me. I pray that I can remove those objections."

I paused, waiting for a response. There was none. "If you allow us to marry, I agree to be wed by your rabbi in your synagogue. My family will pay for the wedding." I didn't know what Poppa would say about that. "I agree to raise our children as Sara decides. I agree to sit with you in your synagogue for Rosh Hashanah and Yom Kippur." I was running on energy, mindless of anything except getting out the words I had rehearsed.

He looked down at his empty glass and filled it part way. He poured it down with one gulp. His hand clutched the empty glass.

"We will not require a dowry," I went on, hoping his financial situation would persuade him if nothing else would. "We will live with my family," another financial incentive. Usually new husbands moved in with the wife's family, at her father's expense.

My voice was coarse with tension. I don't remember what else I offered or how long I talked. He didn't look at me or move even a whisker except when he took another swallow of vodka. There were no more concessions for me to make and I could think of nothing more to say. It was my last chance, and I was losing.

So I sat down in the chair opposite him, desperate, and wrapped my small hands around his big, calloused ones. I stared into his eyes, my eyes unblinking and unflinching like his. Every muscle in my body engaged him. He made no effort to pull away.

"Reb Kravetz, I love your daughter and she loves me. If you give us your permission to marry, the only purpose in my life will be to make Sara happy. I will wipe away every tear. I will provide well for her every want. And I will protect her with my life and my love."

His eyes glistened. Was it an emotion stirring, or was it the vodka?

"Please, Reb Kravetz, please. Give her a chance to love me and to take my love. Give her a chance to be happy. A life she will never know without me. Please. Tell me what else I must do and I will do it."

I slumped back in the chair, done in. I had tried my best. There was nothing else to offer. I didn't know where Sara was. It wasn't such a big house. I hoped she heard what I said to her father. I looked into Reb Kravetz's eyes, searching for some sign, both of us locked in place. The only sounds were his labored breathing and the thumping in my own head.

"You may see Sara." He said it so quietly I wasn't sure I heard him right. "After six months if you still want to marry, you will have my permission."

I was too worn through to feel what he had said. "Thank you," I murmured my hoarse voice barely a whisper.

He pushed back his chair and stood. "Sara," he bellowed out. I jumped. Sara emerged in seconds, like an apparition. She must have been listening from the other room, and heard everything. She rushed to Reb Kravetz, grabbed his vest in her two hands and leaned her head against his chest.

"Thank you, Father. Thank you." I could see her back heaving and heard her weeping.

They stood there that way, his arms hanging at his sides. He raised them half way in the air as though to embrace her. He held them there for a moment. Then they fell back to his sides. His eyes watered.

"You will visit her here." He clenched his fists, his voice strong, like a beating bass drum up close. "One Sabbath dinner here, the next at your house. You will get to know each other." He left the room and a moment later the door to the house slammed. Then his heavy steps banged down the front steps.

Sara turned to me with an unearthly smile like I had never seen before. She was thin and frail. Her clothes hung on her. Her once-wavy hair lay flat, as though it hadn't been washed in a long time. Her eyes were rimmed with deep red, her skin white as chalk. Sara looked pitiful, just like her mother. This had happened in little more than a week.

I held out my arms and she collapsed into them. I pulled her to me, burying my head in her rank hair.

"You came for me. You came for me," she sobbed.

"I love you," I said over and over. I held her close until she stopped weeping, her chest heaving against mine.

When she pulled away, the sparkling smile of my Sara was back. "I am going to be your wife," she said with a certainty I had never heard before.

"And if after six months he still says no?" I was not confident Reb Kravetz had given up.

"I won't lose you again," she said. "No matter what he says."

"And I'll never let you go."

I had nearly forgotten Momma's locket in my pocket. I pulled it out and put it in her hand. Her eyes opened wide. I told her where it had come from. She hugged it to her face.

"Tell Momma thank you. Many times thank you." It was the first time she called her "Momma."

I took the locket from her hand and placed it around her neck. The long black ribbon hung below her waist as it did on Momma for as long as I could remember.

How I did it I don't know. I ran all the way home, shouting out loud and laughing. I passed a few people. They must have thought I was a crazy man. I didn't care. I wanted the whole world to know.

When I burst through the door, everyone was waiting, holding their breath: Lieb, Ester, Zelda, Markus, Momma, Poppa, Uncle Yakov and Simon. I didn't need to say a word. They burst into applause and laughter.

"You have my blessing," Poppa said. "*Mozel tov*." Later, in a quieter moment, he said, "I wish you didn't have to give up so much to that bastard."

"I'm sorry Poppa. But I can't believe God cares who's Hassidic and who's Haskalah. Or even who's Jewish and who's Christian."

"Of course you're right," he said.   And that's the last we talked about it.

No words can describe love, particularly that born in the innocence of youth.   In the following days I thanked God, Reb Kravetz, Poppa, and everyone else.   Mostly I thanked Momma. Life couldn't be any better.   But my resentment of Reb Kravetz didn't go away, ever.

I can understand why someone who sinned like me was put through such an awful test.   But why did God put Sara through it? She was so good, such an obedient and devout servant of Him.

I made a promise to Reb Kravetz to make Sara happy all of her life.   It was a promise I intended to keep, not for him but for Sara.   And I tried.

Winter came but it wasn't a bad winter.   Maybe it was because we were in love.   The affects of her ordeal disappeared quickly.   Sara had this special way of putting bad things behind her.   She was now more radiant than any picture that can be painted with words.   She looked adorable dressed up against the cold, her nose shining and her eyes sparkling like diamonds.   We made plans for our wedding though our engagement was not yet official.   She felt badly she would bring no trousseau or dowry.

Reb Kravetz allowed us to see each other frequently, though always with an escort.   Now and then we went to the Yiddish theater on Alexandra Street, and musical performances in the other end of the village.   I always bought a ticket for Havol or Josef.

Sara and I played in the snow in front of her house or in front of mine.   We built a little ice house and pretended it was our first home together.

Visits to her house were strained.   Her father and I had little to say to each other.   Havol showed her resentment in her every word. Her mother said little, more a servant than the wife and mother. Josef tried hard to make up for the others. Sara was so happy to have me there with her she didn't even notice the mood. I guess this was the way it always was in her house.

Momma and Poppa adopted Sara as though she were their own. Sara plunged right in, helping Momma in the kitchen. She quickly became Ester's best friend. Markus and Josef became brothers. Only Zelda held back, for reasons I will never know. She couldn't diminish my reverie.

Uncle Yakov and Simon often joined us for Sabbath dinner. Simon was at our house all the time now, a reliable if unexciting friend. When it wasn't Uncle Yakov and Simon, it was Lieb and Golde. The Schneider family was growing and Momma and Poppa loved it.

Momma took pleasure seeing Sara wearing the locket. At first she wore it only when she came to our house for Sabbath. Hassidics frowned on such ornamentation. Her plain Hassidic clothing did not change, but she got brave enough to wear the locket in public on special occasions. "I want everyone to know I'm Avi's woman," she joked, hugging my arm.

Though I tried to suppress it all the rest of my life, the horror of Sara on the day I rescued her was engraved on me. She looked like a prisoner from the Tsar's Siberian gulag, gaunt and lifeless, a red rose crushed under the boot of a tyrant. How awful her life might have been if I had not pleaded for her. Her father was willing to destroy her for the sake of his religious dogma.

I had nearly done the same for the sake of my own obstinate pride and mindless convictions. I had to nearly lose Sara to learn there are more important things about a person than whether they can read and write, how they talk, or how they worship

What moved Reb Kravetz in that instant to think first of his daughter, I wonder? Sara believed he gave in because deep inside he loved her more than anything, even though he never showed it. Josef insisted it was all the vodka he had drunk and the money arrangements that turned his head. "And maybe he enjoyed seeing a smart Haskalah like you begging a poor bastard like him."

No matter. He did it, if only this once.

In the end I slew the dragon, the white knight who rescued the fair young maiden. It was now my duty to make sure we lived happily ever after.

FOURTEEN

April 1903

Through his network of army comrades all over Russia, Uncle Yakov knew what was going to happen before it happened. That's how, many months later, we learned the full horror about Kishinev.

Discontent with Tsar Nicholas intensified during the winter. When the spring thaw came, riots and protest rallies began again. And like before, Jewish workers joined the gentile workers, peasants and students in the marches. The government struck back hard. The Tsar's Minister of the Interior, Vyacheslav von Plehve, took charge of the crackdown. He, the Tsar and many others in government either believed Jews were at the heart of the rebellion, or would make convenient scapegoats. In either case, Plehve launched an Anti-Jewish campaign using government controlled press and propaganda. The Kishinev *pogrom* was one result.

Kishinev is a town little more than a hundred miles southwest of Uman. Many Jews lived there. Uncle Yakov never could say for certain whether the government instigated the *pogrom* or merely took advantage of it. Someone murdered a little boy. A rumor started that Jews killed him in a ritual murder, his blood used to make *matzo* - unleavened bread - for Passover. Even

Minister von Plehve later acknowledged it was a false rumor. The police quickly caught the murderer, a relative, who was a Christian man. But the leading newspaper, Bessarabets, continued to print stories that Jews did it. Most gentiles accepted the stories as fact since the newspaper was supported by the government, and subject to government censorship. They convinced themselves these newspaper stories must be a secret message from the Tsar calling for a *pogrom.*

The riots started on Easter Sunday just after mass. It was also the last day of Passover. The whole thing started with boys throwing rocks through windows. Next, Jewish shops were looted and vandalized. The first day might have been a spontaneous religious fervor resulting from Easter sermons preaching about Jews killing Christ. But the next morning the *pogrom* turned more violent, more organized. Hordes of Christians terrorized the Jewish neighborhoods, murdering, torturing, mutilating, and gang-raping women and young girls.

This went on for three days, the police and army standing by and watching. A few individual policemen tried to help the Jews. But most policemen stepped in only to disarm those Jews who formed self-defense units and tried to fight back. After three days of destruction, Minister von Plehve sent orders to the military and the governor to stop the *pogrom.* It ended immediately. Word spread throughout the Ukraine that the Tsar had given the *pogromists* the three days to wreak havoc, and that everything had been done in service to the Tsar.

News of the Kishinev *pogrom* circled the world. At the end of April a reporter's account appeared in The New York Times. Our local Uman Yiddish newspaper then published it.

According to the article, Jews were taken by surprise. One hundred twenty were slaughtered and five hundred wounded. The mobs destroyed over 1,500 Jewish stores and homes. Many were left homeless, their means of income gone. A lot of them left Kishinev. The article said it was a well-planned massacre led by priests:

> *Babies were literally torn to pieces by the frenzied and bloodthirsty mob. The local police made no attempt to check the reign of terror. At sunset the streets were piled with corpses and wounded. Those who could make their escape fled in terror, and the city is now practically deserted of Jews.*

When the Kishinev *pogrom* ended, the newspaper Bessarabets claimed the Jews were actually the ones who attacked the Christians. The government later declared the Jews responsible for their own misfortune. The pogromists were never punished.

In late April, refugees from Kishinev passed through Uman on their way to who knows where. A few who had relatives in Uman stayed.

They came in horse carts, on foot, and by train. Many had only the clothes they wore. One woman who looked like Momma screamed at anyone who tried to help her, foaming in anger. She needed to tell someone about her tragedy. So we fed her, gave her clothes, and listened. But some of the other stories were too horrendous to believe.

One day a small crowd gathered in front of the butcher shop. A crazed old man with a thin grey beard shouted and waved his arms in all directions. "I tell you I saw them drive spikes into the legs, hands and head of this one poor Jew. They said it was God's vengeance, may He be praised, for the crucifixion of Christ."

A mother with a mole on her chin wearing a torn dress told the crowd about a gang rape next door to her house. They killed a pretty young woman when they were done with her. This mother had a young daughter and when she heard what was happening next door, she ran in back of her house with a knife and made a cut in the side of her cow. She sopped up the blood with a rag and put the bloody rag between her daughter's legs. The rapists came to her house but the daughter's supposed condition disgusted them. So they stomped out angry. Before they did, one of the rapists smashed the daughter in the face breaking her nose and knocking out some teeth.

The threat of someone raping Sara made me so insane I wanted to kill someone. There's no way out for Jews, I thought after hearing the stories of the crazy old man and the mother. They will find us and kill us all. We have to leave for America as quickly as we can. There's no other choice.

In the meantime we had to defend ourselves. I would talk to Uncle Yakov about that. Then I had to sit down with Sara and the family to plan how we were going to get to America.

First I had to see Jeremiah. He had to explain to me again why it is that the gentiles hate us so much they want to kill us. So I walked around the corner from the tailor shop and into the door of the school. It didn't look any better than it had those years ago when I sat in Jeremiah's classroom learning my alphabet. It was in even more dismal condition, still dark with peeling paint on the walls, uneven planks in the wooden floor, crowded desks, and the smell of stale body odor. Usually I saw Jeremiah in the tavern or in synagogue, but for this his classroom felt more appropriate.

He was sitting at his crude wooden desk reading. He looked up when I walked in. "I was wondering when you would come," he said without his usual smile.

"I came to see if you've learned anything in the last twelve years," I said, sitting on one of the small work desks in front of him.

"We've all learned something from this Kishinev thing," he

answered. The lines on his face were beginning to show as he got older. He looked as worried as I was, his brow creased and dark eyes strained.

"Remember when I came to you as a young boy after the Haidamacks marched down our street?"

"You had some big questions for such a little boy."

"My question is still the same," I said. "Why do they hate us so much?" My eyes bore in on him, pleading for an answer.

"I don't have a good reason, Avi, any more than you do. Maybe it's the Devil loose in the land. It's about as good an explanation as any other I can think of." He looked away, carefully closing the book he had been reading.

"Aren't you going to tell me about all of the good gentiles like Madame Shumenko and her son Sergey?" I said sarcastically.

"Not this time."

"Mrs. Shumenko and Sergey did stop by the tailor shop to offer their regrets about Kishinev. That's something."

"I guess there really are evil people who are beyond God's reach," he said. "And then there are all the others; good people who let bad things happen."

"Do you think they will ever accept us? Even the best of them. Madame Shumenko, Sergey. Your woman?"

"Keep her out of it," Jeremiah snapped. "You don't know anything about her."

"Sorry." He was right. I didn't know anything about his gentile lady friend or what went on between them. But they had been together a long time by now.

Jeremiah hung his head for a moment. Then he looked up. "Yes, I do believe our Bund and their Social Democrats together can change Russia. I have to believe it. It has to happen." But he didn't sound very convinced himself.

"No, Jeremiah. The only way is to go to America or Palestine or somewhere else that wants us," I said.

"The devil is everywhere, not just here. And maybe if there's a devil there's a god right there fighting him every moment." I didn't have any more faith in that than he did.

I left disappointed. Jeremiah had always comforted me, but not this time. I had to do something. I couldn't wait around for another Kishinev.

So we talked about America over Sabbath dinner. There was no more arguing. Poppa agreed. Momma, Ester, Markus and Zelda were excited. Lieb and Golde said little. Nor did Uncle Yakov. I never realized America would not let him in because of his withered arm. He knew.

The whole idea of leaving Uman scared Sara. She worried her parents wouldn't go. But she would be the dutiful wife and follow me wherever I went. I tried to cheer her with wonderful tales of America. I took on the role of chief planner and promoter for the family, with a solution to every problem, and an inspiring story of the Promised Land to balance every apprehension.

Simon told us one night he was going to join us in America. He and his family were already making plans. Now I would have two friends in America. Duv had left in March, before the Kishinev troubles began. Even Duv would have had trouble finding anything to joke about with this.

The night before Duv left, Simon and Lieb met us in the tavern. We had too much whiskey to drink. Duv and I staggered home, stopping in front of his house.

"I hear American girls are easy." A sly grin lit his glazed eyes. "But you're not going to need that for awhile," he said, referring to Sara.

"I'm never going to need that," I answered. "Not after August." That's when Sara and I planned to be married.

Duv turned serious for a rare moment. "I hope some day I

find what you have."

"You will, in America."   But I wasn't sure he ever would.

"I'll write as soon as I can and let you know where I am. You must come to America. I'll meet you at the dock. I'll help you get started. I promise." I could feel his dark brown eyes on mine even in the dim glow of the street lamp. He hugged me. "You're the only friend I have." He turned and went in his front door. I didn't know if I'd ever see him again.

After he left, I thought about him every time I walked by his empty house. I needed Duv to confide in, to bring some light to the darkness of Kishinev, to share my happiness with Sara, and to tell me what I was supposed to do on our wedding night. I was still a virgin. I didn't hear from him for a long time, and wondered if he made it to America.

The biggest problem about going to America was money. We didn't have enough. Our wedding would take some of the family's savings even if we kept it simple. There would be no help from Reb Kravetz.

So the plan we settled on was for Markus and me to go first and get set up, then send for everyone. We would spend this next year working harder, selling things we didn't need, and skimping. Poppa would keep the tailor shop going until the last moment to continue to earn money in Uman. In the end, he would sell the shop and our house.

I didn't know if I could stand to be apart from Sara but there was no other way. I hoped it wouldn't be for longer than a few months. She cried and clung to me when I told her the plan. But we had a year before we had to worry about that. In the meantime, we had our wedding before us.

Many of our friends decided to leave, most to America but a few to Palestine. Kishinev convinced everyone there would never be a place for Jews in Russia free from persecution.

Debates raged all over town about arming ourselves and forming self-defense groups. A few men were ready to do it right now. Others found a million and one excuses to do nothing. Some fiercely opposed it. These people warned it would only make things worse, as though things could get any worse than Kishinev.

When we gathered at the tavern, more of the men were willing to listen to Gersh Leibowitz's call for action. One day in late April, he was in full oratory as Simon and I entered the tavern. His booming voice could be heard even from down the street. Simon poked me and smiled as we made our way to our usual table. One of Gersh's performances was always as good as the theater.

He paced back and forth across the raised platform in the back of the tavern, punching his fist in the air to punctuate each of his points. "The Tsar and the capitalists will kill us all," he bellowed. "The only answer is a socialist revolution, Jews and gentiles fighting together. Let me die like a martyr at Masada, not a slave in Babylon."

Uncle Yakov sat at his usual table toward the dark corner of the tavern and didn't see me come in. Most of the time he ignored Gersh, but something Gersh said must have interested him because he kept his eyes on him while he sipped his glass of vodka. A few of the men paid attention to what Gersh was saying but most went on talking among themselves until Zimil Straussman spoke out.

"You and all your kind will be arrested and sent to Siberia," young Straussman shouted back at Gersh. He was the worthless son of one of the richest Jews in Uman, and one of the most disliked. The father was president of the Jewish City Council with business and political connections to the gentile powerful. The council was supposed to be responsible for coordinating all Jewish

affairs in the village and interacting with the Uman city government. No one trusted them. The government funded them with
taxes so everyone looked at them as nothing more than tools of
the Tsar.

Gersh stopped in mid-sentence, his arm thrust in the air. He
turned toward the weasel-looking Straussman as though stung by
a bee. He glowered at his new-found adversary. "Is that you
talking, Straussman? Or are you doing your father's bidding
again? You have no idea how those men in the factories work till
they die."

"And you will have a revolution that will bring nothing but
shame and death to Jews." Straussman may have been a small,
insignificant rodent but he wasn't afraid to argue with Gersh
despite the physical menace he presented. "Arming. Fighting.
That's not what Jews do. People like you will bring down the
wrath of God on us."

Gersh glanced over at Uncle Yakov briefly. Was I mistaken,
or did I see my uncle give him a slight nod of the head, as though
granting approval? But Uncle Yakov hardly knew him.

"When the revolution comes, people like you and your father
will be the first to pay the price. To the workers and to the Jews."
Gersh moved toward Straussman with his right fist cocked. Now
everyone in the tavern was watching, silent, afraid to take a
breath.

Straussman thrust out his chin, turning his nose up as those
born in privilege do when looking down at lesser beings. "The
council has voted to forbid Jewish self-defense groups." He spoke
with authority. "If you so much as touch a gun, you will be arrested and sent to Siberia," he warned again.

Then he leaned back in his chair, satisfied with himself and
defiant of Gersh's approaching threat. The beams of sunlight
through the small tavern windows converged on him. Two other

men at his table pushed their chairs back to distance themselves.

Gersh now towered over the seated little man. He reached down and grabbed Straussman with both hands, jerking him upright, nearly tipping over his chair. "Your father and that whole damn council are nothing but donkeys for the Tsar. You're weaklings. Appeasers who betray your own people. No one gives a damn about those worthless proclamations you pass, so you can go to hell."

He spit in Straussman's frightened face and threw him back in his chair. The spittle ran down Straussman's cheek. Then Gersh glanced over at Uncle Yakov, who gave him the slightest shake of his head as if to say "enough." He grabbed his hat from a table and stormed out. Straussman sat silently long enough to be sure Gersh was gone. A rumble of chatter crossed the tavern as the others digested what had just happened. When he thought no one was watching, Straussman slunk out the door, his fine linen shirt a rumpled mess.

We needed to arm and no one would pay any attention to the council vote, I hoped. It could be disastrous if they did. I got madder at the old men on the council than I did at the gentiles. Some like Reb Straussman acted from self-interest and power. Most of the others were just too frightened to do anything but serve our powerful oppressors.

While all of this was going on, I still had business with Reb Kravetz to finish.

FIFTEEN

May 1903

During the six month trial period Reb Kravetz imposed, I worried he would not honor his promise to give us permission to marry. And I worried Sara was not strong enough to defy him if he broke his word. In May, exactly six months to the day, I climbed the steps to his front door to ask again for his permission and blessing.

Reb Kravetz sat alone at the table, vodka bottle and empty glass by his hand. He looked as fierce as that day six months earlier. He had just come from a construction project and his body odor filled the room. The fibers of his dust-covered hair and beard tangled in all directions. His heavy breathing was the only sound in the house.

When he saw me, he motioned to the chair across the table from him. "Sit," he growled. He's not going to make this easy, I thought.

Sara heard me come in and joined me, taking a chair beside me. She looked solemn. His eyes flashed across the blemished table. Sara shifted uncomfortably in her chair, its uneven legs rocking against the floor. She studied her hands clasped tightly in her lap. Anxiety pricked my belly.

I coughed, rested my hands on the table between us, and began my rehearsed speech.

"You said if we still wanted to marry you would give your permission." My voice quavered." It is six months and we still want to marry."

"I made no promises." His huge hand thumped down on the table. He stared at Sara but she didn't look up. I held my breath and my tongue.

She slowly raised her head to look in her father's hard face. She smiled a simple smile and placed her hand in my hand. "I love him. I want to marry him."

He must have heard the determination in her voice. He looked at her, then at me. His body relaxed, as if in surrender. "You have my permission. But you must keep your bargain. I insist." He was salvaging his wounded pride, and I let him.

"Yes, of course."

Josef rushed in and threw his arms around Sara, then around me. *"Mozel tov,"* he said over and over. It was the only congratulations I would get until I got home. Sara's mother gave me a mechanical embrace and whispered in my ear: "If you ever betray her, I will come back from the grave and haunt you." I believed her, but I thought it a strange thing to say.

We set the wedding date for the first day after the first Sabbath in August. Our wedding would be smaller than Lieb and Golde's wedding. Momma and Poppa thought this would be easier on Reb Kravetz since he wasn't paying for it and everyone knew it. There were no secrets in the village. A big celebration was inappropriate anyway in the wake of Kishinev. Everyone in Uman was saving his money to go to America, except Reb Kravetz. He would have nothing to do with America, asserting himself with his obstinacy.

Momma and Poppa did whatever they could to get along with Sara's parents but they were icy. I wondered how Sara could float in the sunshine, far above her family's darkness.

Hassidic superstitions and mysticism repulsed me, but I had promised Reb Kravetz we would be married in his synagogue under Hassidic law. It was worth it to marry Sara. The hardest part was Hassidic custom preventing the groom from seeing the bride the entire week before the wedding.

We were married under a canopy in the courtyard of the Pushkin Street Synagogue. Momma cried and laughed all day. Sara's mother seemed satisfied, and Reb Kravetz resigned. Poppa was serene, but he looked tired and older than his years.

Parts of our wedding day are like photographs, there in my mind to take out when I choose. Other parts drift through a mist. I can hear the rabbi reading the blessing of God to Abraham, promising his seed would be as numerous as the stars. I had been thinking about that almost from the instant I first met Sara. I wanted this day over so we could get started on the multiplying.

When I lifted Sara's veil, I looked on her pure face and for the moment believed it was God who blessed me. It was a hot day; the glistening moisture above her lips was like the dew of an enchanting morning's dawn. We sipped the wine. I broke the glass, and placed a simple gold band on her finger. We signed the *ketubah*, our marriage contract, and Sara was my wife.

I was relieved more than anything, and very hungry. The Hassidics required the bride and groom to fast all day and ask forgiveness for past sins, like a private *Yom Kippur*.

I might have passed out from starvation except for one little Hassidic tradition every wedding should have. Immediately after the ceremony, Sara and I were taken to a small room in the back of the synagogue. There was a table heavy with mounds of food for us to break our fast, alone together. I didn't know which I wanted to do first: Kiss my wife passionately or gobble down a loaf of the challah bread. I decided to kiss my wife.

We pulled back and looked into each other's eyes. "I am your husband," I said.

"And I am your wife."

We kissed, then dove into the food with equal enthusiasm. Between mouthfuls, I thought about what was coming tonight with equal parts lust and apprehension.

The reception was Hassidic, the men and women segregated into separate spots. It pronounced the submission of wives to their husbands. This is not what Momma and Poppa had taught me, but it was all Sara knew. I wondered if Sara could ever take her place alongside me.

I was allowed to hold Sara's hand when we danced. Custom required we also dance with others, but men and women couldn't touch. The man held on to one end of a scarf while the woman held the other.

I wanted the reception to end so I could have Sara alone, but the celebration went on and on. Sara was having such a good time I was getting annoyed. She was not as eager for the night to come as I was. My impatience was rising inside my pants. Uncle Yakov saved the day.

"You're a very lucky man," he told me for the fifth time, slapping me on the back. He put his head close to mine as though to reveal some deep secret, the smell of wine and vodka on his breath combustible. "You treat her well."

"I will. I promise."

"It's time for you to get your bride alone." He winked and jabbed me in the ribs, mischief in his grin. "Come, let's end this. Go over with Sara."

He wobbled to where the band was playing. When the song ended he took command.

"It is time to send Avi and Sara on their way." His voice boomed across the courtyard like he was on a drill field in front of his troops. Everyone stopped talking. "But first, lift your glasses." Everyone lifted their glasses like soldiers lifting their sabers. "To Sara and Avi. May you know a love and a life like no other. *Le Chiam*! To life!" Everyone shouted "*Le Chiam*."

He lifted his glass and poured it down in one gulp. Then he raised his glass over his head in his good right hand and threw it to the ground in front of him, shattering it into a thousand pieces. "Come," Uncle Yakov motioned Sara and me to follow him.

He gave us the most wondrous wedding present: a one night honeymoon at a famous inn on the edge of town. Neither Sara nor I had ever been to an inn before. Uncle Yakov escorted us through the crowd to the street in front of the synagogue.

A fine-looking horse and buggy waited for us, with a driver in lush dark green livery clothes and top hat. The buggy was of highly polished mahogany etched in gold, pulled by a handsome brown horse. In the back behind the seat were our two cardboard suitcases.

"Will this do?" Uncle Yakov grinned like a monkey. He bowed flamboyantly toward the carriage.

"It's so nice," Sara kissed him on the cheek. He embraced her hard, and she embraced him. He held on for a moment. I heard a single sob.

"I've never ridden in anything like this. Thank you," I said. Then he and I hugged. He held on to me like he wouldn't let go, and kissed me hard on the cheek.

"Have the life together..." He paused as though starting a thought, then thinking better of it. "For me," he said softly.

He helped Sara up the step into the cab. Then he helped me. "Take good care of my precious ones," he said to the driver. The driver tipped his hand to his hat. With a crack of the whip, we

were off. I carry a photograph in my mind: The beautiful carriage, the fine horse, the driver in his fine garb, the setting sun, the
slight breeze, and the happiest bride and groom the world has ever
known.

I remember every detail of our wedding night. It is bitters-
weet to recall such a time which can only be lived once.

The horse's hooves clopped on the hard packed street. The
sun glowed orange behind us, casting deepening shadows. The
distance to the inn wasn't far but it was beyond where we ever
traveled. I blathered on to Sara, trying not to think too much
about what was coming. She was unusually quiet.

I looked at her. "Are you nervous?"

"Yes," she said so softly I could barely hear her over the
horse's noisy footsteps. She turned away.

"So am I." That seemed to help her.

"I am so happy." Her soft blue eyes fell on me, a shy smile
on her lips. I kissed her gently. When I touched her I could feel
her tension.

The carriage crossed the river and pulled up in front of an
elegant inn. I climbed down from the carriage. The driver helped
Sara.

A tall well-dressed man in a tailored black suit and vest came
out to meet us. "Welcome to the Sofiyivka Inn, Mr. and Mrs.
Schneider." He shook my hand and bowed to Sara. "I am Gavril
Gergiev, the proprietor. Congratulations on your marriage."

I had never seen such a place. The inn looked like one of the
wealthy merchants' large mansions across the river on the gentile
side of Uman. It was three stories tall, the pristine wood siding
painted a pale blue with white trim and white shutters over big
glass windows. Steps led up to a large veranda. Double front
doors with leaded window panes opened to the inside. A chorus
of birds sang as dusk fell. Overflowing flower beds scented the

evening with the sweetness of honey.

"Do you like it?" Mr. Gergiev asked with obvious pride.

"It's nice." Sara looked all around, eyes wide and mouth hanging open.

"Yakov Schneider is a dear friend," the proprietor said. "Please let me know if I can be of any assistance while you are with us. The driver will return tomorrow at five o'clock to retrieve you."

We walked through the door gripping each other's hand for support. The dark wooden floors, molding, and staircase were polished to a high sheen, contrasting with the white walls. A finely-dressed older gentleman and woman were ensconced on a floral sofa in the front room. They smiled politely at us. The gentleman nodded. There was no hiding the fact we were newlyweds. The proprietor pointed out the restaurant. "Breakfast and lunch are included in your stay," he said.

The thick carpets comforted my tired feet. The chandelier and wall lamps cast a mellow glow. Sara squeezed my hand. "Heaven must be like this," she whispered in my ear.

Mr. Gergiev led us up the stairs to our room. We passed a well-dressed couple on their way down the stairs. The man winked at me and twisted his lips in a lecherous leer.

Our suitcases waited by our door. Mr. Gergiev unlocked it and carried the suitcases inside. He handed me the key and bowed formally. "You will not be disturbed. Please let me know if you want anything at all."

As soon as he was gone, I grabbed Sara and started kissing her all over. She kissed me back. The big double bed loomed over everything in the room.

"Not yet," she said shyly, pulling away.

I didn't want to force myself on her but it took rabbinical restraint. I took my coat off and put it on the chair next to a little table. "We'll go slow. We have all night."

"I won't make you wait all night," she said seriously. That was a comfort. I had heard tales of such tragedies.

Night fell and the light from the lamp played across the ceiling. There was a big basket of food on the table with fruits, nuts, breads, pastries, cheeses, sweets, and dried fish. There was a note from the proprietor telling us everything in the basket was kosher, blessed by a rabbi.

"Can I fix you something to eat?" she asked.

I wasn't hungry but I nodded "yes," not sure what else to do.

I had fretted about this first night for weeks before the wedding. I didn't know what I was supposed to do or how I was supposed to do it. If only Duv were still here, he could have explained it all to me. I certainly couldn't talk to Poppa or Uncle Yakov about it. Lieb should have known. After all, he was married. I was embarrassed even with Lieb, but I forced myself to ask.

"You'll know what to do when the time comes," was all Lieb said. He was as uncomfortable talking about it as I was. I hoped he was right.

We sat in seats next to the table, munching on the food, afraid to look at each other. "It's a very nice room," I said, looking around. A painting of Madam Sofia and Count Potocki hung on the wall. Two windows looked on Sofiyivka Park, dim in the fading light.

"Yes it is. It's very nice." She fidgeted with her food. "I like the blue wallpaper."

We avoided looking at the big bed with its puffy pillows, flowered lavender spread and pale blue sheets. Sara concentrated hard on a spot on the wall across the room. I didn't know what to do next.

Then she jumped up and turned her back to me. "Alright,"

she said. "Help me unbutton my dress."

It seemed like there were a hundred of them, but it was probably more like five or six. My hand began to shake. I fumbled with the first two. Now I could see her undergarments. The back of her dress fell away. I nestled my lips on her white shoulders and smelled her perfume. I could feel her body tense as I unbuttoned the rest.

Sara's eyes narrowed and her jaw set, a picture of determination. She picked up her suitcase. "I will put on my nightgown now," she announced. Then she stepped behind the embroidered changing screen in the corner of the room.

I took off my dress shirt, grabbed my night shirt from my suitcase, and pulled it on as fast as I could. I turned my back away from where Sara was behind the screen, and yanked off my pants and undergarments. I felt so exposed.

When I turned around, I saw Sara had taken off her dress and thrown it over the top of the changing screen. I began to harden. I wished I had some experience at this. I didn't want to embarrass myself or disappoint Sara. A thought of Bayleh Zuckman flashed in and out of my mind.

Now what do I do? I wish she would hurry. I went over to the table and turned down the lamp to a faint twinkle, then sat on the bed and waited.

Sara emerged from behind the screen, a fairy princess wearing the dearest smile. "Do you like it?" She turned around to show off her delicate dressing gown of white with embroidered blue spots.

"It is beautiful. You are beautiful." I was almost afraid to touch her, afraid of what might happen too quickly if I did. I embraced her and kissed her, running my fingers through her soft golden hair. She hugged me hard and pressed her lips against mine. I could feel her warm body through her nightgown.

I guided her to the bed. I will not say what happened next. Some things are best left to the privacy of one's imagination. There was kissing, moaning and eagerness, our hands exploring each other all over. There was the frustration of inexperience as I fumbled and poked. When I entered, Sara let out a high pitched squeak. Her body froze. I thought I killed her. Then she started thrusting with enthusiasm. It was over too fast.

We kissed, snuggled and clung to each other. I loved the taste of her hearty breath and the smell of her sated body.

"Were you satisfied?" I asked, kissing her forehead. I wanted her to tell me I had performed well.

"What?" She was taken aback, maybe surprised or embarrassed.

"Were you satisfied?" I repeated.

She nodded, shy.

She snuggled back in my arms. We lay quietly for awhile. "Momma said it would be terrible," she said.

"Was it?"

"Oh no. I want to do it again."

So we did.

The next morning I awoke with the sun shining in our windows. Sara was staring at me with a playful smile and blazing blue eyes. She was as eager as I was. This time there was no first-time awkwardness, only passion and tenderness. And that's the way it was every time after.

When we left the room, the evidence from the night before was on the sheets. I had no doubt the entire village would know it before the day was finished.

We ate breakfast in the restaurant, a first for both of us. We were ravenous. Then we walked through Sofiyivka Park.

Gavril Gergiev, the proprietor, told us Count Felix Potocki constructed it a hundred years ago, at incredible expense, for his exotic young wife Sofia. He had his architect travel all over Europe before he began building the park.

"I have visited the magnificent gardens of Versailles," Mr. Gergiev said. "And can assure you Sofiyivka is even more splendid." When he finished his description, he whispered to me: "Unfortunately, their marriage ended when the old Count found his young wife in bed with his twenty-two year old son committing all the crimes of Sodom and Gomorrah."

Sara and I held hands as we wandered the sculptured walkways among the aged oaks, graceful linden and elm trees. We stopped and kissed beside clear ponds, fresh streams, delicate gazeboes, waterfalls and grottoes.

We came to marble statues of Aristotle, Socrates and Plato. "Who are they?" she asked.

I was surprised there was anyone who didn't know Aristotle, Socrates and Plato. "Oh, they're just some old Greeks," I answered.

Could anyone have had a more perfect honeymoon than the one we had at Sofiyivka? When the carriage pulled up to take us home, we were husband and wife. I was madly in love with Sara. I would protect her and make her happy. To do that, I had to get us to America.

The morning after we returned, Poppa pulled me aside to tell me Victor Askinov left me a wedding present of sorts. The day of our wedding, while we were all at the Hassidic synagogue on Pushkin Street, Victor Askinov was busy at our Haskalah synagogue. The following day, when Jeremiah came into the courtyard to open the school a dead pig lay by the door, its throat cut. The note around its neck read: "This wedding present is a pig for a pig." He used the blood of the pig to paint a large cross on the front door. His harassments had escalated.

I wanted to tear his heart out. This had to stop. I went to Uncle Yakov. "What can I do," I demanded.

"Nothing for now." He patted the back of my hand. "I need you by my side, not in some jail or hospital. Your time will come."

This thing with Viktor Askinov wasn't going to end until one of us was dead, or I was in America. I pushed everyone in the family to work harder, save more, and get ready to go.

Sara and I moved in with Momma and Poppa. A couple of weeks before the wedding, a neighbor with the skills of a carpenter helped us build a lean-to attached to the front room. It reminded me of a *sukkah*. It was only big enough for the two of us to sleep in, and offered little privacy.

"Wow, you two sure made a lot of noise last night," Zelda teased one morning.

"Shush." Momma gave her a stern look.

Sara and Ester grabbed each other's hands and giggled like schoolgirls. Markus was so embarrassed he looked like he wanted to hide under the table, and I wanted to crawl under with him. But no amount of embarrassment stopped us.

Momma and Poppa were in raptures to have Sara living with them. She took her place like another daughter, helping with cooking, laundry, tending the chickens and the vegetable garden. Ester was glad for the help but Zelda showed flashes of jealousy. Markus was shy at first.

Sara saw less and less of her parents. Josef became a fixture at our house and the tailor shop. He liked our family a lot more than he liked his own. We still went to the Kravetz house for Sabbath dinner every two or three weeks. It was as dark as it was before we were married.

The more distant Sara became from Reb and Rivka Kravetz, the more Momma adopted her as a daughter. Respecting how religious Sara was, she had her say the blessings over the Sabbath candles. This was an honor the woman of a Jewish home did not normally surrender. Momma explained to Ester and Zelda they could say the Sabbath prayers once they were married. Ester did not have long to wait. Zelda was another matter.

SIXTEEN

September 1903

A month after our wedding, Simon and I were having a beer with Poppa and Uncle Yakov in the tavern. Gersh Leibowitz was always excited about something, so only a few men looked up when he burst through the door brandishing Uman's Yiddish newspaper.

"Gomel. There's been a *pogrom* in Gomel!" he shouted., his face ripe as a beet.

About twenty of us huddled around. Gersh read the newspaper aloud as dramatically as a Shakespearean actor.

At one paragraph, he stopped reading and waved the newspaper in the air as though in triumph. "They fought back. Can you believe it? Jews fought back with pistols. The Bund was right in the middle of it."

We cheered, raising our. A few burly gentiles drinking at a table in the corner stared grim-faced.

Gersh resumed reading, his voice quieter. "Eight Jews were killed. A hundred were wounded. The police and army did nothing, just like in Kishinev." He scanned the remainder of the article while the rest of us waited restlessly. "One Russian was killed.... Not much damage to Jewish homes and businesses."

Everyone started talking at once.

"But not so bad as Kishinev," one man said.

"Because they fought back," another answered. Many mumbled their agreement.

I sat back down at the table with Uncle Yakov who had stayed seated when everyone else huddled around Gersh. "You don't look happy," I said.

"Those asses in St. Petersburg." He shook his head, disgusted. "The Tsar thinks Jews are the instigators. This makes it worse."

"So would you have them not defend themselves? Like Kishinev?"

Uncle Yakov looked at me through eyes solemn as a gravedigger's. "You better get ready to fight," he said. Then he drained his beer and left.

Two days later Uncle Yakov reported the details to the men in the tavern, gathered from his network of army comrades. "The *pogrom* started over a fight in the market place between some Jews and some railway workmen. No one knows what they fought about but word spread there was going to be a *pogrom*. A rich gentile handed out guns to the pogromists."

Uncle Yakov paced back and forth as though briefing his troops. "On our side, a couple hundred Jews had armed themselves after Kishinev and were ready. A Russian might have been killed that first day but no one knows for sure. Some Jewish homes and businesses were destroyed. The police put down the disturbance. The police chief asked for help from a nearby army detachment. They didn't help."

Everyone in Gomel knew it wasn't over yet. A few days later a crowd of about four or five hundred railway men marched through the Jewish village, attacking people and ransacking businesses and homes. According to Uncle Yakov, the head man of

the Gomel railroad had organized and armed them. The Bund led
the Jewish defenses with their pistols. It would have been much
worse if they hadn't. Even some women fought.

The army, instead of putting down the riot, stood by and
watched. Some protected the pogromists from the armed Jews. A
few joined the attacks. Those on horseback chased down some
Jewish men, swatting them with their swords. Another group
fired a few volleys at the Jews.

There was confusion about the number of casualties, Uncle
Yakov said. Maybe only four Jews were killed, but maybe ten.
Many were injured. Some said no Christians were killed; others
said it could have been ten. The next morning the police chief
persuaded the army to end the riots, and they did.

One thing Uncle Yakov learned about Gomel worried him
most. The Okhrana, the Secret Police, had declared war on the
Jews, particularly the Bund. They were putting Jews on trial for
starting the riots. Gentile newspapers said the *pogrom* was the
logical reaction of the Russian people to the disobedience of unci-
vilized Jews who dared fight the government of Mother Russia.

Uncle Yakov stopped by the tailor shop early the next morning. "Let's go for a walk," he said to me. I looked over at Poppa,
feeling guilty about all of the time I missed at the shop while in
pursuit of Sara. Poppa nodded approval. Whatever Uncle Yakov
wanted to talk to me about, I guessed he had already discussed it
with Poppa.

He wasn't the ram-rod straight, commanding military man he
was when I first met him six years ago. His withered left arm was
a constant embarrassment, but he still looked tough, if older and
more weathered. His eyes could flash between warm and gentle
one moment, cold and hard the next. It all depended on who he
was talking to and about what.

He continued to share his bed with his gentile landlady,

Leitz. He spent much of his time gambling and drinking with his army comrades. He frequented our tavern by day and the gentiles' tavern long into the night. But he was always with the family for the Sabbath, holidays and every other important time.

We talked idly as we walked along the wooden sidewalk toward the synagogue, but he looked serious. He told me how lucky I was to find love with such a special young woman like Sara. "I have never known what you have," he said. "Don't let anything happen to her." I assured him I wouldn't. But this wasn't why Uncle Yakov was taking me for a walk.

When we got to the synagogue courtyard, he motioned with his good hand toward the alleyway. Then when we reached the edge of town, he motioned again toward Sukhi Yar. He looked around as we walked as if to see if anyone was following us.

"Things are getting worse," he said, eyes fixed on the golden wheat fields nearing harvest.

"What do you mean?"

"Avi, where have you been?" His sarcasm stung. "While you were busy falling in love, things in Uman are falling apart. More Jews, more peasants can't find work."

"I heard some went to jail for stealing."

"Can you blame them? They're desperate. Jewish Welfare is flooded."

"What's the Tsar going to do?" I asked.

"That worthless son-of-a-whore! He doesn't know what to do. And doesn't give a god damn about Jews." Uncle Yakov's nose always flared when he mentioned the Tsar.

I listened, no idea where this conversation was leading. We stopped at the top of the rise where you could see across the immense flat plain of the Ukraine. A train crossed the distant tracks, the black locomotive burping puffs of smoke into the blue September sky.

Uncle Yakov grimaced, then reached across his chest with his right hand to massage his left shoulder. "More riots everywhere. Terrorists. Government reprisals. People marching, demanding democracy. Now Gomel."

We tramped along the path through the woods to the clearing. Dry leaves and dead branches cracked under our feet. The morning breeze off the plains swished the pine tree branches high above us. Uncle Yakov wiped his sweaty forehead with a handkerchief. He pointed across the clearing to the spot where he taught me to shoot a gun. It seemed so long ago.

He fixed on me with the imposing bearing of a leader in the Tsar's army. "Can you still fire a rifle?

I hesitated. "I think I can. Why's it important?"

He turned his head toward where his target had once been. "Because you'll need to. Soon."

"What's this about?" His expression set me on edge.

"The Tsar's in big trouble with everyone. The peasants and workers are angry to the point of rebellion." He slapped the side of his leg a few times. "So he'll blame all their problems on the Jews. Push the blame away from himself. And they'll believe it. Peasants. Workers. All of them."

My first thought was to protect Sara. "What do we do?"

We sat down on the huge trunk of a fallen oak tree. "This time the *pogroms* will be worse than ever."

"It will never be any different for Jews here. I'm going to America."

He nodded. "But first you must help your people here. This time we will fight back. I'm picking three people to help me build a group of fighters. You, Jeremiah, and Gersh Leibowitz. A good man, a tough man."

"Does Poppa know?" He nodded. "What can I do?" I felt a rush, proud Uncle Yakov picked me. A fighter like Joshua, Gideon and Judah Maccabee.

"Show Jeremiah and Gersh how to fire a gun. I teach, you show. Then we recruit some more who want to fight."

"Jeremiah firing a gun?" I couldn't imagine this gentle man as a fighter.

"He's strong minded and he's smart. Watch him; you'll learn something."

"Can we get enough guns?"

"We'll get enough guns."

"General Petrov?"

He didn't answer.

On our way back, a pair of huge black birds, maybe hawks, glided through the blue sky, circling. "Turkey vultures," Uncle Yakov said. "Looking for a wounded prey - like the Tsar."

We stopped in front of the tailor shop. He wiped the sweat from his forehead and behind his neck with his hand, then wiped his hand on the front of his shirt. He stood at attention, deadly serious. "You are a soldier now. You have responsibilities!"

I wanted to salute. Instead I took his hand and shook it. "You can depend on me."

For several days, it's all I thought about, sometimes to the exclusion of Sara. I turned over in my mind how to fire a rifle, even practicing with a broomstick. I was ready to begin, eager to fight Viktor Askinov again, only this time with a gun.

I didn't want to live in a country like this. I wanted to take Sara and go to America as fast I could. But was I being a coward, running away like all the Jews did? Would I be letting Uncle Yakov down after he put his faith in me? I hoped when the time came he would understand.

Soon after the Gomel *pogrom*, a new kind of threat appeared. A series of articles called *The Protocols of the Elders of Zion* were published in a prominent St. Petersburg newspaper, Znamya,. Years later they were proven to be a forgery put out by the Okhrana. The Protocols were supposedly the minutes of secret meetings of international Jewish leaders plotting to dominate the world. It described how Jews would take over the media and financial institutions. Governments all over the world would be replaced with a Jewish theocracy. Christianity, Islam and all other religions would be destroyed. It said the Freemasons were already being used as unwitting tools of the Elders. The Protocols spread across Russia in print and word of mouth, confirming the Christians' worst fears of a Jewish conspiracy to overthrow the government, seize power and enslave the gentiles.

Jeremiah and I were two of the few Jews in our village to read the Protocols in their full form. After Sabbath we stood under the oak tree in front of the synagogue and talked about it.

"These articles scare me," I said. "Do you think there's any truth to it?"

"There couldn't be. Just look at this." He swept his hand around the village in front of us.

"I hoped there was maybe a little truth in it."

"This is a new kind of propaganda," he said. "It's going to be very effective against us."

"So what can we do about it? We're helpless."

"The revolution will come and it will take care of the Tsar and all those like him." Jeremiah was sounding more and more the radical Bund member. He told me he even attended a few meetings with Gersh of that Marxist party people were starting to talk about.

"Do you really believe that? Do you believe the revolution is going to change people's hearts?"

He shrugged his shoulders and didn't answer. He didn't believe it any more than I did.

I wonder how we lived through all we did and still found such joy in the everyday passages of life. When I think of those times, I remember the good as much as the bad, like they weren't happening at the same time to the same person.

About a month after the Gomel *pogrom*, Simon stopped me as we were about to go into the tavern. "I need to talk to you." He grabbed me by the sleeve, his face contorted. He shifted nervously from one foot to the other.

"You look like you're constipated," I teased.

"Do you like being married?" He took off his hat, then put it back on.

"That's a strange question. Of course I do."

"I want to marry Ester. I love her. Do you think your father will say yes? I think Ester will say yes. Did I say I loved her? She's the most wonderful person ever. I want to marry her."

Quiet Simon was speaking, and now he wouldn't stop. I laughed and answered in kind. "Yes, I like being married. Yes, I think Poppa will give you his permission. Yes, I think Ester will want to marry you. Yes, I want to have you for my brother-in-law. And, yes, you said you loved Ester twice." I slapped him on the back several times and laughed. "Come. Let me buy you a drink for courage. Then I'll walk you over to talk to Poppa."

All those times my good friend Simon came to our house weren't to see me, I realized. It was to be with Ester. He had been smitten for a long time. So Poppa said yes. Ester said yes. And everyone else in the family agreed it was a wonderful match. He was already part of the family. I had never seen Ester so happy.

A few weeks later Golde and Lieb had a baby girl. Momma and Poppa's cup runneth over, I thought. Zelda was the only one of their children they still worried about.

Winter came early this year. By the first day of December

we already had our first snowstorm. The drifts, piled against the buildings and doors, turned to a grey, freezing slush. It chilled the passions of protests and *pogroms* until the spring.

A letter finally arrived from Duv. It had been nine months since he left and I had wondered if I would ever hear from him again. I tore open the bulky envelope filled with ten pages of Duv's scrawl. Alone in the tailor shop, I sat down in my padded chair to enjoy it in solitude.

His words were excited, as Duv's always were.   They sounded just like him. I missed my friend more and more with every word I read.

> *I am living in New York City.   America is an amazing place with tall buildings, people from all over getting along fine.   There are more Jews here than in Uman.   A lot of them live in a part of New York called the Lower East Side but I live in a better place called East Harlem.*
>
> *There are all kinds here, even people whose skin is black as coal.   I rubbed a black man once thinking the black would come off on my hand, but it didn't.   The black man laughed at me.   Some buildings are as tall as six stories high. And more whore houses than in all of Russia.   I tried a few of them.   Nice!*

The best part, he wrote, was you could make as much money as you were willing to work for, and you can work at anything you wanted to, even if you were Jewish. Duv worked at a place called the Becker Garment Factory, a large plant where they made women's dresses. Then came the shocker:

> *Avi, I am married.   Can you believe it?   Her name is Rebecca and she is from Kiev.   She is very nice.   You will like*

her. I can see you now sitting in the tailor shop wondering what crazy thing happened to your friend Duv. So let me tell you about it.

He was right. I couldn't believe Duv was married. I always wondered if Duv could ever settle for one woman. Committing adultery was one commandment he was sure to break many times, and I got upset with Duv whenever I thought about it.

> *Life on board the ship to America was very dreary. We were stuck in this crowded place called steerage and only got to go on deck to get some fresh air once a day. I gambled all the way across and won some big money. There were a lot of losers on the ship and I was happy to take whatever they had.*
> *Everyone on the ship got bored after a few days. Especially the girls. And a wonderful thing happened. As soon as they got away from the village, and out from under their mommas, some of them went wild. I sampled a few and they were delicious. But then Rebecca caught my eye. Not bad looking either even if she's a little skinny. She was only sixteen years old then. Young and fresh, just the way I like them. She couldn't get enough of me. There wasn't much room for privacy in those steerage quarters so sometimes other people watched. Rebecca didn't seem to mind.*

I couldn't believe Duv was talking this way about his wife. I couldn't imagine ever sharing such things about Sara with anyone else.

> *When we got to New York I said goodbye to the girl and told her I would come to see her, but I never intended to. A few weeks later she discovered she was pregnant. I should*

*have known better. So her father came calling on my father.
He was ready to kill me! Father was as angry with me as
Rebecca's father. Between the two of them they gave me no
choice. It was that or death. So we were married immediately and now live with her mother and father. I expect to have
our own apartment before you get here. It's not so bad.
She's a nice girl, even if she's got a big belly right now. For
awhile I have to get my satisfaction elsewhere, but that isn't
hard to find in America, even with Jewish girls. The baby
should come any day now.*

He never once said he loved her. He urged me to come to
America as soon as I could. He told me I was still his best friend
and he couldn't wait to see me. We would have such fun again.
He promised to be waiting at the dock whenever I came and that I
could live with Rebecca and him until I got settled. Maybe he
could get me a job in the Becker Garment Factory. He told me
how much he enjoyed all of the girls who worked there.

Looking out the window, I stared at the market square, ugly
in the afternoon gloom of a cloudy winter's day. Then I read the
letter again. Duv was still Duv, fun to be around but sometimes
he knew no limits of human decency. That part of Duv disturbed
me. He was a loyal friend, as loyal as any friend could be. Maybe that was good enough. But I thought about his wife and the
baby. I couldn't see Duv as a father. I hoped he would be more
faithful to his child than he was to his wife.

Maybe it was Duv and maybe it was the picture he painted of
America. I had to go to America and go soon. Enough waiting.
By the time spring, we should have sufficient money.

I stuck Duv's letter in my pocket, bundled up in my heavy
wool coat and stepped out into the cold. I fumbled locking the
door to the shop, my hands covered in bulky knit gloves. I pulled

my cap down over my ears and hurried home, exhaling puffs of white cotton balls, thinking on what I was going to say to Sara to make America more appealing to her. Even though she would go wherever I said, she was not eager for America, and hated the idea we might be separated for even a little while. I thought I had found the right argument to appeal to her.

The best part of every day was when I came home to Sara. She was as eager to see me as I was to see her, throwing her arms around me and giving me a big kiss no matter who was watching. So I was surprised when Sara wasn't there to greet me at the door. Ugly noises rolled from Ester and Zelda's bedroom. I found Sara hunched over a bucket retching, her body heaving in agony. Mother was holding her, a wet rag on her forehead. Ester watched from the doorway, her faced screwed up with concern. Something was dreadfully wrong.

I knew Sara didn't feel well when I left this morning. She looked pale and said she was a little dizzy and tired. I thought it was only a bit of a cold. Momma knew how to take care of that.

Momma heard me come in and turned. She must have seen the panic in my eyes. I thought Sara was dying. Momma's smile settled me. "So. Sara is going to have a baby," she said, never letting go of Sara.

Sara looked up from the bucket and gave me a tired, endearing smile. "We're going to have a baby, Avi," she said. My heart melted. My brain exploded. Given all of our activity, I shouldn't have been surprised. Momma wiped Sara's mouth and gave her some water.

I hugged Sara and kissed her as tenderly as I could, given the repulsion of her vomit. "I love you," I said in her ear. She pulled away and turned back to the bucket, retching.

Sara was gorgeous before she was pregnant. Now she twinkled like a bright star on a dark night, when she wasn't retching.

Nothing bothered her, not even her miserable mother and callous father. Havol was harder than ice over the winter's pond. How had those two produced children like Sara and Josef?

Ester insisted we move into her bedroom; she and Zelda would sleep in the lean-to. Zelda pouted for a few days, but even she got caught up in the excitement of a new baby. Markus liked the idea he was going to be an uncle. Lieb, the new father, warned me to get lots of sleep because I wouldn't be getting much once the baby came. And to get lots of Sara because I wouldn't get much of that either once the baby came. He was wrong.

I loved touching Sara's tummy as it grew, and she loved having me touch it. When I felt the baby kick, my heart told me there was a real baby inside there. And this baby was ours, together.

"It's going to be a girl," she said one night as we lay in bed. "Can we name her after my grandmother, Yakira? She brought you to me." Sara believed such mysticism in a very personal way.

"What if it's a boy?"

"It will be a girl," she said with certainty.

"Yakira is a fine name."

Whatever plans I had to leave soon for America disappeared. Sara and this little baby were going to depend on me to provide for them, take care of them, and protect them. But how was I supposed to do that in Uman? I wasn't going to have my little girl grow up in such a place.

I was trapped. America would have to wait. Still, over the next few months Duv's letter was not far from my mind. When I wrote him back I told him our baby was coming. I would join him in America soon after she was born. Months later I still hadn't talked to Sara about my new plan. I didn't want to upset her while she was in this way.

SEVENTEEN

February 1904

Winter put a stop to the rioting and demonstrations. Everyone in the village hoped Kishinev and Gomel were the last of the *pogroms*. Uncle Yakov had no such illusions.

So I taught Jeremiah and Gersh Leibowitz how to shoot a rifle, sometimes in the freezing cold and snow. Within a few weeks we had them firing well enough, but not yet as good as me.

Uncle Yakov told us to think of others to recruit to our little band. We would train them how to shoot and how to fight. I thought of Simon, Markus, and several of my old school friends, like Moishe Stepaner, Chiam Chernoff, Meier Braun, and Shlomo Zilberman. But not my brother Lieb. Lieb was not a fighter.

Gersh Leibowitz was a big-muscled man, a few years older than me, always ready for a fight. Clean-shaven with sandy brown hair, he was not bad looking except for the missing eye tooth. I was a little jealous of his easy rapport with Uncle Yakov, but he also got under Uncle Yakov's skin.

"Let's give our group a name," Gersh said.

"No." If you knew Uncle Yakov, you'd know he was dismissing the idea with finality.

"How about something like Yakov's Warriors?" Gersh continued as though he hadn't heard him.

"No!" Uncle Yakov leaned his head close to Gersh's. "There... will... be no... name. There will be no mention of our group to anyone for now. Do you understand?" A little of Uncle Yakov's spittle sprayed Gersh.

"Yes." Gersh lowered his head.

"Do you all understand?" Uncle Yakov stared at Jeremiah and me. We both nodded. "Say it!" he commanded.

"I understand," I said.

"I understand," Jeremiah said.

"I understand," Gersh mumbled.

After that there was no doubt Uncle Yakov was in command. But we still called ourselves Yakov's Brigade when he wasn't around.

Soon after, we met to report our recruiting progress. "I've had some trouble getting a couple of men I wanted," Jeremiah said. "Aharon Ackerman and Koppel Geftman. Good men. Zimil Straussman paid them both a visit. He threatened they'd be arrested if they joined a self-defense group." Zimil was the son of the Jewish Council president, Reb Straussman. I remembered him from his confrontation with Gersh in the tavern months back.

Uncle Yakov asked each of us a few shrewd questions about our recruiting. "They already arrested three men in the other end of the village and threw them in jail. Make an example of them," he said. "It seems Zimil Straussman and a couple of his friends are doing the Council's bidding." He and Gersh crossed eyes as though acknowledging a secret they wouldn't share with Jeremiah and me.

Only two days later Zimil Straussman had an accident. Not a serious one, but enough to scare him. I saw him crossing the market square soon after, his right arm in a sling, a purple welt on his cheek. His insolent stride had turned into the creep of a hunted prey. He kept his head down and didn't acknowledge me when I greeted him in passing.

We didn't have any more trouble recruiting after that. Aharon Ackerman and Koppel Geftman joined. Jeremiah and I had our suspicions about what happened but neither Gersh nor Uncle Yakov would confirm them.

Jeremiah was troubled we not become vicious like our oppressors. I had no such reservations. We had a choice: fight or submit. For me, that choice had already been made.

In February 1904 Japan and Russia went to war. The Russians wanted a chunk of Manchuria so they could have a warm water outlet at Port Arthur. It would connect with their new Trans-Siberian railroad. And Tsar Nicholas needed an easy victory in war to gain stature and turn attention from the spreading unrest. The Japanese shouldn't be hard to beat. Everyone thought a European power couldn't lose to a yellow nation.

The Japanese attacked first, at Port Arthur. The Tsar rallied the patriotism of the Russian people. In Uman, crowds cheered as troops marched off to the front, joining an army 300,000 strong. More than 30,000 of them were Jews.

They drafted most of the Jewish doctors and sent them to war. Soon there weren't many Jewish doctors left in Uman. Gentile doctors wouldn't treat us. They were afraid to. So we were left to use veterinarians and dentists.

I worried if anything happened to Sara or the baby there wouldn't be anyone to take care of them. We enlisted the same well-trained midwife who had taken care of Lieb's wife Golde. Fradel Grunwasser's greying hair and deepening wrinkles inspired confidence in me and in Sara. She adored Sara, but she was all business when the time came.

General Petrov was promoted again, this time to a key position on the General Staff. He was stationed in St. Petersburg, and was now an even better source of information for Uncle Yakov. The General predicted from the beginning this war was going to be bad for Russia. "Plehve says we need a small, victorious war to avert a revolution," he wrote. But Tsar Nicholas was incompetent, the army and navy weak and corrupt.

The Japanese fleet bottled up the Russian fleet at Port Arthur. Then they overran the Korean Peninsula and drove the Russian army back toward the port.

By May, it was clear to everyone the Russians were in a difficult fix both on land and sea. The government and the rest of the world were surprised by the Japanese superiority. By August, the Japanese laid siege to the large Russian army force at Port Arthur. The Russian fleet tried to break out but the Japanese fleet stopped them. The battleship Tseararevich was hit by gunfire, killing the fleet commander, Admiral Vitgeft. Heavy Russian casualties mounted. The Russian people were stunned by this turn of events. Disgust with the government replaced the initial burst of patriotism, followed by revolutionary contagion.

Uncle Yakov hurried plans to get our little fighting brigade ready. He warned the government would vent the people's anger on the Jews.

In the next few months, I juggled my time between Sara, working for Poppa, and Uncle Yakov's increasingly urgent demands. He drummed fundamental military leadership into Gersh, Jeremiah and me. Sometimes we met in Jeremiah's darkened classroom, stealing in one by one so no one would see us. Other times we met in the clearing in the woods at Sukhi Yar. No one in Russia was getting better military training than we were getting from Uncle Yakov.

He taught us basic military tactics, how to give clear orders, build barricades, and position our fighters. When we were alone, Uncle Yakov praised me and told me I was the best of his lieutenants. This raised my confidence, but in truth he probably said the same thing to Gersh and Jeremiah.

When he thought we were ready, we recruited a cadre of three men each. Uncle Yakov wanted only young people, preferably without families. He said those were the easiest to train and feared nothing. I picked Simon, Markus and Moishe Stepaner. Uncle Yakov was so intent on our little army remaining secret he threatened to boil any of them who talked. They believed him.

We made regular trips to Sukhi Yar to train them how to fire a pistol. Uncle Yakov couldn't get enough rifles. We rarely practiced with live firing because we didn't have much ammunition. We always had someone on the lookout for intruders but I think Uncle Yakov knew our secret couldn't be kept, not with all of the noise we were making. Before long we had a core of fighters.

In April, May and June, there were four more *pogroms*, but none closer than seventy-five miles from Uman. Altogether, twenty-five Jews were killed and another 150 injured. Businesses and homes were ransacked, a few set on fire. Propaganda spread that Jews started the war, Jews deserted the army by the thousands, and Jews now worked to undermine Russia. There was one rumor of American Jews donating money to buy Japan a new battleship. It was a complete fabrication.

In early June, after the latest *pogrom*, Uncle Yakov summoned Gersh, Jeremiah and me. We joined him at the school just as the shadows of dusk slid in.

"Keep the lamps out and the noise down," Uncle Yakov ordered. "No drawing attention to ourselves." I sometimes thought Uncle Yakov was being melodramatic.

"We have to organize the whole village," Gersh said after

Uncle Yakov described the latest *pogrom*.

"Our mission is to defend our families."   Uncle Yakov wrapped his knuckles on the desk in front of him.

"But…." Gersh started.

"That is the mission." Uncle Yakov slapped his hand on the table. "Do you understand?" He looked at Gersh. Gersh nodded. Jeremiah and I glanced at each other. I think we were both getting impatient with Gersh. "We'll coordinate with other groups in the village. But most don't think fighting back is a good idea."

"What do you think?" I asked.

"We're not ready yet," Uncle Yakov said. "We need more men, more guns, more training."

"We don't have the money for more guns," Jeremiah said.

"We can get it," Uncle Yakov answered. A year later he told me the money came from Reb Henkel and, of all people, Madame Shumenko.

"What now?" I asked.

"We recruit more men. Immediately." He grimaced and rubbed his left shoulder with his right hand. I had gotten so used to his limp left arm I didn't notice it except at times like this. "Fifteen or twenty men each."

He instructed us how we were to select the new men and how we were going to train them. He also laid out the additional training to come for Gersh, Jeremiah and me. "By the time we're done, you will be better trained than any lieutenant in the Tsar's army."

After every *pogrom*, people in the village were on edge. Squabbles and arguments disrupted our tavern every night. Gersh Leibowitz was often in the middle of it. One night Uncle Yakov motioned him to join him outside.

"You are making yourself the center of attention. Stop it!" Uncle Yakov poked him in the chest with his finger. Gersh started to argue and looked like he was going to poke him back. But Uncle thrust out his jaw, his eyes unblinking. "Stop it or go find another self-defense group. Not mine. Do you understand?"

Gersh nodded, then hung his head. "Yes sir."

More and more I saw that look and heard that bark from Uncle Yakov. Yet when he was with the family, he was a warm puppy again.

Uncle Yakov kept an eye on Viktor Askinov. He told me Viktor Askinov had been expelled from the police academy because of his sadistic use of force. Since then he and three others had been attacking people on the streets. It was mostly weak Jewish men and women, but it was also some gentiles who were known to be kind to Jews. Sometimes they robbed them but often it was just for their pleasure. They broke one old man's leg with a club. Viktor's father, the Constable, didn't do anything to stop his son.

In the early summer, Uncle Yakov took Gersh, Jeremiah and me separately on tours of our neighborhood, scouting for places where we could put up a defense. He pointed out possible strategic positions and strong points. He showed us where we could build barriers. One by one, I then took those in my squad on the same tour. It seemed to me all of this walking around would draw attention. Uncle Yakov wasn't concerned.

Little by little Uncle Yakov created pride and confidence in each of us. I began strutting when I walked. Sometimes he praised us; sometimes he criticized. He reminded us we came from a nation of biblical warriors. And if we had to fight, we would be doing it to protect ourselves, not for vengeance. But when I thought of Viktor Askinov, I was thinking of vengeance.

The more the tension grew, the more desperate I was to take Sara to America. But I couldn't leave until after the baby was born. So I had to stay and fight. I still dreamed childish dreams of glory, fighting heroically in a noble cause. I still wanted to make Gideon, Joshua, King Duvid, and Judah Maccabee proud of me, as well as Uncle Yakov, Momma, Poppa and Sara.

Sara knew what I was doing, even if not the details. But she had a way of putting unpleasant things out of her mind. Summer came again. Flowers bloomed, birds chirped, and Sara's tummy grew. She looked adorable. Sometimes I still couldn't believe she was mine.

We took strolls around town so Sara could exercise. One market day we were examining some fruit at a stand in front of the general store. She squeezed my hand. "This is where I was stand-ing when I saw you for the first time," she said. Her perfect smile enchanted me, like on the first day I saw her.

"I wasn't going to let you get away," I said.

"It was only two years ago." She patted her stomach. "Now look at me."

I shielded her from a group of aggressive women jostling to get around us in the crowded market.

Duv wrote every three or four months urging me to come as soon as I could. But sometimes America seemed further and further away. The money we saved was growing but wasn't enough. Now there was a new hole in our bucket. Sara asked cautiously if I could give a little money to Reb and Mother Kra-vetz. How could I refuse? They had much less than we did.

In July, Minister of the Interior von Plehve was assassinated by a Jewish revolutionary. Nothing happened. There was no immediate retribution. It did, however, strengthen Tsar Nicholas' argument Jews were behind the rising unrest.

Ester and Simon were married in August. Sara and I were their attendants. Sara was a beautiful sight with her swelling belly and such radiance she threatened to eclipse the bride. Or so it was in the eyes of her smitten husband.

Momma and Poppa were satisfied three of their children had married well. But rumors about Zelda didn't stop. Men whispered about it when they didn't think I was listening or changed the subject when I sat down at their table in the tavern. Something had to be done. A few weeks before their wedding, I suggested to Ester she talk to Zelda before she brought disaster on the whole family.

Ester and I were alone in the house. She was peeling the skin off potatoes to put in the stew for dinner. I stood nearby, examining the cover of a book Poppa was reading, then flipped through the pages. Ester glanced at me a couple of times, curious, but said nothing. I closed the book and put it back on the table.

"What are we going to do about Zelda?" I blurted out.

"What do you mean?" Ester kept her eyes fixed on the potato she was cutting up.

"She's a sinner."

Ester looked up at me. "Because she made a mistake?"

"Why is she doing this?"

She put her knife down on the cutting board. "Why? Let me tell you why. Because she's the lost child. Lieb's the first born son. Markus is the baby. I'm the dutiful oldest daughter. And you? You're the hero. Momma and Poppa's pride and joy. Everybody's favorite."

Ester's words stung and I was getting mad. "I couldn't have married Sara if she ever did what Zelda did."

"Would you have been better off?"

"Yes, if she did it with another man."

"Zelda didn't hurt you."

"She's embarrassed the whole family." Ester didn't see the damage Zelda was doing. "She hurt Momma and Poppa."

"And maybe they had a hand in it. They can take the hurt,

but Zelda can't take their rejection. And she surely can't take your condemnation."

I picked up Poppa's book and slammed it back down. "She's a whore!"

"You men don't know how hard it is for us women to be good!" She leaned against the table separating us.

"And you don't know how important it is for a man to be the first one." I was frustrated by Ester's narrow-mindedness. "She sinned!" My teeth ground against each other, locked.

"Didn't you ever do anything bad?"

"Not a sin."   Kissing Bayleh Zuckman, and peeking at the naked women in the bathhouse were hardly sins.

"Well, I hope the great Avi Schneider never sins."   She dripped with sarcasm.

"This is pointless."

I was angry at Ester for the first time in my life. How dare she defend Zelda? The thought of Zelda with men was disgusting, an unforgivable sin. Zelda would feel my cold shoulder.

I stomped out of the house. Ester and I didn't talk any more about it. She got over her anger more quickly than I did. She didn't hold grudges. And today, her wedding day, she was as happy as any bride could be. But I still thought about our conversation once in a while.

Late in the day, Uncle Yakov pulled me away from the music and dancing. He led me into the school where Jeremiah and Gersh were waiting.

"Two more *pogroms*," he said. "One in Kerenski, fifty miles east of here. One in Chermanskav, seventy five miles southwest."

"How bad?" I asked.

"Not so bad. No one killed so far."   He twisted his left shoulder trying to find some relief. When he realized what he was doing, he stopped. He never liked showing pain.

"So what do we do?" Gersh asked.

"We don't know if it's organized. It could spread. So alert your people just in case. Except Simon. Let him have a couple of days."

Nothing more happened, but we got a good training drill out of it. We were prepared to fight, but we didn't have a perfect plan yet. We were still vulnerable, and only Uncle Yakov knew how to fix it.

A few weeks later, Yakira came into the world as easily as can be. At least that's the way it was for me, the proud poppa. Like on my wedding day, I only have fragmented pieces in my memory of what the day was like. Yakira had the good graces to enter the world in mid-morning. Sara was marvelous, uncomplaining but eager to have it over with. I was mystified and scared by it all. We men were kept at a distance and knew only vaguely what happened when a baby was born.

The house was full of women: our midwife Fradel Grunwasser, Momma, Mother Kravetz, Ester, Zelda, and later Golde. Poppa had been through this many times before and was a comfort, but he didn't seem to have any more idea of what was happening than I did. Momma came out several times to reassure me, smiling and telling me Sara was doing fine. I had nothing to do but pace back and forth. Poppa paced along with me. I heard a scream from Sara and made a bolt for the bedroom door, but Poppa grabbed my arm and hung on. Then I heard the cry of a baby.

I have this picture in my mind of Momma coming out of the bedroom with the biggest smile I ever saw on Momma. Tears were rolling down her face. "You have a baby girl," she said. "Sara is fine. The baby is beautiful." Momma put her arms around me and squeezed as hard as she could. "My little boy is a father." I was a father! Nothing prepared me for that first rush of realization: joy and fright in equal measures.

It seemed I waited a long time until I could go into the bedroom but it was probably only minutes. I swear when I saw Sara with Yakira for the first time I saw a yellow glow of bright light around them that could only have come from God, my angel holding our angel. My eyes were fixed on Sara and this little bundle she cradled in her arms.

Much as Sara and I loved each other before, it was different now. We were a family: Sara, Yakira and me. When I watched Sara nursing Yakira, it was as though we were Adam and Eve, the first to know the wonder of a baby together.

In the following weeks, the ranks of our brigade swelled to forty-five. Uncle Yakov gave clear direction about what type of men Jeremiah, Gersh and I were to recruit. He examined each one carefully. Then he had us recruit four men who could play the trumpet so we could communicate with each other by sound as well as messenger. When we were done, we had a group of young men willing to be trained and unafraid of fighting. My best people were Simon, Markus and fellows named Moishe Stepaner, Chiam Chernoff, Meier Braun and Shlomo Zilberman.

One day Josef, now sixteen, asked if he could join. He became my most loyal follower. He was rebelling against his father. He hid his side locks of hair behind his ears, and tried not to dress like the other Hassidic men. Reb Kravetz must have thought I was the instigator. I took satisfaction in that.

Uncle Yakov set up his command post in the school. We only assembled in small groups so we wouldn't attract attention, never more than five or six of us at a time. We took our recruits to Sukhi Yar and taught them how to fire guns - mostly pistols. I asked Uncle Yakov if the noise wouldn't alert the gentiles. "Yes," he said. "So they know there are Jewish fighters in Uman. Just not our names." When winter came, we worked on other military skills we would need, like following orders. That was never easy for a bunch of *shtetl* Jews.

Uncle Yakov's got most of his intelligence from a couple of gentiles inside the police department he had bribed with money from old man Henkel. A few other groups of Jewish fighters formed in Uman. They wanted Uncle Yakov to command all the Jewish groups. He declined, but agreed to coordinate with them and share intelligence.

There were thirty or forty *pogroms* the fall of 1904. Jews were injured and property destroyed but there were no deaths. Many attacks were carried out by army troops on the way to the front, angered by rumors Jews were undermining the war effort. In Mohilev, north of Kiev, over a hundred Jews were wounded. The police chief knew it was going to happen but wouldn't help.

There were no *pogroms* in Uman. Viktor Askinov harassed Jews now and then but it was random and unorganized.

When we gathered in the tavern, most of the talk was about the war with Japan, the bad economic times and the workers' marches in Uman. The newspapers reported similar demonstrations all over Russia. Everything bad that happened was being blamed on the Jews, even the famine that winter further south.

A river of Jews now flowed out of Russia bound for America. A few of the hardiest and most idealistic Zionists set out for Palestine. Many trooped through Uman in their carts, or walking on the way to the train station, carrying all of their belongings with them. This flock looked more like victors off on a new campaign than did the desperate ones who stayed behind.

Duv seemed to know more about what was happening to Jews in Russia than I did. Every letter from him pleaded with me to join him. He promised again and again to help me any way he could. I didn't need much encouragement. I used his letters to reassure Sara everything would be good for us in America.

I told her about the *pogroms* to convince her of the urgency to leave Uman. But Sara had no interest in anything political.

"In the spring Yakira will be six months old," I said. "It will be time I left for America."

"Don't go without me," she pleaded.

"You'll have the family to take care of you." I grew impatient with her. "I will send for you as fast as I can."

"Bad things will happen if you go," she said quietly.

"Enough already. Worse things will happen if I stay here."

Sara didn't say anything. She looked down at Yakira in her arms, sad.

"I have to go. For all of us," I said.

She nodded. I put my arms around both of them and kissed Sara on the top of her hair. She looked up at me and I kissed her sweet lips.

I couldn't stand to make her unhappy, and I couldn't stand the thought of being away from her and Yakira. But I had to do what needed to be done. If not for me, Sara would never leave Uman. So when the snows came again, I began the practical tasks of learning how to get tickets, transportation to a port, visas, and passports. Duv would be there to help me when I got to New York.

EIGHTEEN

January 1905

In January, the whole country went into a convulsion. On the second day of the new year, the Russian forces at Port Arthur in Manchuria surrendered to the Japanese. In the process, the entire Russian Pacific fleet was destroyed. Nearly 50,000 Russian army troops surrendered. This stunned everyone from the Tsar to the lowliest peasant.

Uncle Yakov explained what was happening in the war all along, often with inside information, so this surrender didn't come as such a big surprise to me. Still, I felt apprehensive. No one knows how a wounded bear is going to react.

Bloody Sunday came next. Uncle Yakov never said so but I suspect General Petrov was somehow involved.

By January 22, St. Petersburg had been on edge for weeks. Nearly 100,000 workers were on strike protesting working conditions, pay, the war with Japan, and demands for a parliament. Many couldn't clothe or feed their hungry families. But they believed in the Tsar, their loving father who would take care of them if only he knew what was happening to them. What idiots!

So on this Sunday a priest led thousands of workers, their wives and children on a march to the Winter Palace to present a petition to the Tsar. But the Tsar was in his country home. He left his uncle, Grand Duke Vladimir, in charge.

Hoping to gain sympathy from the Tsar, the women and children were in front.   Everything was going peacefully when they reached the courtyard of the Winter Palace. The commander of the troops surrounding the palace ordered the group to disperse. The soldiers fired warning shots and tried to scatter the crowd with cavalry. Nothing stopped them. So the soldiers fired on the crowd, unleashing volley after volley. The marchers scattered in panic. The dead and wounded laid all over the courtyard - men, women, children, infants - their blood staining the snow crimson.

Word of the massacre galloped to every city and village in Russia, and carried around the world. I read about it in our Uman Yiddish newspaper and in the Russian language newspaper. The press reports all agreed: The people were demonstrating peacefully when they were murdered.   The leftist newspapers said thousands were killed or wounded, many of them the women and children in the front rows. But the government newspapers said the official count was a little more than one hundred.

We Jews always knew the Tsar wasn't our friend. But after Bloody Sunday a lot of Russians no longer believed the Tsar was their spiritual father and protector either. The peasants and workers were hungry, confused, angry, scared and desperate. They were looking to lash out at someone. Who was it who did this to them? The Jews.

At the same time, Uncle Yakov heard from General Petrov how badly the war with Japan was going. Commanders were confused, the government was confused, and the troops were disheartened. The Government's desperation compounded.

In the weeks after Bloody Sunday, strikes in St. Petersburg, Moscow and other cities grew bigger and nastier. Demands for political reform intensified. Workers in Uman marched as often

as anywhere else. The Jewish Bund linked with the Social Democrats hoping they could bridge the gorge between gentile and
Jewish workers. Gersh and Jeremiah marched with them.

Uncle Yakov was certain more *pogroms* were coming, worse
than before. So he increased the training of our little brigade. We
met more often. We worked out more detailed plans about how
we would respond in an emergency. We began taking our guns
home with us, except for the rifles which remained hidden under
floor boards in the school. We got better and better as a fighting
unit.

His training preoccupied me. Everywhere I went, I found
myself searching for strong points, thinking about how to deploy
my squad, and scanning for fallback positions. Most of all, I
thought of how I was going to protect Sara and Yakira, if it came
to that.

The burden of protecting the village fell mostly on Uncle
Yakov. He was the one who understood matters of war. He took
care of the supplies, intelligence, communications, and strategies.

The more threatening the situation, the stronger Uncle Yakov
became. He was firm, energetic, encouraging and tireless. He
inspired us. I think he was in league with Rabbi Rosenberg because the rabbi's Sabbath readings and sermons now frequently
came from sections of the Torah and haftorah about wars and
Jewish victories.

Uncle Yakov demanded more and more of everyone in the
brigade, particularly Gersh, Jeremiah and me. He spent most of
his time working on our defense. He still visited the taverns often,
but he wasn't drinking as much. He was forty-five years old but
looked younger every day. His penetrating brown eyes and firm
jaw now dominated his air, rather than his greying hair and deep
wrinkles. He reminded me of the younger Uncle Yakov I met
nearly nine years ago.

The first *pogroms* started soon after Bloody Sunday.   They didn't flare everywhere in the Ukraine until spring.

I tried to get Sara ready for me to leave for America.   It was the only way out of this.   Since Yakira was born, her thinking had changed.   She worried about keeping her little baby safe.   But she also worried about her mother, father, sister and brother, and wanted them safe in America too.

We visited the Kravetz household for Sabbath dinner less and less frequently.   Sara knew it was not my pleasure, and Reb Kravetz let us know we were eating his scarce food.   This February evening we came with our usual two bundles, Yakira in Sara's arms, and a course brown cloth bag in mine full of breads, smoked fish, beets, potatoes and a bottle of vodka.

The street was clear of snow, but the air cold and the night dark.   When we walked in the door, Mother Kravetz stopped setting the table and ran over to take Yakira from Sara.

"My precious little baby."   She hugged her, cooed and grinned at Yakira, one of the few times I ever saw her smile.   Reb Kravetz waved a hand and grunted but didn't get up from his chair by the fire or stop reading his newspaper.   Havol barely looked up.   Joseph shook my hand, gave Sara a kiss on the cheek, and stroked Yakira's soft rosy cheeks.   The bare walls provided little shelter from the blowing February wind.   The smell of cooked cabbage putrefied my nose.

We performed the same play every time we had dinner at the Kravetz's.   The meal was sparse.   Tonight it was a watery cabbage stew with some carrots, potatoes, and a few stray shreds of chicken and goat's meat.   Mother Kravetz served Reb Kravetz first with a healthy helping.   Mine was also substantial, Joseph's meager.   Havol's, Sara's and Mother Kravetz's was little more than a few spoonfuls.   As I did every time we visited, I took a few bites and said "I'm not very hungry."   I passed my dish to Joseph who took a little and passed it to Havol and Mother Kravetz. Sara would eat when we got home.

Usually Sara helped clean up after dinner but tonight she sat with the men. "Father," she said. "Avi and I are going to America. We want you to come with us."

"America. Who needs America."

Sara was not going to be silenced tonight. "There have been pogroms. Uncle Yakov says there will be more in the spring."

"So, does Yakov know everything? Pogroms, pogroms. All anybody talks about is pogroms. We've survived them before; we'll survive again, God willing." He grabbed the bottle of vodka and filled half a glass. He held the bottle out for me but I declined in another of our rituals.

I wanted to jump into the discussion but this was Sara's fight, so I sat and listened, hands folded on the table. Josef stifled his urge to join, finally standing up and retreating to a corner of the room, his jaw locked.

Sara went on: "It's not safe for any of us here any more and we can't have Yakira growing up with this." Sara fixed her eyes on Reb Kravetz. Havol ignored the conversation. Mother Kravetz glanced over as if looking for some sign of hope.

He threw the vodka down his throat and lowered the glass to the table. "What do you know about America? Nothing. This is your place."

"We will be going, Father. I will be lonely there without you." She reached out her hand for his but he ignored it.

"I will be buried here in Uman, next to the famous Rabbi Nachman."

"Well I won't be," Josef said from across the room, arms folded in front of his chest. "I'm going with you, Sara." Reb Kravetz stared at his son but said nothing. He filled his glass with vodka and threw it down.

Mother Kravetz looked away as though the last hope was ex-
tinguished. When we said goodnight, she squeezed Yakira and
held her a little longer than usual. She kissed her cheek.

On our way home, Sara walked fast with a determined stride.
Carrying Yakira, I struggled to keep up. Pillows of our cold
breath smoked the air. "He will die here in Uman just like he
wants," she said bitterly. "So what about Mother and Havol? Do
they have to die here with him?" We both knew the answer was
yes. Sara gave up trying to persuade her father after that, but she
didn't stop worrying about them.

"At least Josef will come," I said. "Maybe he can travel with
you when you're ready to join me." I don't know whether the tears
in her eyes were from the brisk pace in the cold night, or something else.

My problem now was I didn't know how to tell Uncle Yakov
I was leaving for America. He needed to find a replacement for
me. Simon could do it. So could Moishe Stepaner. But Uncle
Yakov said I was the best leader he had, better than Jeremiah and
Gersh. He wasn't going to like it no matter how I justified it.

He and I were alone in Jeremiah's classroom, finished briefing my squad on the new pistols Uncle Yakov secured for us.
These simple six-shot revolvers had a very limited range, but they
were small and cheap. As everyone left, the frigid February night
penetrated through the open door. Uncle Yakov stood behind
Jeremiah's old wooden desk, staring down at a map of the streets
surrounding the synagogue. He had drawn it himself. I shifted
from one foot to the other, waiting for him to finish.

"Something on your mind?" He didn't look up from the
map.

"We need to talk about my replacement," I said as firmly as I
could. "I'm going to America in a couple of months."

"You can't go now." He raised his right eyebrow, but kept looking down at the map. "Hand me that ruler." He pointed at the one lying on the adjacent desk.

I handed it to him. He's going to tear my head off, I thought.

"They say love makes cowards of us all." He raised his head, his eyes accusing me. I squirmed, searching for the right words.

"My duty is to Sara and Yakira." I rested my hands on the desk and fixed my eyes on his. I was not backing down.

"Your duty is to the Jews of this village." He smacked his hand on the desk. The crack startled me. "Are you afraid?"

"I need to protect Sara and Yakira and I'll do what I need to do."

I grabbed my coat and stomped out of the school into the snow, slamming the door behind me. I struggled to put on my wool cap and gloves, the pistol in my pocket an uncomfortable weight. Light snow was falling, putting a new layer on the ugly grey undercoat.

I was ready to fight. But Uncle Yakov challenged my courage and that was unfair. It hurt. He never had a love like Sara and Yakira so how would he know what it was like? But maybe I hadn't picked the right words to explain to him why I had to leave right now. I had to make him understand. I would go see him again in a couple of days. For now, it was best to let us both simmer down.

When I was near our house, my thoughts shifted to Sara and Yakira. Sara jumped into my arms and smothered me with kisses. Momma and Ester turned away to give us a private moment, but Zelda always had a comment: "Someone get a pail of water. The dogs are in heat again." We usually were.

Yakira was a happy little bundle of joy. And she was very smart. Here she was, only six months old, standing up, answering when I said her name, and laughing when I talked to her. She loved it when I got down on the floor and played with her.

Yakira looked more like Momma than like Sara, with her dark hair and dark eyes. Nevertheless, she was the most adorable baby God ever created. I made a point to thank God every Sabbath for bringing Sara and Yakira to me. I asked Him to help me shield them from the ugly world around us, and bring them hope and happiness. That meant America, no matter what Uncle Yakov or anyone else said.

The day after my argument with Uncle Yakov, I burst into the house as usual. Sara came toward me but she moved slowly. She looked pale. She threw her arms around my neck and kissed me hard on the lips. I smelled the vomit on her breath and felt tension in her body. She pulled away from me a little, her arms still clasped behind my neck. She looked like she had something unpleasant to tell me. "We're going to have another baby," she said. "In November."

I grabbed her and kissed her passionately. She relaxed now and pressed herself against me. "Are you happy?" she asked.

"I love you," I said, and kissed her again.

This was a disaster. All of my plans for America evaporated. Now it was going to be another year until the new baby came and was old enough for me to leave. How was I going to protect them in the meantime? Sara would have two babies to take across the ocean by herself. We needed a new plan. And we had to find a way to stop producing babies until we were in America. Now I was going to have to stay and fight whether I liked it or not. Uncle Yakov tried not to look too pleased when I told him.

That night we lay in bed, Sara cuddled in my arms, Yakira snoring in her crib next to us.

"This time it's a boy," she said.

"Are you sure?" But who was I to argue? She had been right the first time.

"Can we name him Itzhak?"

"For my grandfather?" I squeezed her and kissed her fore-head. Momma and Poppa would be pleased. But I was thinking when we got to America we would call him Isaac. Duv wrote me how names were Americanized. He now called himself David, or just Dave.

Sara snuggled deeper in my arms, her voice unearthly. "Do you remember the Book of Genesis. How God blessed Avraham and Sara with a son named Itzhak? He will bless us with a son named Itzhak."

"And just like you, the Sara in the bible was beautiful," I said.

"We begat Itzhak. Just like Avraham and Sara." She giggled.

"But there will be no Hagar," I laughed.

"I pray not." She was more earnest than she needed to be.

On March 10, Japanese forces defeated Russian forces in a major battle at Mukden in Manchuria. The fight had raged for three weeks. The confused, retreating Russian units disintegrated. We had over 300,000 men in the battle, and lost about 90,000 dead and wounded. Uncle Yakov said it was a horrific slaughter. The Russian army was collapsing.

Every defeat shook the government and shocked the people. Agitation in the streets grew larger, louder and meaner. The Tsar's ministers knew the government was in trouble. So they adopted the use of *pogroms* as official policy, maybe convincing themselves Jews actually were the source of all their problems.

One day in April, shortly before the start of Passover and the Christian holiday of Easter, I was in the tailor shop working on a suit for Boris Prutko, a rich boorish gentile. He hated Jews but liked my work.

Markus rushed in, out of breath. "Uncle Yakov needs you, Jeremiah, Gersh.... Meet him right now.... In the barn behind the blacksmith's shop. He said to drop everything and get there fast."

I grabbed my hat and coat and went. The abandoned barn had deteriorated more since the time I met Bayleh there for my first kiss. The walls sagged, the wooden boards black and rotting. The spaces between the planks let in sunlight, the holes in the roof a sieve.

Uncle Yakov was inside, draped in sun and shade, pacing back and forth. A big rat strolled across a big beam near the ceiling as I walked in. Uncle Yakov had a piece of paper in his right hand he kept slapping against his leg. Then he would stop and read it again.

"Look at this proclamation," he said, handing it to me. "I picked it up at the gentiles' tavern." Gersh hurried in, then Jeremiah. They looked over my shoulder as I read.

> *To all those of faith who worship Jesus Christ on this Easter season. We salute and celebrate those brave brethren who last year brought retribution on the Jews of Kishinev for killing our lord. You brought glory on us all. The Jews are Satan in our midst. They drink the blood of our children, and poison our holy Russia. They work with America and England to help the Japanese crush us. We must battle these serpents. People! Rise up in defense of mother Russia! The government alone cannot protect us from this scourge of the Jews. We must rise up and kill them. It is the Tsar's plea that we help him. He sanctions our holy war. Kill them. Give no quarter. Every one of them is a traitor. Make them pay with their blood for their treachery.*

"When did you get this?" Gersh asked, taking the paper from

my hand and reading it again.

"Last night. Copies are all over Uman. And all over the towns around here." Uncle Yakov couldn't stop pacing.

His spies told him it was printed in the police station but had come originally from the publisher, Pavel Krushevan, in St. Petersburg. Propaganda in Krushevan's newspapers instigated the 1903 Kishinev *pogrom*. And he was the one who published The Protocols of the Council of Elders.

"This is a call for a *pogrom*," I said. "Here in Uman."

"Let 'em come." Gersh was on fire.

"Don't be so eager for a fight," Uncle Yakov said. "For now we need half a dozen men on guard all the time up till midnight. Everyone else needs to be on alert, ready to assemble in fifteen minutes."

"Armed?" I asked.

"Armed," he answered. "But no firing without my orders. Do you understand?"

"I understand," I answered. We had all learned how to respond to Uncle Yakov's orders.

"I understand," Jeremiah answered.

"I understand," Gersh answered. "But I think we should attack them before they attack us."

"No attacks!" Uncle Yakov got right up into Gersh's face. Sometimes I wondered why Uncle Yakov put up with Gersh's constant questioning. "Because he will fight like hell when the time comes," Uncle Yakov once told me.

That afternoon we each assembled our squads, briefed them, and issued a guard duty schedule. A trumpeter was on hand all the time in front of the synagogue to sound the alarm if any threat arose. Everyone in the brigade was to come running when they heard the trumpet call. My sector to guard was the southern approach to the market place from Nevsky Street and the river. I knew every building and every rock in the road.

Three days later, we were sitting down for supper when I heard the trumpet sound. "Alert," Markus shouted. "Let's go!"

Sara screamed, the whites of her eyes stretched wide. Yakira started crying.   Momma, Poppa and Zelda sat fixed to their chairs.   I threw on my coat and grabbed my pistol, my mind already on my job. I gave Sara a quick hug, stroked her hair once and ran out the door.

Markus and I charged down the street. The trumpet sounded over and over. "Get Simon," I ordered as we approached Simon's house. Markus broke off while I ran on. I saw men ahead of me, and others in back of me. They were gathering under the big oak tree in the synagogue courtyard. Uncle Yakov was already there. Josef had grabbed my rifle from beneath the floorboards in the school house. He handed it to me. Gersh and Jeremiah pulled up right after that.

Uncle Yakov stood ramrod straight, his voice composed. "Don't know how big a force. Don't know where they're coming from." His demeanor settled me and everyone else.

"Avi, take five men and set up on Nevsky. Gersh you cover Pushkin. Jeremiah, Potocki Street. Just like we practiced. I'll keep a reserve force here and send more men wherever they hit first. Questions?" No one responded. "Then Go!"

Markus, Simon, Josef, Moishe Stepaner and Chiam Chernoff followed me across the market square toward the opening onto Nevsky Street and the river. Meier Braun and Shlomo Zilberman were already there, huddled together in the doorway of the dry goods store. They had been on guard duty when the trumpet first sounded.

"What's the situation," I asked.

"All's quiet. Nothing's moving," Braun answered, his voice so strained he could barely speak. I patted him on the back.

We spread out on both sides of Nevsky Street, hidden in a doorway, behind a wagon, or behind a barrel for protection. I stayed low to the ground, like Uncle Yakov taught us, and went around to each man to make sure we had clear fields of fire and crossfire. They were good.

The street in front of us curved down at the end, toward the river, so we wouldn't be able to see them coming until they rounded the bend about a hundred meters away. That wouldn't do. Meier Braun crouched next to me behind a wagon. "Go down there till you can see around the bend. Get back here as soon as you see anyone coming." He nodded and charged off.

Meier was a skinny little guy who could run like the wind. I'd known him since our first day of school. His father was a kosher butcher and Meier was learning. Their shop was close by, along one side of the market place.

Sunlight was fading, shadows creeping across our field of fire. I hoped they would come in daylight when we could see what we were firing at. Any advantage we had would fade as night came on.

A few shops stood on each side of the street, then some houses. They all looked much like our street and our house, weathered grey but solid. One store to my right had a balcony. I sent Chiam Chernoff up there to provide us some high-ground advantage. A man and woman who looked like peasants came out of one of the shops, saw us and hurried on.

I looked behind me at the open market square, trying to imagine what it would be like if we had to retreat across the wide expanse to the synagogue. On market day this would be crowded with stalls and pushcarts. But today there wasn't anywhere to hide. I would need to leave at least two men at our current position to cover the retreat. I picked Shlomo and Markus.

Markus was now nineteen years old. He was built like Uncle

Yakov, squat and powerful. He was smart and handsome, his curly brown hair, big brown eyes and shy smile tempting women to hug him. Young or old, they all wanted to take care of him. He was attracting lots of attention. With an older brother like me, he knew more about copulation than I had at nineteen. I teased him but he wouldn't tell me if he had found someone like Bayleh Zuckman to teach him. He was a smart, brave fighter I would have wanted by my side even he hadn't been my brother. I couldn't let anything happen to him.

I could see Uncle Yakov in front of the synagogue. He looked taller from here. The rest of the reserve force was concealed somewhere. I hoped they were there. We would need their covering fire if we had to retreat.

When everyone was in position, exit routes checked, and weapons inspected there was nothing left to do but wait. I went down to the bend in the street to check the visibility for myself. Nothing was moving. As night began to fall, it got more and more difficult to make out the bridge over the river. The temperature began to drop. None of us was warmly dressed.

After all the training, I was ready to fight. I wondered if this was how Uncle Yakov felt in his first battle. Time was distorted. Every object and shadow was crisply outlined. Shlomo Zilberman's breathing thirty feet away sounded loudly in my ears. I could taste my own excitement and smell the tension in the men. The nubs and curves in my rifle comforted me.

I thought of nothing but how to direct my troops if the mob moved up Nevsky Street. I hoped Viktor Askinov would be in the lead so I could shoot the Tsar's bastard. I didn't even think to be afraid. I concentrated so hard on the task at hand I barely thought about Sara and Yakira.

We crouched in our positions, trying to conceal ourselves. Uncle Yakov, on the other hand, marched across the market square in plain view as though he was out for a walk. He wanted the gentiles to know we were here in force, ready to defend ourselves.

As the night turned dark as coal, muscles cramped and apprehension rose. Uncle Yakov crept up beside me. "It's over," he said. "They're not coming. Go home. Make sure everyone retires in order. Good training."

He de-briefed Gersh, Jeremiah and me before sending us on our way. He reported that a small group lead by Viktor Askinov struck the other end of the village, many blocks away. Nobody was hurt but two businesses were ransacked, one house burned, and a Jewish goat clubbed to death. "Wouldn't have even been that bad if they'd defended themselves." He frowned, slowly shaking his head. "You all did well tonight."

As we were leaving, Uncle Yakov slapped me on the shoulder with his good right hand, a sarcastic smile on his face. "Don't look so disappointed," he said. "You'll get another chance to kill the son-of-a-whore." How did he know that's what I was thinking?

I walked home alone in the cool, black night, thoughts and feelings swirling like a thousand moths. I had been ready to kill, and hadn't even thought much about it.

Two days later, Uncle Yakov called Gersh, Jeremiah and me together to review our performance. "It was good," he said, "but we wouldn't have repelled a full assault. Tomorrow we get to work making a better plan. I want it in place in two weeks."

Uncle Yakov walked part way home with me after the meeting. Dusk flowed over the soggy earthen streets, dampening the grayness of the storefronts and houses. Laughter from the tavern across the street disturbed the quiet. More men started their drinking early these days.

"We've got to do something about Viktor Askinov," I said.

"He's not just my problem, you know. And I'm not sure I can handle him by myself. He's got his own little army, protected by his father."

"Yes, he's built quite a following, hasn't he? Mostly cowards and fanatics." His detachment frustrated me. He didn't seem to understand what I was telling him.

"He has me in his sight," I said. "He's lurking there all of the time. He doesn't get too close, but he wants me to see him."

"Don't worry; I'm keeping an eye on him." He continued his slow march down the sidewalk, looking straight ahead, his voice even.

"I heard the other day they beat up a couple more old Jews who couldn't defend themselves. They break windows. Burn a building now and then. When are we going to do something?"

"Not yet." He kept walking.

"I'm afraid he's going to hurt Sara one of these days. Sometimes he watches her from a distance. I warn her but she says she can't stay locked up all of the time."

He stopped walking and put his hand on my arm. "If he gets near Sara, I want to know right away." That got to him, I thought. So I pressed on.

"Are we going to wait until he hurts her? Let me take Gersh and a couple of others with me. Let him know who he's dealing with."

He moved his arm to my shoulder and let it rest there. "No. Not yet."

"So what do we do? Nothing?" I pulled my shoulder from under his hand. My irritation with Uncle Yakov's inaction climbed. But in truth, I wouldn't have welcomed the confrontation with Viktor Askinov to follow if Uncle Yakov had said "yes."

"For now we watch him and learn more about him. How he thinks. Acts. Who his subalterns are."

"Enough! I already know more about Viktor Askinov than I ever want to know."

Getting nowhere with Uncle Yakov, I turned and stomped off toward home, boots thumping on the wooden sidewalk, hands jammed in my pockets. He watched me go, and then crossed the street toward the tavern.

Uncle Yakov wasn't going to help, that was for sure. It troubled me. Maybe he had lost his stomach for fighting. Maybe that wound to his arm had killed his courage. But I had a wife and baby to defend, no less myself. I had to decide whether to deal with Viktor Askinov in my own way, or listen to Uncle Yakov. But who was I to challenge the wisdom of my uncle? You have to put your faith somewhere, and mine was in him.

I took a deep breath when I reached our front step, put a smile on my face, and prepared myself for Sara's welcome. I turned the door handle and walked in.

NINETEEN

April 1905

Even terror takes a break. The next couple of weeks were beautiful April days, spring days that give hope and bring love. Sara wanted to go to the square on market day to celebrate the day we first met. The mid-morning sun shined as it did three years earlier, turning Sara's hair to gold.

"This is the last April we will be in Uman together," she said wistfully. She turned and smiled the gentle smile that melted my heart and buckled my knees. I put my arm around her and kissed the back of her neck for the entire world to see. The old women in the crowd were so eager to grab their fruits and vegetables from the stalls and pushcarts they didn't even notice us.

"You are more beautiful than ever," I whispered. Her belly had begun to swell, our son growing inside.

"I'm Avi's woman." Her smile glistened. She grasped my arm.

"Next April in America," I said.

"I want Yakira to see Sukhi Yar."

"She's only seven months old. She'll never remember."

"I'll remember."

So the next day we took Yakira to Sukhi Yar. Wild flowers

bloomed, bees flitting from one to the other. The apple trees were so laden with budding white blossoms they looked like they were covered by a heavy snowfall.

We strolled to the edge of the ravine and into the clearing in the woods. Yakira babbled, pointing at the squirrels, the butterflies and the feathered shadows the sun cast through the leaves. Sara told our story to Yakira. "This is where your father kissed me for the first time.... This is where we held hands.... This is where he felt my breast and made me tingle," she giggled. I kissed both of my women. I wanted this day to go on forever.

At the end of May, the Russian fleet was annihilated in the Battle of Tsushima Straits, between Korea and Japan. The Russians had sent their large, prestigious Baltic Fleet around the world to reinforce their crippled Pacific Fleet. The Japanese fleet intercepted them, sinking eight Russian battleships. Over 5,000 Russian sailors lost their lives. The Japanese lost a few small torpedo boats and little more than a hundred men. Of the thirty-eight Russian ships that started out, only three made it through to Vladivostok.

For all practical purposes, the Russian army and navy had been defeated. The government staggered. Violence and revolution surged everywhere, including the streets of Uman. No one could tell who was fighting who. Anarchists, Marxists, students and peasants each had their own grievances and demands.

In the countryside, former serfs protested by burning farms and fields. Some days we could see the black smoke, especially when we stood on the hillcrest of Sukhi Yar and looked across the plain. The monarchy, government, aristocracy, and new industrialists held the power and they were going to defend it. The Okhrana, the secret police, were given more authority. Their savagery produced results. A regular stream of revolutionary activists filled prisons. Meaningless political reforms accompanied the hammer. Gersh and most socialists weren't satisfied.

A few days after we learned of the defeat at the Battle of Tsushima Straits, Uncle Yakov stopped by the tailor shop. With all of the turmoil, our business was down so I was taking my time cutting out the material for the one order we had for a new suit. Uncle Yakov looked magnificent. He had on his riding boots, shined to a mirror-like gloss. And he had on his brown serge riding breeches even though it was a hot June day. Up above, his immobile left hand tucked in the pocket of a well-cut civilian jacket Poppa had made for him. The red, white and blue medal he won at the Battle of Mangidia was pinned to the lapel. From that day on, he wore those riding boots every day.

After some harmless gossip, Uncle Yakov asked me to come outside. "I'm leaving by train for St. Petersburg in a few hours," he said.

"To see General Petrov?"

He nodded. "I need to get better information. Directly. No more letters and messengers."

"But if there's an attack?"

"You're in command. Can you handle it?" He put his good hand on his hip.

"What about Gersh and Jeremiah. Are they okay with it?"

"You earned it. Everyone knows it."

"Yes, sir. I can do it." I think I snapped to attention. A salute would have been too much.

"Don't look so surprised. And close your mouth." His lips curled in a satisfied smile. Uncle Yakov couldn't have honored me more if he'd pinned a medal on me. But I held my breath for the nine days he was gone.

Uncle Yakov wasn't a young man any more and the train trip alone took more than thirty hours from Uman to St. Petersburg.

His body sagged with fatigue when he assembled Gersh, Jeremiah and me in the school late in the afternoon of his return. He still wore the uniform he wore when he left for St. Petersburg, only now it was all rumpled and dirty from the trip. He leaned against the table in front of him, struggling to focus on the notes in his hand. He put them on the table and took out a pair of glasses from his jacket. This was the first time I saw Uncle Yakov with glasses.

He cleared his throat. "The war is lost. The government will sign a peace treaty as soon as it can do so without losing further face. The terms the Japanese extract will embarrass us, and the Russian people will be furious. All those deaths for nothing. Nothing!" He whacked the palm of his hand on the table, his mouth taut. "A few old comrades lost their lives in those battles. A waste!" He smacked the table again. Gersh, Jeremiah and I sat quietly, our fingers interlaced, elbows on the desks as though we were all in prayer.

His voice rose. "The *pogroms* have already started. There's going to be a lot more. It's now official policy. The Tsar actually believes Jews are behind the commotion. If only we had such powers. His ministers feed him this shit to cover themselves. They know it's not true, but it gets the attention off their own mistakes. But that son-of-a-whore doesn't have a brain to think for himself." Uncle Yakov put his notes down and rubbed his chest with the palm of his hand. He took off his glasses and laid them on top of the notes.

"Are you okay?" Gersh asked, getting up from his seat.

Uncle Yakov stopped him with a flick of his hand. He went on. "Some powerful people started a secret society called the Black Hundreds. It's a paramilitary force backed by the Okhrana. They have the support of monarchists, clergy, land-owners, and businessmen. They call themselves a holy brigade. Their target is

Jews and revolutionaries. They'll destroy us if they can." Uncle Yakov caught his second wind. He paced back and forth. We sat rigid, breathing hard like children listening to a scary fable.

"They've used their money to recruit thousands of the toughest anti-Jew gangsters in Russia. Expect lots of propaganda from the churches, and the right-wing press."

"Some more good news," he said sarcastically. "Viktor Askinov is now one of the leaders of the Black Hundreds in Uman. They bought him off." When he finished, he sat down slowly, exhausted.

"How about the local army commander?" I asked. "Can we expect any help from him."

"He's a young colonel named Baranski. General Petrov doesn't know much about him. I'll try talking to him when the time comes. But who knows?"

"Can General Petrov persuade him?" Jeremiah asked.

"Not this time." Uncle Yakov closed his eyes and rubbed the bridge of his nose.

I left discouraged. Uncle Yakov hadn't brought back any good news. We were on our own, as always.

Just as Uncle Yakov predicted, *pogroms* poured down like the plagues of Egypt on the Pharaoh. Riots erupted in Elizabeth-grad in the last days of April, then Kiev, Shpola, Ananiev, Wasilkov and Konotop. Some were within thirty miles of Uman. In six months, a hundred and sixty *pogroms* drenched the southern Ukraine in places like Zhitomar, Bialystok, Yekaterinoslav, Theo-dosia, Simferopol, Kalarash, Vitebsk, Belostok, Odessa, Gomel again, and Kiev again. Thousands were killed, many of them women and children.

In late June, the crew of the battleship Potemkin mutinied, killing seven officers and taking command of the ship. They sailed it to the Black Sea port of Odessa, a hundred fifty miles

south of Uman. There they joined with sympathetic revolutionaries on land in demonstrations and strikes on the streets of the city.
The ship, flying the red flag, fired into the city but didn't do much
damage. Loyal troops struck back hard, killing many of the de-
monstrators. The navy sent other ships to sink the Potemkin but it
sailed away, eventually turned over to Romania.

The international press spread news of this rebellion on one
of the Tsar's naval vessels. We heard about it in Uman almost as
soon as it happened. The Potemkin rebellion triggered new fears
in the government of the military turning against the monarchy.

The one thing in our plan none of us wanted to think about
was what we would do if the pogromists broke through our defenses. Time permitting, we were supposed to retreat into the
synagogue where we would make a stand with whatever force we
had left. But what would happen to Sara, Yakira and the family if
there wasn't enough time to do that?

So one evening we assembled in our house: Momma, Poppa,
Sara, Ester, Simon, Lieb, Golde, Markus, Zelda, me, and Uncle
Yakov. The family saw a different Uncle Yakov than our kindly
old uncle. He was the military commander I had become so familiar with, blunt and direct in the measures to be taken. Sara's lip
quivered; she grasped Yakira tightly.

Markus, Simon and I would be on the barricades with the
brigade. The rest of the family were to fortify themselves inside
our house. The women would arm themselves with knives and
sulfuric acid to throw at the pogromists if they came through the
door. Poppa had a pistol. Lieb would use the old axe that still
hung by the woodpile behind the house. Lieb couldn't bring
himself to use a gun no matter the circumstance. It wasn't that he
lacked courage. It's that he abhorred violence to an extreme I
couldn't comprehend. My brother was a very good man.

The plan comforted the women somewhat but the truth was if

the pogromist mob got by the main fighting force, the women wouldn't be able to stop them either. I wasn't going to let that happen.

Sara surprised me with her fearless determination to defend Yakira and herself. She worried more about me, her mother, father, sister and brother. Reb Kravetz was stubborn beyond all logic. He refused to have anything to do with the defense of the village, or himself. He was one of those who thought fighting would only make things worse. He intended to wait in his shuttered house, depending on God for his protection.

I tried to get Uncle Yakov to push our Pushkin Street defense line further out to encompass Reb Kravetz's house, but Uncle Yakov refused. "It will weaken our position," he said. "It is indefensible." I encouraged Sara to keep trying to persuade Reb Kravetz. He wouldn't listen.

Every day groups of men gathered in the market place and the tavern to get the latest accounts of the *pogroms* from the newspapers, letters, and refugees passing through town. Some had desperate relatives from destroyed villages move in with them, crammed together in their overcrowded houses.

The mobs always ransacked and burned the synagogues first. Smashed windows in homes and shops were the least of it. The gruesome murders terrorized. One pregnant woman had her stomach cut open and her baby torn out. An old man had his hands tied behind his back and his beard set on fire. Rapes were so common they no longer shocked anyone. The entire village of Kalarash was burned to the ground, one hundred killed and eighty wounded. There wasn't a building left untouched. Not even a dog or a goat was left alive. They say the odor of burning flesh was so putrid the air was green.

The anti-Jewish press kept up an unrelenting stream of incendiary filth. Flyers and proclamations urging gentiles to join the *pogroms* were everywhere. City governments did little and in at least one instance the mayor and a priest visited neighboring villages together to rouse the peasants to enlist in the *pogroms*. Police were often among the pogromists. The Black Hundreds provided the muscle, money and weapons.

Some days I felt overwhelming fear and desperation. Other days I was so angry I wanted to kill. We trained more and more, refining every detail. It kept us from sinking into despair. Our bodies grew harder, our minds sharper. Uncle Yakov carried the whole cargo on his back. We became a tight brigade of sixty tough, trained, disciplined young fighters ready to battle ferociously to protect our families.

More men clamored to join our brigade. "It's too late to train them and integrate them," Uncle Yakov said.

"Maybe we can use them as a reserve force," Jeremiah suggested. "A last line around the synagogue."

"Agreed," Uncle Yakov said. "But only clubs and knives. No guns. And keep them well back from the barricades."

In the end there were about twenty-five of these auxiliaries. Uncle Yakov put Zubin Skolnick, Golde's older brother, in charge of them and left it to him to give them a little training. Uncle Yakov wasn't counting on this reserve for much, but the added bulk impressed the village.

The stream of Jews to America turned into a gusher. Every day more load-heavy wagons headed out of town. The wealthier ones crowded the train station. The others walked.

In early August, Ester announced she was pregnant, and two weeks later Golde told us she was pregnant again too. Six months along, Sara's tummy swelled. I tried to be happy about all this proliferation but these pregnant women would be an added problem when we were attacked.

The following Sabbath, a muggy August morning, Poppa, Markus, and I rounded the corner into the courtyard. A dozen men huddled under the oak tree gawking up. A pair of turkey vultures circled low above the tree.

A corpse hung upside down from the biggest limb. The man's hands were tied behind his back, his tongue cut off and hung around his neck on a string.

TWENTY

August 2005

The sign around the man's neck read: "Judas." His eyes bulged out of his head like two big white marbles. A small pool of blood stained the ground beneath him. A crowd of Sabbath worshippers gathered around the tree, men and women with a few children. A mother covered her children's eyes and led them away. The men cursed and prayed.

Chiam Chernoff climbed the tree and cut the rope tied around the corpse's feet while two other men guided the body gently to the ground. "He's not a Jew," someone said.

Uncle Yakov slammed his hat down on the ground, a scowl on his face, and pushed his way through the crowd. I followed.

"Who is he?" I asked him.

"Who is he? Who is he?" he screamed. "Who do you think he is?" Heads turned in our direction. "Can't you read the sign around his neck?"

Judas. "Your spy inside the police department?"

"For god's sake! Why don't you tell everybody!" I didn't think I was talking that loudly. The word flew through the gathering crowd. A couple of sinister looking gentiles watched from the edge of the courtyard. When they saw me looking at them, they walked away. One of them bared his teeth in a contorted smile. I thought they might be Okhrana.

Uncle Yakov's spy inside the police department had been caught and killed. This could cripple us, but we still had another spy inside. Uncle Yakov's loss of composure unsettled me.

Rabbi Rosenberg told us to treat the body with respect. This was the first dead body I had ever seen up close. I was fascinated. It didn't look real to me.

"Doesn't that look like Viktor Askinov's friend Pyotr Panasenko?" Markus said, pointing to the chalky white corpse. I smiled and nodded.

Markus and I hurried around the corner and into the tailor shop. Then we both doubled over laughing. That's the way Poppa found us when he came in. He was horrified.

"What's going on here?" he demanded.

Markus muffled himself enough to answer. I held both hands over my mouth. "Our uncle's a sly old fox," Markus said, then started giggling again. "The police must have suspected there was a spy. So Uncle Yakov set up one of their own people."

"One of Viktor Askinov's friends." I added. "It's so sweet."

Poppa shook his head. He wasn't laughing. "God help us. You think a dead man is something funny? Have you both lost your humanity?" He turned and walked out, slamming the door.

The police conducted nothing more than a hasty investigation of Pyotr Panasenko's death. They decided Jews were the likely murderers but, with no evidence, they did not charge anyone.

In Uman, the socialists and democrats clashed with the police almost every day. The police were having a harder time controlling them. One sweltering day in late August mill workers marched to city hall on the gentile side of the river. They made speeches in front of a statue of the martyred Tsar Alexander II. When they threatened to storm city hall, mounted police charged across the square. One man was trampled to death underneath the horses' hooves. Others were injured.

Disorder spiraled across Russia. Demands for economic and political reform kept escalating. What would have been accepted three months ago was now no longer enough.

The Tsar's government was in a corner. They were forced to accept peace with Japan no matter the terms. So in early September the American president, Theodore Roosevelt, mediated. The two sides met in New Hampshire and agreed to a treaty. Japan got rights in Korea, Manchuria, and Port Arthur – the prize Russia had originally been after in this war. Russia was not only badly defeated; it was humiliated before the entire world, and the Russian people knew it. Two of Russia's three fleets were sunk and some say as many as 70,000 were killed. Every Russian lost someone.

Viktor Askinov and his gang intensified their attacks on Jews in different parts of Uman. They turned their black truncheons on people at the slightest provocation, picking on the weakest men, the women and children. They harassed and scared them until they wet their pants, then rolled over in laughter.

At last Viktor Askinov focused on me. One night he smashed the front windows of our tailor shop, carefully knocking out every piece of glass. When I came in that morning, the malodorous odor of feces assaulted me. Pig droppings covered the inside of the shop. Garments we were working on were destroyed. It took days to clean up. The whole family worked hard at it, even Zelda who always found a way to escape any form of work.

The next Sabbath afternoon, we walked by the shop on our way home from synagogue. Our windows were smashed again. I ran in. There were no feces this time. Instead there was a big note for me nailed to the center post:

THE TIME IS COMING.
I WILL HAVE YOUR HEAD.
THEN I WILL HAVE YOUR WIFE.

I went crazy. I threw anything in the shop I could get my hands on. Poppa and Simon tried to hold me but I kept struggling free.

"I'm going to kill him! I'll kill him!" I hollered.

"Get Uncle Yakov," Poppa yelled to Markus. Uncle Yakov, on his way to the tavern, came at a run.

He gripped my shoulder in his one good hand like a vice. "This is the buildup to the attack." Uncle Yakov was firm and loud. "He's trying to goad you."

"Enough!" I shouted. "No more. I've had a lifetime of him." I felt hot all over, not from the outside like on a boiling day, but from the furnace inside.

"You're the best we have. He knows that. He wants you out of the fight." He put his face so close to mine I could see every river of red in his eyes. "You're putting Sara and Yakira at risk. Now stop it."

My chest heaved. He bore into me, not letting go of his grip. Then I took a deep lungful of air and moved back, nodding to him as my racing heart slowed. He was right. "It won't happen again," I said.

"He'll try again. Don't let him beat you."

"I promise." And I meant it. I couldn't let Uncle Yakov lose confidence in me, and I couldn't let Viktor Askinov blind me. Anything I did from here on had to be cold and calculated.

Sara grew large, now in her seventh month. She had me place my hand on her stomach to feel the baby's kicks. That made it real in a way even her expanding tummy didn't. Her back often hurt and she wasn't sleeping well. Some of it was because she had to make trips to the privy every hour. I went with her to guide her in the dark. But much of her restlessness, and mine, was because of the dread we were trying to hide from each other. We were bringing a baby into a nightmare. I tried to help Sara by telling her marvelous tales of America. I showed her our passports as proof we were going, and read her the good parts of Duv's letters again.

My prayers to God became more fervent and pleading. I wasn't asking for much. Only for him to keep Sara, Yakira and the new baby safe. But He didn't seem to hear.

I didn't see much of Viktor Askinov in the following weeks except in the distance, watching me. I didn't take his bait. Then he began stalking Sara whenever he saw her on her occasional trips to the market square with Ester. Once he got close enough to touch her, staring at her until she looked his way. He spooked her badly. From then on Josef, Simon, Markus or I tried to be with Ester and Sara whenever they went out, but it wasn't always possible.

October is a beautiful time in Uman. The leaves on the trees begin turning color. The last of the summer heat departs, replaced by brisk mornings, cool evenings and perfect sunny days. Peasants in the countryside harvest and in the village everyone picks their fruits and vegetables in preparation for the harsh winter that's coming.

This October was different from any other. Apprehension clutched the village. There were demonstrations and strikes every day. Police on horseback were everywhere. No one knew whether it would be a revolution or a *pogrom*, but something bad was brewing. Speeches and proclamations urged the overthrow of the Tsar. Only a few months earlier such heresy would have been unthinkable.

The militants demanded a democratically elected national assembly, reforms to limit the Tsar's power, and economic relief for the poor. Anger over loss of the war with Japan didn't go away with the signing of the peace treaty. General Petrov wrote Uncle Yakov about troubles in St. Petersburg, Moscow, and other cities. In some places, revolutionaries tried to set up their own governments. Petrov also wrote there was a lot of disagreement among the Tsar's ministers. Some thought the Tsar must grant the reforms. Others resisted to the last. The Tsar himself seemed ready to give in.

The day after *Rosh Hashanah*, the Jewish New Year, Uncle Yakov had Gersh, Jeremiah and me meet him at the school. He stood erect behind the table at the head of the classroom. We sat on the desks in front of him. How many times had we been there by now?

Uncle Yakov was solemn. "The time is here. Soon we fight."

"You've said that before," Gersh said.

Uncle Yakov ignored him. "The government is trapped. No options. So they're starting *pogroms* everywhere."

"How soon?" Jeremiah asked.

"As soon as they announce the reforms," he answered. "Within days."

"Can we win this?" I asked, begging for reassurance.

"Stick to the plan. No one has to die." Uncle Yakov fidgeted with the red, white and blue medal in his lapel.

"Well, I want to kill the son-of-a-whore," I said, referring to Viktor Askinov.

"Your job is to make sure no one dies." He slapped the palm of his hand on the table.

"I know. But I'd still like to kill him." I forced a smile so Uncle Yakov knew I was in control of myself.

Uncle Yakov went over the plan one more time. It was masterful. We all believed it would work, mostly because Uncle Yakov said it would. But there was a little tickle in my brain. Everything had to go perfectly if it was to come out the way we hoped it would.

Ten days later, October 12, Markus and I quit early at the tailor shop. It was never very busy right after the high holy days.

When we walked in the door, the house was unusually quiet. Momma wasn't in the kitchen like she usually was. I heard some commotion from our bedroom. Uncle Yakov stood outside the doorway like a sentry on guard duty. I heard a moan, a little cry and a whimper. It was Sara.

I rushed toward the bedroom but Uncle Yakov stood in my way. "Sara's okay," he said. "But she's had a little accident."

"Let me see her." I tried pushing my way past Uncle Yakov but he wasn't moving. My heart stopped.

He didn't budge from the door. "She fell down. But there's no harm to her, or the baby."

He wasn't telling me the whole story. "How did she fall down?"

"She and Ester were walking to market. On the sidewalk. Viktor Askinov came around the corner and stood in their way. Ester says he stared at Sara even after she looked away. Then he shoved her so hard she fell off the sidewalk into the street."

"I'm going to kill him," I screamed. "I'm going to kill him right now."

Uncle Yakov squeezed my forearm so hard my anger shifted from Viktor Askinov to Uncle Yakov. "Vengeance can wait. Right now comfort your wife."

"The devil has got to die." I pulled my arm away. He let go.

"Your job is to protect this family. This village."

"I want justice!"

"You want blood!"

We faced each other like a pair of snarling pit bulls ready to fight. Neither blinked.

"Aviiiii," Sara's screech vibrated the windows.

I pushed my way through Uncle Yakov into the bedroom. Momma, Ester, and Fradel Grunwasser, our midwife, gathered around Sara lying in bed. She was pale and sweating. I rushed over to her. I should have protected her better.

She held up her hand to me. "Don't kill him or they'll kill you," she said weakly.

I took her hand, bent down and kissed her gently on the lips. "I won't leave you," I said. "He can wait." Sara's frail look scared me. I glanced over at Fradel Grunwasser.

"The baby could come at any moment," she said, wiping sweat from Sara's brow. She held a cup of water to Sara's lips and held her up to sip it. Then she gently laid her back down. The room was dark and damp though it was still warm and sunny outside.

Momma stood in the corner wringing her hands. "We'd better send Markus to get Mother Kravetz," she said.

Sara screamed, her faced coiled in pain.

"The baby is here," Fradel Wasserman said as calmly as she could, but she was tense. It was too early. We were supposed to have a month more.

Sara screamed again.

TWENTY-ONE

October 12, 1905

Itzhak was born at almost the same instant as the Tsar's pitiful constitution, October 12, 1905. Inside the house, Sara lay in bed too weak to raise her head or eat. Fradel Wasserman assured me she was going to be alright, though at times she lacked conviction. Itzhak struggled, breathing with difficulty. He was so tiny and feeble he had trouble nursing. "It's because he came too soon," Fradel Wasserman told me. "He will get stronger in a day or two."

I stayed by Sara's side, holding her hand, washing her warm brow with cool water, or feeding her some clear soup. She looked as pale as whitewash and as fragile as a butterfly. She moaned in her sleep, sending a shiver up my spine. In the quiet moments of the dark night, I prayed and prayed to God to spare Sara and Itzhak. I trembled when I thought I might be left to raise Yakira by myself.

Momma was with Sara every waking moment. We took turns sleeping. Everyone tiptoed around the house. Uncle Yakov stopped by several times a day, no doubt waiting for some upturn that would allow me to resume command of my squad. He put Simon in charge temporarily but neither Uncle Yakov nor the others had the same confidence in Simon they had in me. And I wouldn't leave her in this state.

Mother Kravetz was there much of the time, helping whenever Sara would let her. Sara wanted Momma, and Mother Kravetz deferred to her. Reb Kravetz came by once to see his first grandson.

Poppa, on the other hand, was exuberant at the arrival of his first grandson. "A Schneider to carry on our name," he said, as if denying Itzhak's perilous state.

On the third day Sara sat up in bed and ate some chicken. She held my hand tightly. "God has given us our Itzhak." Her smile was weak. "He will not make us sacrifice him." The next day Itzhak started to nurse, move and cry.

Fradel Wasserman had been there most of the time since he was born. "Itzhak will grow up to be a big strong fellow," she said, "A blessing to you and to God." She packed up her belongings to leave. Exhausted as she was, she smiled a lot now. But her tired body flagged.

I walked her outside our front door. "You saved them." My big hug embarrassed her.

"God saved them," she answered. "Thank Him. Then go save our village."

I held Itzhak for the first time that day. Maybe I hadn't wanted to hold him before now because he might die. Sara's color returned. We cuddled - Sara, Yakira, Itzhak, and me. I had a family to save, and it scared me.

On the eighth day, as the Torah commands, Itzhak had his *bris*. We held it at first light at Uncle Yakov's urging. Under the circumstances, only the family gathered, along with Rabbi Rosenberg, Fradel Grunwasser and the Hassidic moyhel there to perform the ceremonial circumcision. There was no big meal to celebrate, only a few bagels and cooked wheat cereal. Ester and

Simon, Itzhak's godparents, carried him into the front room. I held Sara's hand tightly as the moyhel made his cut. Itzhak let out a healthy cry. Sara let out a little scream with him. The moyhel put a drop of wine on Itzhak's lips.

Everyone forced a cheerfulness they did not feel. They had kept me in a cocoon for seven days while I coped with Sara and Itzhak's struggle. But the crisis had arrived outside our door. Those who came in the house wore their worry on their faces, Uncle Yakov most of all.

The night before the bris, Uncle Yakov came by. I took him out back by the well. The damp darkness of October felt like wind blowing on wet skin. A light shined from Momma and Poppa's bedroom window. I could see Uncle Yakov's intensity.

"What's the situation?" I asked.

"Yesterday the Tsar signed this October Manifesto thing. It gives some rights to vote, some civil protections, and a parliament of sorts."

"And what do you think?"

He pulled his pipe from his coat pocket and fumbled to strike a match in the breeze. He gave up and put the unlit pipe in his mouth. "They say the Tsar's lost a lot of power. But I doubt the government will ever carry out these reforms."

"And the *pogroms*?"

"They've already started. Odessa, Kiev and a few other places. You'd better say goodbye right after the *bris*."

One crisis passed into another, my emotions swinging from end to end: love and compassion one moment, hate and revenge the next. I cherished the vision of Sara with Itzhak at her breast, then flashed to Viktor Askinov's steely grey eyes.

Viktor Askinov was coming for me, of that I was sure. He had to kill me if he wanted to get past our barricade and into the rest of the village. And if he didn't kill me, I would kill him.

As soon as the moyhel finished his cut, Uncle Yakov pulled me aside. "Are you ready?" His face was stone.

"Let's go."

"Get your gun and say goodbye to Sara. And bring a warm coat. It's going to be a cold night."

I clutched Sara to me and stroked her hair. She buried her face in my chest. This might be the last time I ever saw Sara, I thought. I felt calm, detached from the possibilities facing me.

Our feet thumped on the wooden sidewalk in unison. My heart pounded in rhythm with the pounding of our feet. The pistol hung heavy in my pocket. The cool breeze of the late October morning didn't stop me from sweating or moistening my dry tongue.

Uncle Yakov looked as grand as General Kutuzov must have looked before facing Napoleon at the Battle of Borodino.   His grey-streaked hair was cut short, his face clean shaven. A new hat with a short leather visor rested on top of his head. His stomach was as flat and hard as it had been during his army days. His riding boots glistened. His brown riding pants were clean, pressed and tucked neatly in his boots. In his lapel, of course, was his Hero's medal.

The streets were nearly empty. Two old women hurried across the street in front of us. An old man pushed a cart stacked with his belongings. The shops along Potocki Street were closed and locked.

"Where is everyone?" I asked.

"They know what's coming. Odessa and Kiev started yesterday. I'll brief you as soon as Gersh and Jeremiah get here."

"Are we going to win this?"

"Do we have a choice?"

"Is Poppa ready at the house?"

"Poppa's ready. But Reb Kravetz won't move." He looked straight ahead and walked. "He's a stubborn, stupid man." Reb Kravetz's house was beyond our perimeter, defenseless.

We turned the corner into the synagogue courtyard. A few of the men were already there. Uncle Yakov had doubled the guard two days ago when he first heard of the signing of the Manifesto. They straightened up when he passed. He nodded to each of them. The *Shamash* held the door open for us as if in a salute. He was an old man when I was a boy. He still looked like the oldest man I knew, hunched over with long, grey unkempt hair.

Gersh and Jeremiah were already inside, engaged in animated conversation. They stopped when we walked in. Both of them were grim-faced and looked tired already. They had filled in for me while I tended Sara and Itzhak, taking turns commanding the guards. One would be on duty for twelve hours, then the other.

Gersh's dark beard, shaggy hair, bushy eyebrows, and wild eyes made him look like a madman ready for a fight. His rumpled clothes hadn't been changed in days.

Jeremiah, on the other hand, was going to war well-dressed. He had on a fresh grey shirt under his dark blue pants and jacket. His face was clean shaven and his hair carefully combed. Grey flecked his thick hair; lines cut across his forehead. He was probably the oldest in our brigade other than Uncle Yakov. His mature presence comforted me like when I was a little boy.

Today Uncle Yakov had the energy of a powerful locomotive. He sported a riding crop, again a cavalry man, only one without a horse. Sometimes he clasped the crop in the armpit of his disabled left arm. Other times he gestured with it to make a dramatic point or to focus on the battle map on the wall.

Uncle Yakov stationed a person at the telegraph office just across the river, as well as his two spies still inside the Uman police department. Couriers could get here from Kiev or Odessa by train in less than two hours. He had better intelligence than anyone in Uman, even the army commander.

He paced back and forth, riding crop in hand. "Here's the situation. *Pogroms* everywhere. They started yesterday as soon as the Manifesto was published. So far forty-three, but new ones every hour. The closest is twenty-five miles from here. There's a big one in Kiev." He stopped pacing and turned to us. "The worst is Odessa. That one started a couple days ago. Atrocities are widespread. Fighting can start here any time, but probably not till tomorrow."

My heart beat harder and louder. "Who's attacking?" I asked.

"Everyone. Monarchists, police, priests, workers, peasants. The Black Hundreds. In Odessa it started with a group of nuns leading their students. They marched through the streets singing, carrying pictures of the Tsar and of Jesus. Priests carrying crosses. They were followed by a mob with crowbars, axe handles, shovels and guns."

It was no longer revolutionaries against the government. The government and radicals supporting the Tsar had turned it into a battle of Christians against Jews. Agitators told the workers and peasants the Manifesto granted Jews power to rule over them. That's all they needed to set them off.

Uncle Yakov looked from Gersh to Jeremiah and back. "Bund connections with the Socialists are gone. Expect no help from the Mensheviks or the Bolsheviks." Gersh and Jeremiah hung their heads. They must have felt betrayed. We were all alone again. Gersh opened his mouth to say something, then stopped, a gurgle coming out his throat.

"These *pogroms* are worse than Kishinev. Raping women. Young ones and old ones. Children thrown out of windows. Babies' heads smashed on the pavement and torn apart. Looting and burning factories and businesses. Synagogues burned. Houses demolished. The mobs are huge." We learned later that in Odessa alone nearly a thousand Jews were killed and 5,000 wounded.

My stomach churned so badly I thought I would give back the little food I had in my stomach. The taste of bile mixed inside with fire. The more we talked the more the bile receded and the fire blazed. There was no where to run and nothing to do but fight. We had no choice left. I looked over at Gersh and Jeremiah. They looked like I was feeling.

"Please tell me the Jews are fighting back," Gersh pleaded.

"They're fighting. Like bears!" His voice rose. He slapped his riding crop against his leg. "But the police and army turn on them. We hear the police are paying some *pogrom* leaders, and spreading rumors about Jews slaughtering Russians. Some police and army try to protect Jews. Not many, but a few."

"And in Uman?" I asked.

"Expect no help from the police. Tonight I'm meeting Colonel Baranski, commander of the military unit stationed outside town. Let's hope I can persuade him." I wondered how many favors Uncle Yakov had to call in from his old comrades to bring this meeting about.

"Fifty to a hundred thugs paid by the Black Hundreds will arrive in Uman some time tomorrow by train. I think they'll wait till then to attack us, but who knows. Anything could set it off."

Gersh, Jeremiah and I said nothing. We must have looked gloomy. Uncle Yakov leaned against the table in front of him. "Come! You're Jewish fighters," he barked. "You're our leaders. Act like it. We have a lot in our favor. We're going to win!" He smacked his crop on the table, a vein bulging out of his right forehead.

He talked at some length about our advantages. We were a well-trained fighting force and they were disorganized rabble. We were fighting on our own territory to defend our families. "And they'll never expect the surprises we have waiting for them." A devious smirk twisted his lips.

He began reviewing our own plan. Whenever we talked about it before, it always seemed like a game. Now it was real. My faith lay mostly in the man behind it. Uncle Yakov never showed the slightest doubt.

Now and then he used his crop to point something out on the map or to emphasize a point. "The objective is to protect our family and our village. It's not to kill Russians. Don't forget that. The more we kill, the more they will keep coming back until they kill us. So drive them off. Scare them so bad they don't come back. That will be victory. Don't... kill... them." He pointed his crop at me.

The excited voices of our men gathering outside in the courtyard infiltrated the classroom. Word had spread even though the trumpet had not yet sounded for them to assemble.

"We don't have enough ammunition for a prolonged fight," Uncle Yakov said. "We have to end it quickly. That means making them believe we have an overwhelming force. They're cowards and bullies. They won't fight against a strong opponent." If that doesn't stop them, I thought, we will have to kill them. I wanted Viktor Askinov in my gun sight, no matter what Uncle Yakov said.

"Any questions?" He had been speaking for probably a half hour.

"What's going on in other parts of the village?" Jeremiah asked. "What are we going to do about those neighborhoods that won't defend themselves?"

"We can only do what we can do." Uncle Yakov showed no emotion. "We can defend our few square blocks of this village. No more. We can't help those who won't help themselves."

"Do you think we should lead the men in prayers?" Jeremiah asked.

"Enough with the prayers." Gersh flung his arms in the air, spit spraying from his lips. "All week long. Prayers, prayers and more prayers. Enough. I'm sick of prayers. It's time to fight."

Uncle Yakov patted the air with his open hand, motioning for Gersh to calm down. Then he fixed his gaze on the back of the school room. " Remember. You are the sons of Gideon, Joshua, King Duvid and Judah Maccabee. You are the finest young leaders I have ever known. When you leave here, show no fear and your men will know no fear. The battle is now in your hands."

A tear glistened in Uncle Yakov's eyes. He came to attention, riding crop at his side. "Go!" he commanded.

I was ready to do battle with the Philistines, Goliath, the Tsar, and all of our other oppressors. I felt like a real soldier leading a real army, not an improbable bunch of poor Semites. I charged out of the classroom and into the courtyard. As we left, the Shamash handed me my rifle.

Uncle Yakov thought of every detail. The moment we exited the door, a trumpet player sounded the call for the fighters to assemble. The other two trumpeters picked up the call. It sounded like shofars on Rosh Hashanah eve. An emotional stew of contradictions jolted through me: pride, anger, fear, determination, confidence, hope, duty. But most of all, revenge.

Men shouted to each other as they ran to the courtyard. Markus, Simon and Josef were among the first to arrive. Loaded carts pulled by horses or oxen rolled across the market square toward the spot where we would erect our barricades. Dust swirled, clogging my nose. The shadows of the fresh October day danced through the tree in the courtyard. It was a beautiful day, if a day meant for killing can be called beautiful.

Finally the full force of nearly eighty-five young men was assembled.   About sixty were well-trained regulars, the rest un-trained reserves we hoped we wouldn't need. I think Uncle Yakov wanted them mostly to give the impression we had more fighters than we really had. If things got desperate, maybe they would be the last hope.

The assembly looked like the tribes of Israel. The few blue-eyed blonds sprinkled the throng of dark hair and dark eyes. Their uniforms were baggy pants, tattered coats, well-worn shoes, and short-billed caps. Only a few had no beards or moustaches. The only grey hairs among them were those of the old Shamash, Jeremiah and Uncle Yakov.

The Shamash handed the fighters white arm bands with a blue Star of Duvid. The reserves got blue kerchiefs to tie around their arms. Everyone looked at their flimsy armbands as though they had just been given fine army dress uniforms.

A trumpet sounded. Everyone stopped talking. The only noise was the creaking cart wheels and a complaint from one of the oxen. Uncle Yakov raised his riding crop over his head. "Men! Assemble behind your squad leaders," he commanded. Eighty-five men shuffled around until the men of each of our squads were grouped behind Gersh, Jeremiah or me, facing toward Uncle Yakov. The reserves gathered to the side.

Our commander stood at attention, his gaze scanning from right to left and back again. They all tried to imitate him, shoulders back, head high, eyes straight ahead. The leaves of the oak tree rustled in the wind. No one moved.

Uncle Yakov's voice boomed, resounding off the three walls surrounding us. He looked to the sky, arm reaching out seeking God's intervention. Then he looked at each of us as though he were talking to that person alone. His voice rose, went soft, then rose again. He made us feel like we were about to fight the greatest battle in the history of the Jewish people. He invoked the names of nearly every Jewish fighter in the bible.

History has never noted what we did in those days. We were only a tiny little skirmish in one small neighborhood in one small village. But for me and everyone who was there, it was the time of times.

"You are fighting for your lives, the lives of your families, and for the people of Israel. You will not fail." In that moment, Uncle Yakov became someone I had never seen before - General Yakov.

As his oration concluded, cheers and shouts erupted. Clubs and guns waved in the air. Uncle Yakov held his hand up for silence. Rabbi Rosenberg shuffled forward, struggling against his arthritic body. He wore his best black Sabbath garb, a big black hat, and a small white *tallis* around his neck. He spoke with the strength of a man who spoke to God on a regular basis. He raised his arms to bless us, looking toward the deep blue sky.

"Today you are on the verge of battle with your enemies. Do not let your heart be faint, do not be afraid, and do not tremble or be terrified because of them, for the Lord your God is He who goes with you, to fight for you against your enemies, to save you." He lowered his arms slowly to his side amidst a chorus of Amen's.

In the years since then, I've frequently read the full passage Rabbi Rosenberg took from the Torah, trying to understand what happened that day and in the days that followed. Between Uncle Yakov and Rabbi Rosenberg, my mind and my soul were ready. I never questioned whether I could kill and whether I should kill.

"Take your positions," Uncle Yakov commanded. Three trumpets sounded, one from the direction of Pushkin Street where Gersh would be, one from Potocki Street for Jeremiah, and one from next to the nearby well, for my squad. Along side each of the trumpeters, a man held a large flag attached to a long pole, the blue Star of Duvid on a field of white waving in the wind.

Uncle Yakov assigned twenty-five men to my squad because he expected the first attack to come up Nevsky Street. Gersh and Jeremiah each had fifteen men. He kept five men in reserve with him under the oak tree in front of the synagogue. They also served as runners bringing messages and orders to the three squad leaders. The five in reserve would be rushed to whichever barricade was attacked hardest. Or they could be needed to cover our retreat.

My squad ran across the market square toward Nevsky Street. Mica Rosenbaum, Meier Braun, and I carried rifles, the rest pistols. The square was as quiet and vacant as a Sabbath afternoon. Only a few stalls were standing and they would soon be turned into material for our barricade. A flock of geese scurried out of our way, the anxious mother pushing her little ones along. The sun had passed its peak and we had much to do before it set. It was going to be a cold night. No one was to go home until this was over. Uncle Yakov didn't want anything getting in the fighters' minds except the battle. We would sleep in our positions and in a few stores along the sides of the square.

We set to work building our barricade on Nevsky Street about ten meters before it entered the square, facing toward the river. Shlomo, the engineer among us, designed and supervised. Carts were overturned. Stalls in the square were torn down, the boards added to the growing rampart. Barrels filled with earth reinforced it and gave stout protection.

More carts pulled by oxen rolled in filled with derelict materials. I recognized some old benches from the synagogue and timbers from the abandoned barn behind the blacksmith's shop.

We worked feverishly. Coats came off as sweat wetted our shirts even in the shadows of late afternoon. The grey pile of weathered wood grew taller and deeper. The barricade grew as thick as two wagons and taller than a man.

It was high enough so from the top we would be firing down on anyone coming up Nevsky Street. Segments of rock gave the wall substance. Nevsky Street was completely blocked. I checked frequently to be sure the firing steps would provide clear fields of fire. As the barricade grew, confidence grew.

"How does the saying in the bible go?" Moishe Stepaner bantered. "May the gentiles see our might and shit their pants."

The final pieces were the ladders on each side of the street so a few fighters could climb onto the roof tops. This was the vital part of Uncle Yakov's plan.

At its core, there were two principles to the plan. First, do everything necessary to keep the pogromists from passing. Second, do everything we could to keep from killing any of them. How do you ask a man to be ready to kill and still think about not killing at the same time? I thought Uncle Yakov was asking too much from us. I hoped he saw us realistically - *shtetl* Jews, not the Tsar's disciplined army of his imagination.

Our strategy was to take the pogromists by surprise, counting on cowardice and confusion to make them flee when faced with strong opposition. I put five men on the rooftops on the east side of Nevsky Street and five on the west. Thirteen men took positions behind the barricade. We would have them in a crossfire contained inside a horseshoe.

Two men posted themselves down Nevsky Street at the bend where they could see to the river. They would give us an early warning, then run back to the barricade. Along the way, they would light six kerosene torches at intervals along the street.

When the mob was inside the horseshoe, we would open fire, yelling, screaming and blowing the trumpet. The risky part was Uncle Yakov's order not to kill anyone. And we didn't have a lot of ammunition for a prolonged battle. We only had three rifles.

The rest of our guns were less powerful, inaccurate handguns. After that it was knives, clubs and crowbars.

We were each to fire only two rounds in the air or at their feet. Uncle Yakov was sure they would retreat when they saw they were boxed in, opposed by strong firepower in front of them and above them on the roofs. If they continued forward, we would fire on the first row of marchers, which is where Viktor Askinov would be. He warned us not to fire at any priests.

Uncle Yakov was thinking of the consequences of actions we took. I wasn't. He was convinced the plan would work. I wasn't. If the plan had come from anyone but Uncle Yakov, I would have thought it a fairy tale.

I hoped the plan worked, but I wanted the chance to kill Viktor Askinov. I was not thinking rationally enough to see the contradiction. This man was the only person in my life I ever truly hated. Certainly he was the only one I hated enough to kill with my own hands.

Before the sun set, I sent Josef to try one more time to persuade his father to move inside our perimeter. "Tell him the situation's desperate," I said. "Tell him to do it for Sara."

When Josef returned, I knew from his long face he had failed. "He's a stubborn goat." Josef spit. "There's no convincing him. But he let Mother and Havol go to your house for now."

By the time we finished building the barricade, the shadows of early evening had seeped in. Carts had been delivering water throughout the day. Now they arrived with a load of food. It was cold but as welcomed as a Sabbath dinner: bagels, smoked fish, hard boiled eggs, cheese and pastries. Kosher.

Uncle Yakov handled these logistics as surely as he handled everything else. The butchers, bakers and fishmongers contributed. Women volunteered their supplies set aside for the Sabbath. Uncle Yakov also sent warm army blankets. God alone knows how he got so many.

He inspected our position every few hours. As soon as they saw him, everyone perked up, worked more feverishly, joked and laughed. "God, I love that man," Chiam Chernoff said. Uncle Yakov examined the construction of our barricade as it was going up, made some suggestions, and complimented each man. Before he left, he pulled Shlomo Zilberman and me aside and told us what really needed to be fixed.

In the early evening, he said he was on his way to meet with Colonel Baranski. "Bed the men down for the night. Half on duty, half off. They will not attack tonight."

Dark nights and uncertainty compound fear. So I made the rounds of our positions every two hours and let everyone know everything I knew, which wasn't very much. I had to climb those ladders onto the rooftops in the pitch black. It seemed I had stepped off into a void. I felt my way along, sure I was going to slip and tumble off the roof. There were only a few lamps burning along Nevsky Street but they provided me a little visual perspective. Without them, I would have had no balance at all.

Mica Rosenbaum, a devout young man about the age of Markus, was the last one to check. He huddled next to a chimney, his rifle sticking out from under a grey blanket.

"Are you scared?" he whispered, shivering in the damp fog swirling around him.

"Of course I'm scared," I whispered back. "Only a fool wouldn't be."

"Do you think they were scared? Gideon, Joshua, and Judah Maccabee?"

"Even them. Uncle Yakov says everyone is afraid before a battle."

"I can't imagine Duvid being scared when he faced Goliath."

"He was scared." I patted Mica on the shoulder like Uncle

Yakov had done to me so many times.

"But the Lord told him he was going to win." Mica's anxious voice rose above a whisper; I patted my hand down for him to lower it.

"He also told Duvid the battle is God's, and God would give Goliath into his hand," I said. That's all I could remember about the Torah's story. I hoped Mica would not press the subject further. "God will deliver Goliath into our hands."

"Are you King Duvid?" Mica was serious, almost reverent. He was looking for a reason to believe our farfetched plan would work, but his mysticism unnerved me. I laughed quietly and shook my head.

"Uncle Yakov knows what he's doing," I said. "His plan is a good one. Put your faith in him." I turned to go down the ladder, not looking forward to negotiating the slippery rungs in the dark.

"Wait, Avi." I turned back. "I don't know if I can shoot someone," he said.

"Mica. What are saying? You're the best shot we have. You must do it, if it comes to that." The sharpshooters on the roofs were critical to the whole plan.

"It's wrong to kill. The Torah says so. The Ten Commandments."

"The Torah says it's wrong to murder. This won't be murder. We're defending our families. Why do you think God made all those heroes? Gideon, Judah Maccabee, Joshua, Duvid? To give us faith in ourselves." My voice got louder, carrying too far in the still night. This could be a disaster and I had to change his mind.

Mica pondered my words, gently stroking his rifle like a man strokes a good goat. "Am I a coward?" he pleaded.

Yes, I wanted to say. Then the picture ran through my mind of that rabbit I couldn't kill when I was a boy and Uncle Yakov was first teaching me how to shoot. Viktor Askinov was a different story. "No," I answered. "But we need that rifle firing from up here. Do you want me to give it to someone else?" In reality, it was too late to train a new sharpshooter.

Mica clutched the rifle to him as though fearing I would yank it from his arms. "No. I'll do it if I have to."

But I was no longer sure he would. "Think about those two younger sisters of yours and what this mob will do to them if they get past us." I leaned close enough for our noses to nearly touch. "They'll rape them. Then they'll kill them. Your momma and poppa too. They'll burn our synagogue and the whole village. Is that what you want?"

Mica set his jaw. "Let's hope the warning shots scare them off," he said with the slightest bit of fire.

I patted him on the shoulder, then turned and felt my way down the ladder. Maybe I was going to have to put someone by Mica's side to take his rifle from him and use it if he wouldn't use it himself.

Half the men went to find a warm place to bed down for a couple of hours. Those on duty were so tired from all the work we had done building the barricade they had to force themselves to stay awake. I couldn't sleep until Uncle Yakov returned from his meeting with Colonel Baranski.

A cold October fog drifted up from the river, chilling me to the bone. The mist cut down visibility and stirred a dread inside me. I felt for the comfort of the rifle in my hands and the pistol in my pocket. I huddled beneath a blanket, thankful for it but wishing I had two of them. My mind poured over the plan again and again, searching for any detail I might have overlooked. Then I imagined what the battle was going to be like. Uncle Yakov told us often enough that the best of plans is up the chimney the minute the fighting starts.

I must have dozed because I jerked when Simon shook me awake. A runner arrived with a message from Uncle Yakov. He had returned from seeing the colonel with promising results. The squad leaders would meet at first light to discuss it.

"Get some sleep," Simon said to me. "Tomorrow we need you awake." He patted me on the arm.

"Wake me in a couple of hours. I'll bed down in the general store." What a rock that Simon is, I thought. I'm glad he married Ester. And I'm glad he's here.

I went into the general store and found a spot in the corner. I stepped on someone in the dark and heard sleepy cursing. I apologized.

"Oh, it's you Avi. Sorry. Find a spot," Markus mumbled.

Keeping Markus out of danger was a priority, so I tried assigning him to the reserves back by the synagogue. He would have none of it.

"I've earned the right to be here." He stuck his nose in my face. "I want to kill the son-of-a-bitch too!" He was right. He had been Viktor Askinov's victim as much as I had.

"I won't be able to keep an eye on you once the battle starts."

"So who asked you to?"

Markus was a good soldier. He was nineteen years old, and as big as I was. But he was still my kid brother, probably still a virgin. I didn't want him to die that way.

The mind plays tricks at times like this. Itzhak's *bris* had only been this morning but it seemed like it was years ago in a different place. I wrapped my blanket around myself and said a prayer for him before I dozed off: May he know in his life a time and place of peace and safety.

During the night someone unfurled the big white flag with the Star of Duvid and mounted it on top of the barricade. I wiped the sleep from my eyes and stretched my aching bones.

A few men looked up at it as they woke. Then more. Everyone was quiet, lost in their own thoughts. To me it said be brave, be proud, and have hope. Not a sound came from anywhere. Then from the back, toward the market square, a single voice began singing Hatikvah. It had become an anthem of sorts all over the Pale of Settlement. I've heard it many times since then but never like that morning.

The reserves gathered across the square near the synagogue heard our singing and joined.

> *Hear, O my brothers in the lands of exile,*
> *The voice of our prophets,*
> *Who declare that only with the very last Jew,*
> *Only then is the end of our hope.*

By the time we finished, tears moistened the cheeks of many men. I wiped the wet from my mine, unembarrassed.

A few minutes later, a hot breakfast arrived in a wagon pulled by an old grey horse, and driven by an even older grey-maned, one-eyed man. A couple of fires burning during the night to keep us warm were converted into stoves to heat the food: a grainy cereal, more eggs, hot goat's meat, warm noodles, herring and coffee. Uncle Yakov made sure we were better fed than we were at home.

I picked at my breakfast, eager to find out what happened last night at the meeting with Colonel Baranski. Then I hurried across the open square toward Uncle Yakov's headquarters. The morning fog lifted, and the grey sky lightened. Shortly the sun would peak through. I had that unwashed feeling from having slept in my clothes all night and could smell my own feet. My mouth tasted like trash even after breakfast and coffee. My beard itched as though it were crawling with lice.

Some of the reserves in the synagogue courtyard were on guard duty while others ate. A few waved to me. They didn't look much like an army. They looked like Mottel the baker's assistant, Saul the blacksmith, Tevye the butcher's helper, and the other sons of the village.

The night before, Beryl Weisman tried to sneak home to see his wife. Uncle Yakov sent three of his largest men to drag him back, humiliated. He locked poor Beryl in a schoolroom closet all night until he begged to be let out to fight. Uncle Yakov assigned him to Gersh Leibowitz's squad. Gersh would have no sympathy if Beryl tried it again. It squelched my own temptation to steal off to see Sara.

Uncle Yakov watched me approach from beneath the oak tree, his good hand on his hip. Gersh stood beside him, looking no better than I felt. Something told me I wasn't going to like what he had to say about his meeting with Colonel Baranski.

TWENTY-TWO

October 21, 1905

Gersh, Jeremiah and I squeezed into children's seats waiting for Uncle Yakov to speak. He took his time, pinching the top of his nose, sniffling, and running fingers through his hair. He looked fresh, clean-shaved, as though he had gotten a good night's sleep. Gersh drummed his fingers on the splintered desk in front of him. Jeremiah yawned and rubbed sleep from his exhausted eyes.

"I didn't get everything we wanted, but I got enough," he said. "A group from the Black Hundreds arrive in Uman by train this afternoon. The *pogrom* starts tonight." The three of us leaned forward, waiting for some good news.

"Colonel Baranski will send his troops in tomorrow if the fighting is still going on," he continued. "But there's one condition." He paused, locking on each of us separately. "One big condition. No Christians can die tonight. If we kill any of them, Baranski will send his troops to fight us and to arrest us."

"That's not fair," I blurted. Gersh studied his black fingernails. Jeremiah said nothing.

"We will not kill any Christians." He shouted, his face turning red. "Do you understand?" He smacked his riding crop on the desk in front of me sending a plumb of dust into the air. I jumped.

"How are we supposed to do that if they overrun us?" I yelled back.

"Use your head! Follow the plan! Then use your fuckin' clubs and fists."

"What if the plan doesn't work and they keep coming at us? There are more of them than there of us."

"You'll follow the plan! Do you understand?" He didn't blink. He didn't move a muscle.

"Yes," Gersh and Jeremiah said softly. Uncle Yakov sunk his stare into me.

"Yes," I mumbled, looking away. But this was personal between Viktor Askinov and me. I had waited a long time to kill that son-of-a-whore.

Uncle Yakov took a deep breath and leaned forward on the table. "The plan will work. We're going to spend the day working on a contingency."

My right hand was shaking; I couldn't stop it until I grasped it with my left. I told myself Uncle Yakov had faced battles like this before and I hadn't. I had to trust him. It was easier for Gersh and Jeremiah. My position was the one the pogromists were likely to hit first and hardest.

I leaned forward to hear Uncle Yakov's plan modifications. Each squad would build another barrier several meters behind the first one in case we had to fall back. The reserves were going to construct strong points across the square for us to use if the pogromists broke through and we had to retreat toward the synagogue. At that point, we would have no choice but to fire right at them.

"Maintain discipline," Uncle Yakov said. "Talk to your men now. If we have to retreat, there can't be any panic. And you can't leave anyone behind. If anyone is wounded someone must pick him up and carry him." He took a deep breath. "If we're forced to retreat, we won't try to defend the synagogue."

"They'll burn it to the ground," Gersh said.

"We will fight to save lives, not buildings," Uncle Yakov answered.

"Does Rabbi Rosenberg know?" Jeremiah asked.

Uncle Yakov nodded, his eyes sad.

If we made it back across the square, the survivors would set up a defensive line blocking Potocki Street. I liked that part of the plan because, if it came to this, I would be closer to our house and Sara. It never dawned on me I might not be alive at that point.

When we left the schoolhouse, makeshift positions were already being constructed by reserves and a few of Jeremiah's squad. Older men not in the brigade helped. A similar position was to be constructed blocking the end of Pushkin Street nearest to the synagogue.

The fog burned off and the glow of early morning sunshine caressed the square. There was much work to be done on these new backup barriers before nightfall. Urgency bordering on panic drove us. Our families trembled behind closed shutters only a couple hundred meters behind us. After all of our careful planning and training, it was coming down to last-minute improvisations.

"At least building these new strong points gives us something to do. It'll keep our minds busy," I said to Shlomo Zilberman.

"Maybe that's just what Uncle Yakov was thinking," he answered, his brain already at work on how to approach this new construction project.

In mid afternoon, Uncle Yakov took me on a walk around the market square, away from the men. "We have new reports from Kiev and Odessa." He gritted his teeth. "It's very bad. Horrible atrocities."

Hundreds of Jews had already been killed in Odessa, their bodies left lying in the streets. Thousands were wounded. They attacked the women and children as brutally as the men. So many synagogues, houses and businesses were on fire the smoke blocked the sun.

Uncle Yakov stopped walking and leaned against the side of the butcher shop, fatigue showing in his face and body.   He winced when a driving pain shot up his limp arm. "One woman was raped right in front of a group of Christian women. She was pregnant. They killed her. Then opened her up with a knife and took out the baby, smashing it against a stone wall until its head burst. The women who were watching stuffed the dead woman's stomach with garbage."

I gagged. Uncle Yakov touched my arm. If the men heard about this there would be no restraining them when the fight started. So I didn't tell them.

"Jews are fighting back hard. They're killing Russians," he said. "Tell your men that."

The whistle in the distance announced the arrival of a train in Uman. The afternoon shadows descended and the chill settled in. Tonight was going to be clear under a full moon. The new construction was finished.   These backup positions were not as substantial as the main barricade we built yesterday, but they would have to do.

The day wound down. Tension overlapped boredom. The men played cards, read books, wrote letters, cleaned guns, and talked quietly. Much of the talk was about going to America when this was over. Mica and two other pious ones spent their time reading from a prayer book, swaying back and forth. It didn't do any harm to ask God for help. I hoped He was listening.

Uncle Yakov sent the wagon with the evening meal around early. This time it was loaded with extra bread, dried meat and water to sustain us through the night. The old man driving the wagon looked down at me from his seat and held two fingers to his bushy grey eyebrow in a salute. He nodded his head. Then he jiggled the reins and the old horse strained, slowly pulling the rickety wagon away. Chiam Chernoff was the only one who did more than pick at his banquet.

Darkness crept in early at this time of year. A few lanterns burned in the distance. A runner scurried across the square with a written message from Uncle Yakov. "The Black Hundreds have arrived," it read. "We counted seventy-one of them getting off the train. Expect an attack at any time." It was signed with his simple "Y."

I took a deep breath and turned to Simon. "Here we go," I said. His shoulders tensed. He nodded, his lips pulled tight.

Three blasts on my whistle signaled an attack was coming. I stood on top of the barricade so everyone could see me, the trumpeter by my side. I kept Markus and Simon close by, for their sake and mine.

Men dashed to their positions like angry bees in a molested beehive. Josef and Moishe Stepaner charged down Nevsky Street to their lookout spot at the bend in the road, a cloud of dust swirling behind them. They would be the first to see the pogromists coming across the bridge.

Meier Braun climbed the ladder to the roof on my right, rifle in hand. Mica Rosenbaum did the same on the left. I'd alerted Chiam Chernoff to be prepared to grab the rifle from Mica and use it if Mica wouldn't.

The ten men on the roofs were the bravest. They were the vital element in the plan, catching the pogromists in a cross fire. But they could get trapped on those roofs if we had to retreat. It gave me little comfort that they had all volunteered. I only allowed unmarried men on the roofs. I didn't want to be responsible for creating a widow or an orphan.

The waiting was nearly over. The light of the full moon against the black night created shadows that danced like spirits. There were moments I was certain the pogromists were sneaking up on us. I ran out three-man patrols a couple of times. They came back with nothing to report. I visited each man and assured him the dancing spirits were only shadows.

Time passed as slowly as a turtle crossing the road. I jumped when a horse brayed behind me in the square. One of the men kicked over a chamber pot. "Sorry," he whispered so loud the pogromists could have heard him from the other side of the river. The taste of metal clung to my tongue. My leg cramped. My elbows got sore from leaning on them, pointing my rifle out of the firing slot. We waited some more.

Uncle Yakov had been right: Whether a battle or a brawl, nothing else focuses you like this. Every detail of the plan passed through my mind again and again. Was I missing something? No, we're ready, I thought.

Only images of Sara penetrated my barriers. And thoughts of the mob coming for us, led by Viktor Askinov. I didn't believe it would really happen, but I admitted to myself the possibility Sara and I might die. Yakira and Itzhak could grow up without us. But death wasn't the worst I imagined.

My horror of horrors was Sara raped and tortured before she died. Visions ran through my head of five or six big, ugly, dirty men with garlic on their breath holding her down, spreading her legs and taking their turns until they killed her. Her screams for help and Yakira's cries pounded in my ears. I wanted to murder someone, and prayed they would attack my barricade first so I could kill them all. Let them come and let them know my vengeance! Please God.

Simon touched me on the arm, bringing me back. "You were

somewhere else," he said. "Are you alright?" Steady Simon gave me a puzzled examination.

"Tonight I'm going to kill Viktor Askinov."

"No you're not!" He snarled, barely above a whisper. He searched my face in the dark for something. "This isn't only about you and Viktor Askinov." His swept his outstretched hand around over all of the men and the village behind us.

I took a deep breath, then chewed on my lip for a moment. "I'll be alright," I said. "Don't worry." I forced a weak smile to assure him I was in control of myself.

Simon was wary. He gestured at the men crouched behind the barricade and on the roofs. "Their lives depend on you. I depend on you." He looked down the street. "I'm staying close."

"That's where I want you."

I knew my duty, even without Simon's lecture. But I wanted my revenge too, biblical justice brought down on Viktor Askinov. Only I couldn't leave it up to God; maybe there was no God.

Not more than an hour after dark I heard the first crack of gunfire in the distance. Then a few more shots. They came from the direction of Gersh's position on Pushkin Street. Others turned their heads like I did. The faint smell of smoke drifted in.

"Markus," I yelled. He was right at my elbow. "Go see where that firing's coming from. If you can't find Uncle Yakov at the headquarters, head for Gersh's position." Markus bolted across the market square. The beat of his feet could be heard well after his black outline disappeared into the darkness.

He seemed to be gone a long time. I turned toward the square every time I heard a sound. Simon put a hand on my hand as if to say "patience." But maybe we were being outflanked and cut off from the others. Uncle Yakov had taught Gersh, Jeremiah and me to think about all possibilities and have a contingency plan in mind. I was considering repositioning a few of the men when I finally heard Markus's hurried footsteps and saw his shadow racing toward us.

He collapsed beside me, gasping to catch his breath. "It's outside our perimeter," he said. "The other end of the village where they're not defending themselves."

"Reb Kravetz?" I asked.

"They haven't gotten that far yet. I went to Gersh's position and looked over their barricade." He breathed a little easier. "But a few of their big guys looked like they were moving toward the Hassidic synagogue with torches."

"Maybe they'll attack Gersh first."

"Uncle Yakov says to be ready. They're going to attack us first. In force."

I was angry at Reb Kravetz. Sara would mourn his death. Well, I had enough to worry about besides him.

I didn't see or hear Uncle Yakov until he materialized alongside me. He presence always made me feel better. He was always so confident we would win. Now he peered over the top of the barricade, his profile low. The only weapon he showed was his riding crop.

"They'll hit here," he whispered. "This is where the synagogue is. They want to burn it down." He looked over at me. "And this is where you are." Even in this cool air, a trickle of sweat ran down my arm. Viktor Askinov wanted me as badly as I wanted him. I wondered if he was as afraid of me as I was of him.

"No one has to die here tonight," Uncle Yakov said. "Just follow the plan." He turned his hard gaze on me.

"I'll try." But I didn't mean it.

"Do it, damn it!" He squeezed my arm so hard I struggled not to cry out. Then he jumped up and disappeared across the market square just the way he came.

We waited.

At last I heard the faint sound of their beating drum. I looked over at Simon on my right and Markus on my left, tightening my grip on my rifle. "They're coming!" Mumbles passed from man to man on the left, right and up on the roofs. Those on either side of Simon and Markus crawled into their firing burrows, braced their pistols on the rubble at the top of the wall, and sighted.

The drum beat louder. The thump of Josef's and Moishe Stepaner's pounding feet ricocheted off the channel of stores and houses on both sides of Nevsky Street as they raced toward us. They slowed to light the torches before scampering over the barricade. "They're right behind us," Josef panted. The torches ignited the night.

When the first of the mob came around the bend in the street, I motioned for the trumpeter to sound the alarm. One short and one long blast disrupted the stillness. "Keep blowing it," I yelled. Trumpets from Gersh's and Jeremiah's positions answered. I hoped Uncle Yakov would get here soon. I needed him. Currents of anticipation gushed through me, wiping out the fear.

Our blue and white flag rippled in the wind. The yelling, screaming mob came into view, illuminated by their torches and ours. Their long shadows and determined strides made them look ten feet tall and as powerful as blacksmiths. There must have been a hundred and fifty or two hundred against our band of twenty-five. God saved us before. I hoped he was watching now. Their voices converged into one big roar. A few stood out:

"Kill the Jews!"

"Avenge the Christ!"

"Save the Tsar."

"Fuck the Tsar," someone on our side of the barrier yelled back. I prayed no one on the roof tops would call out and give away our positions.

The drum beat louder and louder. Their boots hammered the

ground beneath them. There were so many. As they came into the light of our torches, I could see Viktor Askinov clearly in the center of the front row, leading, a club swinging from his muscular arm. A thick black belt cinched his long grey shirt, full black pants tucked into high boots.

To his right was a priest in a black robe carrying a wooden cross and to his left his father, Constable Askinov. He scanned our barricade until his unblinking eyes fixed on me. He bared the teeth and the snarling lips of a rabid dog.

Behind the first row, a line of big, angry men strode step for step with their leader, clubs and crowbars in hand. Others waved pistols and large wooden crosses. A few carried rifles. A few carried torches. I saw some more priests in the crowd and recognized a policeman who only last week was patrolling the square on market day.

The trumpeter ran out of breath, maybe from fear. "Keep blowing that damn thing," I yelled, "Louder! Louder!"

"Fuck the Tsar," Markus yelled. Someone else repeated it. Then everyone took up the chorus, except those on the roofs: "Fuck the Tsar! Fuck the Tsar! Fuck the Tsar!"

The thunderous jeers and tramping feet of two hundred men showered us. The smell of kerosene and tar from the torches soaked my nostrils. My heart hammered. My head throbbed.

I tracked Viktor Askinov in my rifle sight, waiting for him to come so close I couldn't miss. The stock pressed against my shoulder, sweating finger on the trigger, shaking. Obligation to the plan wrestled with the compulsion to kill this man.

In my mind's eye, the mob was ten feet from me. I could see the detail of his face in the yellow glow of the torches. More likely he was thirty or forty meters away. Viktor Askinov stared right at me, those steely grey eyes secreting hate. I savored the bitterness of my own hate.

Their pace slowed when they saw the magnitude of our barricade. It would not be easy for them to charge through it or scale it. And they didn't know how many fighters we had. Viktor Askinov glanced up at the roof tops on his left. I held my breath.

They walked slowly forward, hesitant, one small step at a time. The drum beat continued but the shouts and curses weakened, and then stopped. I took a deep breath when they crossed the designated line, about fifteen meters away.

"Fire!" I screamed at the top of my lungs. The trumpet sounded. I blew a whistle. Our guns boomed.

All twenty-five of us fired simultaneously at their feet and over their heads from all directions. Claps and bangs flashed in the night like violent thunder and lightning. Mica's rifle flashed and banged from the rooftop on my left and Meier's on my right. Men on both sides screamed and roared.

Each of us fired two rounds, and then stopped. Puffs of smoke from the guns floated like clouds. The smell of gunpowder engulfing me still clings to me even now.

Uncle Yakov was a genius. They were caught in a cross fire from above and all around them. They stopped. Most of them crouched down, including Viktor Askinov, the Constable and the priest by his side. A few fired shots aimlessly into the night, but the Constable yelled at them to halt. Some in the rear of the crowd drifted back down Nevsky Street, ready to run. Shock and fear painted their ugly faces. They didn't know what to do. It's working, I thought. Now turn around. Leave.

When our volley ended, unearthly silence followed. Their drum stopped beating. Our trumpet stopped blowing. Shouting stopped. Time stopped. I could hear Simon breathing hard next to me. A dog barked from far away.

Viktor Askinov knelt down on one knee. I kept my rifle sight fixed on his head. His wide eyes darted randomly from one direction to the other, up to the roofs, and back again. He looked confused, scared and as dangerous as a cornered boar.

This was when, in Uncle Yakov's plan, they were supposed to retreat down Nevsky Street, and leave us alone. If they moved toward our barricade, we would have to fire right at them. We only had enough ammunition for a brief fight. Then it was clubs and knives.

I wonder now how much time went by, everyone suspended. I wanted to end Viktor Askinov's life right then and there. I begged him to make so much as a small move so I could kill him.

He rose cautiously from his crouch, his steely eyes staring right at me again. What I see now is him slowly raising his right arm over his head to signal his men to attack. He opened his mouth to shout something.

I sighted down the barrel at his head, took a deep breath, held it - and slowly squeezed the trigger. "Bam!" My rifle roared at the dark, punching my shoulder.

He screeched like nothing I have ever heard, except maybe a goat being slaughtered. He toppled to the ground grabbing his right leg, blood gushing under him. He screamed and screamed. He cursed. He called for his mother. He bled. The fires of Hades surged through me. I gorged on the sight of his writhing body and the river of red flowing from him.

His father and the priest hunched over him. The priest made the sign of the cross, his lips moving in prayer. Some in the back of their pack snuck away, down Nevsky Street; then a few more and a few more. Others called out to each other, confused and terrorized. They all started running as fast as they could. A couple of them banged into a priest, knocking him to the ground. They dropped their clubs and torches. Their drum rolled along the ground and came to rest against the foot of our barricade.

I worked the lever of my rifle, chambering another round,

and again fixed Viktor Askinov's head in my sight. This time I wouldn't miss. His head would explode like a melon. I took a deep breath, held it - and slowly squeezed the trigger.

The rifle was ripped violently from my hands. "Stop! Stop!" Uncle Yakov yelled, throwing my rifle to the ground. "Enough. He's down. Simon. Markus. Get hold of him." Both of them put a firm hand on each of my arms. I struggled for a moment, and then gave in to their determined grips.

Uncle Yakov crawled on top of the barricade and threw some bandages in the direction of Viktor Askinov. The Constable took the rags and wrapped the leg but blood soaked through immediately. His cries pierced the stillness. Two of their biggest beasts put their arms under his arms and carried him down Nevsky Street. He shrieked every time his leg dragged the ground. I savored his every scream.

"You didn't need to kill him," Uncle Yakov hollered, poking me in the chest with his finger.

"He was attacking."

"You've tasted blood." His lips trembled. I didn't understood why Uncle Yakov was so mad at this moment of victory.

Simon and Markus released their grips. Uncle Yakov and I sat on the barricade for a few minutes, neither of us speaking. "Check on your men," he said. "They may be back." Viktor Askinov's screams faded as they rounded the bend toward the bridge.

My fever was so high I wouldn't have even needed the ladder to climb on top of the roofs. "Did we win?" Mica Rosenbaum asked.

"Yes, we won." I patted him on the shoulder, noticing in the moonlight a wet patch on his pants. "But they might be back."

I went down to the bend in Nevsky Street to be sure they were gone. When I returned, Uncle Yakov was no longer so upset

with me. He stayed with me the rest of the night. He kept touching me: on the arm, the back, and the hair. In those touches, he
gave me what I needed.

The plan had been preposterous. There were so many of
them and so few of us. We weren't a real army, just a bunch of
poor Jews led by a worn-out war horse. It shouldn't have worked.
Maybe this is how God does his miracles.

Even then I recognized I had done something important, and
affected many lives. Wounding Viktor Askinov stopped the attack. But I was trying to kill him, not just wound him. If I had
succeeded in killing him, they would have attacked again with
greater force until they killed us. The army would have helped
them.

I've turned over in my mind a thousand times whether or not
I did the right thing. I wanted to kill him, and I could have. If I
had succeeded, maybe more of Viktor Askinov's havoc would
have been prevented. But then maybe some other devil would
have done it anyway.

Just before dawn, Uncle Yakov stood up and stretched. "I
have to see Colonel Baranski," he said. "Keep half the men on
alert until I return." He marched off across the market square as if
he was on parade.

A couple of hours later I watched anxiously as he marched
back toward us. His cadence told me nothing of the outcome of
his meeting.

"It's over. There will be no more attacks." But nothing in
his look or tone suggested victory. "The army will move in immediately to preserve order." He turned to Markus and Simon
who hadn't let me out of their sight all night. "Tell the others," he
said. Their faces questioned, but they followed his order.

"It's over? Are you sure?" I asked.

Uncle Yakov grabbed me firmly by the elbow with his good

hand and walked me away from the barricade. Others watched, waiting to hear what happened. He didn't say anything until we sat down on a pile of dry wood. He put his hand on mine and looked at me.

"Viktor Askinov will live, but they know you were the one who shot him." His eyes were tired and sad.

"But I was defending myself." I needed to convince Uncle Yakov I did the right thing.

"Maybe you didn't need to shoot him."

"He's the devil."

"But now it's you who must pay." His shoulders sagged. His voice softened. He squeezed my hand. "They have given you thirty days to leave Uman. If you don't, they will put you on trial for attempted murder and inciting a riot. You will lose. You have no choice. Leave for America or you will go to prison for twenty years."

It felt like the world had fallen on me. "I must talk to Sara." I got up to leave.

He held my sleeve. "I will protect her and the children until they can join you."

"How?"

"My army comrades will watch over her all the time."

"Christians?" That didn't reassure me.

He nodded his head emphatically. "I promise to God."

I couldn't bear to leave Sara after all we had gone through. But I had no choice.

"I did the best I could," he said. He got up from the wood pile. "Now let's go tell the men of their victory. It's the Sabbath." I had forgotten.

It would be nice to say this was the last of the *pogroms* in Uman, but it wasn't. The last one was years off.

And I still hadn't taken Goliath's head.

TWENTY-THREE

Early November 1905

O nly in telling this story can I grasp all that happened, and all that might have happened. Maybe it's how it always is when we are in the midst of such tribulations. We only see a little bit behind us and a little bit in front of us, too fixed on surviving to ask questions. Maybe it's how we have the strength to get through it.

Walking home, my energy deserted me so completely that by the time I walked in the door I was near collapse. I must have been a sight, covered with two days of dirt and grime, my pants torn at the knees. I still carried my rifle by my side, gripping it tightly in my hand, afraid to let go.

Sara was at the kitchen table feeding Yakira. She screamed when she saw me and threw herself in my arms. I buried my head in her golden hair. We clung to each other, neither saying a word.

I slept for two days after that. Sara told me I tossed and kicked in my sleep, sometimes yelling "Fire, fire." When I did wake, I moved as slowly as if I was still dreaming, unable to shake the feelings of dread and evil.

For a few days I couldn't concentrate. My head ached. I started sweating and shaking for no reason. I had no appetite and felt anxious, as though the battle was going to start all over again. Some nights I was restless and unable to sleep. Sara cuddled me to her like another of her babies. She said little but understood everything. Her touch was the only thing that could drive that demon from my mind.

I took comfort in Itzhak and Yakira. Sometimes Yakira babbled and climbed into my lap as if she knew she was needed. My little boy cradled in my arms, his eyes looking at me. I put my little finger in his hand and he grasped hold of it. I closed my eyes and prayed to God Itzhak would know a better life than the inferno he was born in. And prayed America would give him peace, pride and hope.

"He didn't cry any." Sara smiled. "He was brave like his poppa."

I couldn't sit still so I did anything to keep from thinking about that night and a lifetime leading up to it. I chopped fire wood, fed the chickens, and cleaned the debris from the garden, then went to the tailor shop, but did nothing worthwhile.

I walked around the market square. The barricades had been dismantled immediately and the square cleaned up. In a few days there was no sign of what had happened. I walked over to Nevsky Street where our barricade had stood. Viktor Askinov's dried blood was still on the hard packed street. I bent down and touched it with my finger, examining the leavings on the tip of my finger. I smelled it and tasted it. It brought me satisfaction like nothing else did. Then my conscience forced its way on me. Not for nearly killing a man, but for not feeling guilty about it.

Someone had already mounted a marker on the corner of the building where the barricade had stood: *October 21, 1905* it simply said, with the Star of Duvid engraved on it.

Everyone in the brigade stopped at the tavern most afternoons, except Uncle Yakov. The others revisited every detail of the battle over and over again. I said little, but savored being in their company.

No one in the village gloated over our victory. Uncle Yakov wouldn't have it. Besides, we were all too tired. Yet the crowd at Sabbath services was so large there wasn't room for everyone in our small synagogue. For the only time in my memory, Rabbi Rosenberg refused at the end of the service to give the prescribed blessing "to the good health of the Tsar." Someone had taken down the picture of Tsar Nicholas that had hung by the front door since that son-of-a-whore ascended to the throne nine long years before.

Reb Kravetz survived. The pogromists stopped only a little further down the street from his house, their eyes on the synagogue.   Reb Kravetz, Mother Kravetz and Havol had nothing particular to say to me or Josef.

Momma, Poppa, Lieb and Ester didn't talk much about it but they were proud of their men - Markus, Simon, Uncle Yakov, and me. Zelda said nothing.

I had to prepare to leave for America but couldn't concentrate. So Uncle Yakov took charge, putting everything together for me. I already had my passport but he miraculously produced a visa, train ticket and passage on a ship.

I sent a letter to Duv asking him to meet me at the dock when I arrived in New York. I would be gone before he could reply so there was no way to tell if he even got the letter until I got there.

Every member of my squad came by the house in the first few days after the battle to offer their thanks, sometimes alone and sometimes in groups of two or three. They wished me luck in America and promised to watch over Sara. Most were making their own plans to leave Uman soon.

It didn't take long for the myth of what happened that night to be created, with me again an exaggerated hero. Within days,

the tale was written of how Avi Schneider had defeated the pogromists and shot their leader. The first stories were that there
were 150 pogromists, then 300 and by the time I left Uman everyone was saying there were five or six hundred. My Duvid and
Goliath moment with Viktor Askinov when I was fifteen years old
was told and re-told, integrated into the myth of the barricades.
Maybe this was how the miracles of the bible got started.

Uncle Yakov was the only one not captivated by my heroism.
He looked dispirited whenever I saw him. One day while I was
chopping wood behind the house, he sat down on the old bench.
I stopped chopping, buried the axe in a log, and sat on the edge of
the well.

He told me again Sara would be safe and well-protected until
I sent for her. "Viktor Askinov is out of the hospital. But his leg
is permanently damaged. He will walk with a limp for the rest of
his life."

"I'm glad to know he will always have something to remember me by."

Uncle Yakov smiled. He rubbed his limp elbow with his
right hand. He had aged in just a few days, the lines in his face
deepening into craters. He had carried the full weight of the village on his shoulders. He was the real hero, not me. I will always
see him marching across the market square with such fearless
resolve it moved everyone to be braver, do more and be better.

"You would have made a fine officer," he said. "The Tsar
would have given you a medal." He touched his own medal on
his lapel. He closed his eyes and pinched his nose. "You have
drawn blood." His voice was a monotone. "You can never wash
it off your hands."

"You killed because you were a soldier. Because someone
told you to," I snapped. "I did it to defend my family."

"And for revenge."

"Yes. But it stopped them."

"It was an important victory," he said quietly.

"You don't sound happy about it."

"You drew blood. Now you know you can kill."

"Viktor Askinov is an evil man." I stood up. "So was it a sin?"

"Ask the rabbi." He stood up and put a hand on my shoulder. "You must find peace. You mustn't go through life tormented by this."

"Like you?"

"Yes, like me."

He walked slowly back into the house. He was the only one in the village who understood my guilty satisfaction in drawing an enemy's blood.

Our battle was not in fact victory. By the end of 1905, when the *pogroms* exhausted themselves, as many as 10,000 Jews were dead. Many of them were women and children. They say more than 15,000 were wounded. More than 1,500 sons and daughters were orphaned. Whole villages, like Kalarash were burned to the ground. Countless synagogues were set ablaze. And if they weren't burned, they were defiled and plundered. The number of homes and businesses destroyed were beyond count. There were nearly seven hundred *pogroms* in 1905.

The life of every Jew was shattered in a million pieces. Thousands upon thousands left for America, an endless procession of those with enough courage to overcome their fears. The Pale of Settlement was being drained.

I took a walk with Josef around the part of our village where the people had not defended themselves. "I'll travel to America with Sara when you call for her," he said. I was grateful and told him so.

On Pushkin Street, we poked through the remains of the Has-sidic synagogue where Sara and I were married. There wasn't much left to remind me of that day. The charred remnants smelled sickening. Part of one wall escaped the inferno, maybe like the Western Wall in Jerusalem. Partially burned prayer books littered the courtyard. Smashed glass from shattered windows crunched under my feet. I heard they managed to get the Torah out of the synagogue before the pogromists set their torches to it.

Why had the Christians done this to us? Why didn't all the Jews defend themselves like we did? And why would any Jew stay in Russia after this? Why wouldn't Lieb and Reb Kravetz leave? Well, I was leaving and I was going to take every Jew in Russia with me that I could. Let these Russians rot in hell. Let the Tsar go to hell.

The police kept a close eye on me to make sure I left when the time came. One was often stationed across the street from our house to let me know they were watching.

My thirty days were running out and the closer the day for my departure got, the more I dreaded saying goodbye to Sara. But I was excited about what was coming: Freedom, hope, safety, money, and adventure. I had never been on a train or a boat, and had never even been as far as Kiev or Odessa. I worked feverish-ly learning all I could about America, refreshing my English with the few in Uman who spoke it.

I spent the last few days visiting people who were important to me, and the places I would never see again. Rabbi Rosenberg said a blessing for me on the Sabbath before I was to leave. Old man Henkel, struggling but alive, gave me the equivalent of twen-ty American dollars to spend when I got to New York.

The days of mid-November were growing shorter and colder. I stood in the courtyard of the synagogue, hands in the pockets of my warm coat, examining the stately oak tree. A few yellowing

leaves still clung to its branches. The rest gathered in piles wherever the wind swirled them.

I stopped in the school and examined every wall and plank in
the floor. It never changed. The paint still peeled from the walls.
The desks were still crowded together, the floor still uneven,
crossed with furrows. A rat scampered across and out the door,
maybe an old friend there to say goodbye. The odor of decay
saturated the room.

Jeremiah sat at his desk as he did on my first day of school
seventeen years before. Back then he looked fresh and eager.
Now he looked old and tired.

It was late afternoon. The students were gone. Jeremiah
pushed back his chair and rose to embrace me.

"What are you going to do now?" I asked.

"I'm going to Palestine. We will never know peace anywhere until we have our own country."

"And are you going to marry your lady friend? Take her
with you?" Jeremiah's whole body sagged like a burlap bag emptied of its potatoes.

He looked down at his desk top and ran a finger along one of
the scars. "She won't ever marry a Jew. She can go to hell." His
hurt was written all over his face. They had been together all the
time I had known Jeremiah.

"And what of Gersh?"

"Gersh still believes in his socialist revolution. That Jews
will be accepted like everyone else. Only now he's joined the
Bolsheviks. He's ready to fight again."

"One battle's enough for a lifetime. At least for me."

"And me."

"I have to ask you the same old question. Why do the Christians hate us so?"

"They don't all hate us. Only enough of them to make our

lives unbearable," he said. "You know a lot of workers didn't join in the *pogroms*.   Here in Uman a good number helped us. They've given shelter to some of the Jews who were burned out. In some villages police and army stopped some *pogroms*."

"Will you write to me in America?" I asked. He nodded but I doubted he would.   He was going in one direction and me in another.

When I opened the door to leave, he called after me. "You were the best pupil I ever had." I turned. Our eyes embraced.

"And you were the best teacher."

I walked out with my head down, not looking where I was going. I bumped into the Shamash. "May God watch over you," he whistled through his missing front teeth. I think it was the only time I ever saw him smile.

My last three days in Uman arrived. I played with Yakira, held Itzhak, and clung to Sara.   Then I bundled up against the November cold for a last trip around the village.

Rain fell now and then from black skies. I walked down by the river where I had had my Duvid and Goliath encounter with Viktor Askinov. I was glad I wouldn't have to face him again. Surely one of these times he would win, and if he did, he would kill me.

I paid a last visit to the tavern, the synagogue where I had my bar mitzvah, the ritual baths where Duv took me to see the naked women, and the barn by the blacksmith shop where I had my first kiss with Bayleh Zuckman. I walked out to the inn where Sara and I spent our wedding night. Only three years ago? Impossible.

Markus and Lieb went with me to the cemetery where the Schneiders had been buried for centuries. We stood by Grandma and Grandpa Schneider's graves and recited mourner's *Kaddish*, then put a stone on each of their gravestones.

If there's a God, I asked, why didn't he grant the peace we

begged him for? Instead He brought *pogroms*, and I resented Him for it. Markus and Lieb turned to leave. I lingered a moment longer. I could feel Grandma and Grandpa in this place.

I had a lump in my throat as big as an apple most of the time. I would never know another spring time in Uman. This poor, decaying, pathetic village was my home, the place where I was born. I wouldn't miss this cruel place but I would miss all the other people I loved. It wasn't only family. It was also all the people who had been a part of my life, like Rabbi Rosenberg, Reb Henkel, Madame Shumenko and Sergey, the Shamash, and the men who gathered in the tavern. I wouldn't see them again.

"Why do you torture yourself?" Momma said. She was never one to mope over what she couldn't change. She was still the same strong woman she had always been. She was heavier now and, never a beauty, the years had not been kind. Her hair was almost completely grey and thin. But Momma's mind, if anything, was quicker and wiser.

"This is my home," I said. "I'm leaving it forever."

"So you'll make a new home in America," Momma said. "A better home. You'll see."

"I can't leave Sara. Yakira and Itzhak." I was reveling in my misery, maybe so I wouldn't feel so guilty for leaving them. It tortured me, but part of me was eager to be on my way to America. Was it the hope for the better life this new land promised, or merely the adventure of it?

"When you were a little boy I said you would have to leave Uman. Sara will be fine. Give her credit. She's strong."

I nodded.

"Talk to Zelda before you go."

A shrug of my shoulders was my answer. I had no intention of talking to Zelda. She had disgraced the family. But Zelda was stronger than I was. To my surprise and discomfort, later that day she came into the bedroom where I sorted through the things I would take with me.

My little sister was a beautiful, provocative woman. Where did she get her good looks with parents like Momma and Poppa?

"I can't have you leave without saying goodbye," she said. I looked at her with practiced coldness. We hadn't talked in a long time. What I really wanted was to hug her, but I couldn't.

"Why did you do it?" I asked. My question was partly condemnation and partly a need to understand.

"No explanation would satisfy you." She shook her head, defiant and close to tears.

"Come to America. Start over." I put my hand on her shoulder, the first time I touched her in a very long time. She looked at my hand and placed her hand on top of it.

"I'm going to live with Auntie in Kiev. Maybe some day I can come home to Uman." I rubbed her shoulder gently and kissed her on the top of her head. I loved my little sister but she was right. No explanation she gave me would be good enough.

Simon promised he would leave for America a few months after their baby was born. It would be good to have Simon and Duv together again, but Lieb wouldn't be with us.

My last attempt to convince Lieb to come to America ended like the previous ones. He smiled. "Maybe," he said, but we both knew he didn't mean it. We hugged each other.

"You've been a good big brother."

"Which of us is the big brother?" He laughed. There has never been a better big brother than Lieb was to me.

I was so absorbed in myself I didn't much notice the pain Poppa was feeling. He dealt with it by concentrating on the little work we still had coming into the tailor shop. I sought him out there.

I looked around carefully, trying to engrave it in my memory.

So much had happened here. I sat at the window where I saw Uncle Yakov strutting across the market square the day I first met him. "The shop still looks the same," I said.

"Eh, some things never change." He turned his head to look the shop over. The well-worn mannequin in the back looked like a good friend there to say goodbye.

Poppa wasn't that old but he was starting to remind me of old man Henkel, the oldest person I knew. His hair was grey and nearly gone. His shoulders sagged, he was thinner, and his wrinkled skin was whiter. He must have suffered watching the persecution of his children and the fear of *pogroms*, helpless to protect us. Still, he clung to Uman.

We chatted about this and that, both unable to talk about our love for each other. So instead we talked about how long the trip would take and what it would be like to sail on a ship. He assured me he and Momma would come to America, but it sounded like another one of Poppa's procrastinations.

There is no place on earth that holds so many good memories as Sukhi Yar. On the last day I had to make one final visit, but not without Sara.

"It's prettier in the spring," I said. The grasses were November brown and dead, the black earth damp. It was quiet except for the wind rustling through the bare trees. No birds sang, no butterflies fluttered, and no wild flowers perfumed the air. We walked over to the edge of the ravine and peered into the long, deep gorge. I held Sara close to me to shield her from the cold. This was not the memory of Sukhi Yar I wanted to carry with me.

By late afternoon, I was packed. There was nothing to do but wait. It was how a man awaiting his own execution must feel. I played with Yakira. I held Itzhak. I made small talk with Momma, Markus and Sara.

A determined knocking at the front door resounded like that

day, as a little boy, Constable Askinov introduced me to Viktor Askinov's evil eye. My heart skipped a beat. I opened the door cautiously. My old friend Sergey Shumenko stood there shivering, bundled against the November cold, wearing a grieved smile. He carried something in his gloved hand.

"Come in, come in." I motioned with my hand. I was glad to see him.

"I can't." His eyes dashed from right to left as though he was afraid he would be seen. He didn't need to worry. The cold had driven the policeman watching me to warmer quarters. "Please come outside," he said.

I grabbed my coat and pulled my wool cap over my ears. He handed me a package. "These are cookies from Mother. For your trip. She remembers how much you liked them."

"This time I'll eat them all myself," I laughed. "Thank Madame Shumenko for me." We walked around to the side of our house where Momma planted her beets and potatoes.

Sergey's weary smile turned somber. "I don't blame you if you hate us all. But not all Christians are like Viktor Askinov." He wouldn't look me in the eye.

"I know you're not." I patted him on the shoulder. "But there aren't enough like you and your mother. And too many like Viktor Askinov."

"You and your Poppa are fine men."

"And so are you. Your mother has been a good friend too." I looked down at the package of cookies.

"Russia will be a better place after the revolution."

"And whose side will you be fighting on?"

"Your side." He looked up, his blue eyes embracing mine.

"I'm glad you came to say goodbye." We shook hands. He walked away, hands in his pockets, back hunched against the wind.

Why were Sergey and Madame Shumenko so kind to us? Sergey had to defend himself for having a Jew friend. Madame Shumenko was slandered with rumors about her and Poppa. Maybe some people are born with so much goodness inside them they repulse doctrines of hate, even when they're preached from the pulpit.

Sara and I spent the last night in each other's arms. We talked till dawn, comforting each other, trying to hide hurts and fears.

Uncle Yakov arrived early in the morning with a horse and cart he borrowed to take me to the train. Everyone gathered in front of the house bundled in shawls and coats, enshrouded by the damp and cold of morning fog. Momma held Itzhak and Poppa held Yakira. Simon, Ester and Zelda were there. Lieb and Golde were there. Josef was there. Mother Kravetz, Reb Kravetz and Havol were not.

"We'll see you soon in America, God willing," Poppa said, hugging me hard to him. I nodded but I knew I might never see him again. A tear streaked his cheek.

My last kiss and embrace of Sara was unbearable. Her soft blue eyes glistened. She looked so beautiful, so delicate. I gulped several times, trying to keep control.

"I will send for you as soon as I can," I said.

"I will be waiting."

"I love you."

"I love you."

One last kiss; one final embrace.

Uncle Yakov and I mounted the wagon, just the two of us. It was easier this way. I looked back over my shoulder, waved goodbye and turned away from the house where I was born. We exchanged only a few words as we bumped through the rutted street.

"Watch out for that puddle," he said as we walked along the platform toward my waiting train. "Maybe someday we'll have a big train station in Uman like in Kiev. One where the roof doesn't leak." I had never been in a train station before so I had nothing to compare. We passed the mail car and stopped by the entrance to my passenger car.

"That night at the barricades. You did what you had to do," he said.

"But you said...."

"What you did was very brave. Important. You did it like no one else could." He moved his face so close to mine, our noses were nearly touching. "You stopped him. That's all we can say for sure." He pulled his face back a little

"When I pulled the trigger I wanted to kill Viktor Askinov. Vengeance. That's all."

He nodded nearly imperceptibly. "I'm acquainted with such disaster." All of his life's agonies were painted on him.

"I can kill. How do you live with that once you know?"

"That's between you and God. Atone. Live a good life. Make peace with yourself." His mouth contorted as though feeling his own stab of pain. I feared I would never make peace with it. He understood. No one else ever would.

He fumbled in his pants pocket, and pulled out the red, white, and blue medal he won at Mangidia. He stared at it as if remembering how he got it.

"I want you to have this." He pinned it on my shirt. Then he took a step back, stood at attention, and saluted me. "You are a good man," he said, returning his hand to his side. "I am proud of you." He smiled.

The train horn blared. It was time to go. We embraced hard

and patted each other on the back. He kissed my cheek. I loved this man.

"I don't know if I will ever see you again, Uncle."

A tear ran down his cheek. "That is in God's hands, Avi. Go to America and make your life."

I turned and lifted my two cardboard suitcases onto the top step of the train door and bounded up behind them. When I turned back, Uncle Yakov was trudging away, his shoulders hunched and his good arm limp at his side.

"Goodbye Uncle," I called out. He waved his hand over his head without slowing his pace or glancing back.

When I was seated, I looked out the window and saw him standing there in the distance, looking at me. He waved goodbye as the train pulled away.

AMERICA

July 1907

Just like he promised, Duv met me on the harbor dock when my ship arrived in New York on a cold, bright December day in 1905. Nothing after that was what I expected America to be. When Sara joined me nineteen months later, I didn't dare try to explain what it had been like without her, or the scars left on me.

The July day she arrived was warm and sticky, sun and blue skies after a night of downpours. With a fresh haircut, beard trim, and bath, I went to meet her. Sara's younger brother Josef was traveling with her to help with Yakira and Itzhak. If I was honest about it, I didn't really feel much like a father. Yakira and Itzhak were babies when I left Uman. Now they were only fictional characters Sara spoke about in her letters to me.

As early in the morning as it was, the main harbor terminal already pulsed with men on their way over to Ellis Island to meet their arriving families. A few piers further down, the four gigantic smokestacks of the Kaiser Wilhelm, the ship Sara arrived on, rose above the warehouse roofs. But immigrant passengers were quarantined until they passed through Ellis Island for clearance into the United States.

If her ship was here, she was here. That thought made my insides jingle. I had gotten used to the ache of being in America and Sara in Uman. Anything different felt unreal. After all this time apart, we had both changed.

The ferry ride over to Ellis Island only took a few minutes, but it was long enough to sniff the deep blue water and follow the gulls gliding across a sky punctuated with passing wisps of white clouds. A nice looking Jew with a well trimmed bush of a mustache struck up a conversation. He wasn't much older than me but his hair had already started thinning.

"The name's Mottel," he said offering his hand. "But in America they call me Max."

"Where are you from in the old country?" I asked to be polite.

"Kiev Gibernya." The province of Kiev.

Within a couple of minutes I learned he too lived in East Harlem, was meeting his wife and kids, and worked in a laundry. He hoped to start his own laundry as soon as he saved enough money.

We jumped off the ferry when it docked at Ellis Island and strolled up the brick walkway. When we went through the fortress's giant doors, he went in one direction and I in the other. Too bad. He seemed like a nice man and talking to him would have helped pass the time. I had a long wait.

So I took up a position near the pillar at the base of the double flight of wooden steps down from the Registry room. That big room was the last obstacle before immigrants were cleared to enter America. Someone had dubbed the pillar where I waited for Sara as the Kissing Post.

Other men gathered there to wait, some my age, some much older. They all looked American, no longer the greenhorns dressed in native garb like they were the day they arrived. Now you couldn't tell the Italians from the Greeks or the Russians from the Germans, at least not until they spoke.

A number of passengers came down the big staircase. Women met their husbands, some with passionate embraces, and some with the formality of strangers. I asked a few of them what ship they came in on. None were from the Kaiser Wilhelm. I paced and fiddled, the heat from the warm July afternoon mixing with the heat of the bodies crowded at the base of the steps.

The giant clock at the far end of the hall showed it was past noon. I had been waiting for nearly three hours. A swarm now streamed down the steps. I kept asking until finally one man said "Kaiser Wilhelm." I waited some more, struggling to control my excitement and anxiety. What am I going to do if she didn't make it through inspection, I worried.

"Avi, Avi." I looked up and there she was, bounding down the staircase as fast as she could, her eyes locked on mine. A beam of sunshine followed her, lighting her golden hair.

She dropped her canvas bag and threw herself at me. We hugged tightly, our lips meeting in a long, deep kiss. My heart exploded.

She buried her head in the crook of my shoulder, sobbing. I stroked her hair.

"My darling, my darling," I said over and over.

"Avi, don't ever leave me." Her body heaved.

"Never again."

We pulled away and looked at each other. I was as lost in Sara's soft blue eyes as I was the first time I saw her that April day in the market square. The mixture of tears running down her cheeks and her shining smile made her sparkle, more beautiful than an angel. We kissed again, pulled away laughing, then kissed again, more gently. I touched her hair and her face while I held her close. She stroked my beard, her laugh wrinkling her nose. I had forgotten the gentle touch of her hand.

I hugged her again, this time looking over her shoulder. Josef stood there holding the hands of these two adorable little urchins. Yakira's face wore a shy smile. Itzhak's eyes darted from side to side, up and down, examining everything going on around him. In that instant I fell in love with my children. "Come," Sara said. She took my hand and led me over to them.

"Give Pop a hug," Sara said. I squatted down and Yakira stepped into my outstretched arms. I kissed her hair and hugged her gently. Then I held out my arms for Itzhak to join. He studied me as though deciding whether this was a good idea. Then he moved cautiously into my embrace. Sara bent down and wrapped her arms around all of us.

"Thank you Lord. Thank you," she whispered. I thanked Him too.

There had not been a day for me like this one since the day we were married. No day quite like this one ever came again.

Poppa died the next year, buried in Uman in the cemetery behind our synagogue, next to his mother and father. When Uncle Yakov died a few years later, General Petrov traveled to Uman to honor him. Momma came to America with Ester, Simon, Markus and Zelda. She wasn't the same without Poppa but I think she was fulfilled to see her family safely in America.

Zelda settled in Philadelphia rather than New York. She married a man she met in Kiev, a widower ten years older with two small children. She never had any children of her own. I only saw her once before Momma died. She came to Momma's funeral, but I rarely saw her after that.

Markus, now married, joined me as a partner in the tailor shop I had started on 115th Street a few months before Sara arrived. We made quite a success of it. We said *Kaddish* for Poppa and Uncle Yakov, then for Momma too after she passed on a couple of years later.

My old teacher Jeremiah made it to Palestine, married one of the other pioneers, and lived on a kibbutz. He helped build the Jewish homeland but didn't live to see the creation of the state of Israel.

The freedom of America released the worst of Duv's compulsions and excesses. They are best not talked about here. No one should have expected him to be a good husband and father. I expected him to be a better friend.

My greatest regret was my failure to convince Lieb to come to America. He and Golde had three children, two girls and a boy, who in turn blessed them with many grandchildren. We wrote each other often, every letter touching me with a longing for him. Even after the Bolshevik revolution and the death of the Tsar, life for a Jew in Uman didn't get much better. I tried to help him by sending money regularly. His life was hard but Lieb seemed to accept whatever came, just as Poppa would have, taking his sustenance from his family and the certainty the Messiah would find him in Uman.

Reb Kravetz got his wish to die in Uman and be buried in the same cemetery as the famous Hasidic, Rabbi Nachman. Mother Kravetz joined him. Havol married the rabbi's son Reb Kravetz had intended for Sara.

Viktor Askinov didn't bother Lieb again after I left Uman. In his letters, Lieb talked about him hobbling around the village on his damaged leg. It never healed right, a lifelong souvenir from me. I was never sorry I gave it to him. Even hobbled, he continued to dispense pain and trouble to everyone weaker than him, Jew or gentile.

Lieb said he had a way of sniffing out who was going to win the shifting battles for power in Uman and Russia. First he was a monarchist supporting the Tsar. When the revolution came, he joined the Bolsheviks early, but never earned more than a minor position in the Uman bureaucracy.

It's not hard to imagine Viktor Askinov joining in the Nazis' atrocities when the Germans arrived in Uman. So should I have taken Goliath's Head and damn the consequences? Maybe so.

We never talked much about the old country. It was a misery we all wanted to forget. My blessed children Yakira and Itzhak grew up as American as any American children, with no memories of Russia - no Tsars, no *pogroms*, and a good life they would not have known in Uman. The years with Sara that followed were the best of my life, and of hers.

ACKNOWLEDGEMENTS

My wife Ann had the hardest job in bringing this book to life - living with me. She left me alone to write when that's what I needed. She gave me encouragement when that's what I needed, a kick in the pants when that's what I needed, and wise counsel when that's what I needed. She read bits and pieces over and over again, and the final manuscript when I could no longer stand to look at it again. Her edits were always the right ones, and her proofreading sharp-eyed.

From beginning to end, my good friend George Marcellino offered the wisdom and compassion I've come to expect from him. He lent unfailing support and enthusiasm from the beginning when the very idea of me writing a novel seemed most preposterous. He was there when I finished writing and needed to know whether I had achieved anything worthwhile.

My wonderful daughter Beth did a splendid critique in her always-professional manner, even though her loyalty to her father precludes criticism. She was delicate with her touch, ever-mindful of her father's fragile ego.

Grace Davis-Brooks, with a writer's sensitivity, interjected herself at critical moments when I was befuddled about what step to take next. The copy she gave me of Anne Lamott's book, *Bird by Bird*, lit my way. Friends Tom Kearns and Andy Weir read Goliath's Head when it was in its crudest form, yet they still found something positive to say about it. My cousin Ted Blumenstein, with whom I share our Fleishman grandparents, provided valuable commentary on the book's Jewish authenticity.

When Tom Brunner, Wallace Brunner, Bob Berkowitz and

Barbara Berkowitz read the finished Goliath's Head, their thunderous applause gave me confidence to move forward.

Earning Lynda Steele's enthusiastic support was an unexpected gift. Lynda read Goliath's Head, and its still-maturing sequel, and became my champion. Her insights were always good ones. She presented her wise thoughts clearly and more humbly than necessary. Then she proselytized with enthusiasm.

To all, a grateful thank you.

ALAN FLEISHMAN

Afterward

My father, Ben Fleishman, was ten days old when the worst of the 1905 *pogroms* swept the Ukraine. Shortly after, my grandfather Max led the family to America. A hundred years later, I returned to the Ukraine. I paid my respects at a tombstone honoring the victims of the 1905 *pogroms*, and stood in the square where the Nazis in 1941 rounded up thousands of Jews and marched them off to be executed. My need to write Goliath's Head arose from those moments.

So how much of Goliath's Head is a true story? All of the historical references to events are factual, like the Haidamack uprising that killed 8,000 Jews in Uman, and the importance of the Hassidic Rabbi Nachman who is in fact buried in Uman. Thousands of Jews from all over the world still make their way to his burial site every Rosh Hashanah to honor him and celebrate his life.

My research has been meticulously documented through books, historical records, and internet sites. It surprised me to see in original documents how much the rest of the world knew at the time about the *pogroms* going on in Russia. The New York Times and other international publications had first-hand accounts from reporters on the scene in Kishinev, Odessa, Kiev and other *pogrom* locations. In fact, pressure from other parts of the world brought upon Tsar Nicholas and his government may have had something to do with the cessation of the *pogrom*s. The U.S. president and Congress condemned them.

The works of Sholem Aleichem, the most famous Yiddish writer of the time, were an invaluable source. Aleicheim wrote

Tevye The Dairyman, upon which the Broadway show *Fiddler on the Roof* was based. He gave me a feeling for the everyday lives of the people, their attitudes, customs, language, and the setting of the Jewish *shtetls* in a way historical non-fiction could not possibly do.

My father and his family did not want to talk about the old country, only about America. Maybe it was too ugly for them to want to remember. So I had little to go on other than that they were from Uman and that my father was born there on October 12, 1905. He came to America in 1908 with his mother and his sister Jean. His mother Taube took the name Tillie, and his father Mottel took Max as his name. Max, like many husbands and fathers, had come ahead to America earlier to get set up before sending for the family.

In Goliath's Head, only those key family dates and the Uman setting are based upon my known family history. Everything else about Avi, his family, and friends is fictitious, as are all events surrounding the Uman *pogrom*. I could find no direct reference to a 1905 *pogrom* in Uman, though surely there must have been disturbances. Uman was a reasonably large town with a large Jewish population. *Pogrom*s raged all around Uman. It is unlikely this town would have escaped. There was a serious threat of a *pogrom* in Uman in 1906, and a devastating one happened there a few years later, after my father's family had departed for America. These are documented.

In Goliath's Head, Momma gives Avi a silver locket - a family heirloom - to present to Sara when he goes to plead with her father for her hand. The locket described in the book is the locket my grandmother is wearing in the only picture I have of her. Taken in Russia, the photo shows her with my two year old father and three year old aunt. My guess is she sent it to her husband Max shortly before she joined him in America.

Though all of the most grotesque incidents of *pogrom*s used in this story are true, in a few instances I transposed them from one *pogrom* to another to facilitate the flow of the story. But they are all true. Other incidents, like the Haidamack near-*pogrom* in Chapter Two, were inspired and fictionalized from similar incidents that took place elsewhere in the Pale of Settlement.

The Jews' journey to Uman began when the Romans conquered Palestine in the first century A.D. and expelled the entire Jewish population from their homeland. Most of them trekked first to Spain and Italy then, over the centuries, into France and Germany, often chased at the point of a sword.

By the Middle Ages, the largest concentration of Jews was in Western Europe, but persecution had reached horrifying proportions. Knights of the Crusades on their way to free the Holy Land from Muslim control found it only logical to attack the Jews, the killers of their lord Christ, along the way. They drove many Jews eastward. The hostile Christian communities segregated and tormented those Jews who stayed.

The Black Plague which swept Europe in the mid-1300's killed a third of the population. Jews were blamed for the plague, though it killed Jews as often as it killed Christians. The Europeans responded by slaying the remaining Jews or hounding them out.

Those who were expelled moved into Poland, leaving much of Western Europe devoid of Jews by the end of the 15th century. They were welcomed into Poland by King Kazimierz the Great who needed the skills they brought. Though they remained despised, isolated outsiders, over the next few centuries they established a society in Poland.

In the sixteenth and seventeenth centuries, the Polish kingdom expanded through a series of successful wars with their neighbors, conquering everything between the Baltic Sea in the north and the Black Sea in the south. Some of the Jews became merchants and innkeepers in these new territories, while many others were employed to manage the large estates of the aristocracy in the lands the Poles had conquered.

Thus Jews administered much of the agricultural economy in the Ukraine. But they were both aliens and infidels. The Poles themselves were Roman Catholic while the Ukrainians were Eastern Orthodox, adding fuel to the boiling cauldron of resentment. As overseers and tax collectors, Jews were often caught between the Ukrainian peasants and the Polish aristocracy, attracting the animosity the peasants might otherwise have directed at their foreign landlords. It was almost certainly during this period that Jews first came to Uman in large numbers. There was a Jewish community there as early as 1620.

In the late 1700's, Russia conquered Poland and took all of the lands Poland once owned. Catherine the Great, and the tsars that followed her, held a very different attitude toward the Jews than the Polish kings had. She believed, as did the Russian Orthodox Church, that God tormented the Jews in retribution for killing Christ, and that it was the Russian monarch's job to help God in this work. So she did. From the moment of Russian conquest, horrid Jewish oppression began. All Jews were confined to an area called the Pale of Settlement running along Russia's western frontier, on into Poland. They were restricted in where they could live, what they could own, what occupations they could pursue, and the education they could receive.

The large majority of Jews in the world now lived under Russian rule, perhaps as many as four to five million, an estimated seventy percent of all Jews in the world. They were poor, crowded, and oppressed beyond salvation. Largely isolated, they developed their own culture. The life as I have depicted it in

Uman is reasonably representative. But the Pale of Settlement covered a large area and Jewish sub-cultures varied considerably from place to place. There were Jewish doctors, teachers, restaurants, music, literature, and theater. A small number of Jews were wealthy and well-educated by the standards of the time.

If things were bad for the Jews in Russia, they were little better for everyone else except the aristocracy. Smoldering rebellion was punctuated by periodic acts of terrorism, invariably followed by stiff government reprisals. The government blamed the troubles on the Jews and often used the gentiles' animosity toward the Jews to rally the country to their side.

Tsar Alexander III died unexpectedly in 1894 leaving his son Nicholas II to ascend to the throne. Only twenty-six years old, Nicholas was ill-prepared in training or in temperament to rule in tumultuous times. He was both a stubborn and incompetent autocrat who continued to believe in the divine right of the Tsars to rule. This was at a time when such thinking was out of step with the wave of democratic liberalism sweeping the Western world.

It's around this time that our story begins.

The Russian *pogrom*s of the late nineteenth and early twentieth century were of biblical importance to world Jewry today, yet does not seem to have received the attention this period warrants. Until then, the Pale of Settlement was the religious, cultural, and population center of the Diaspora. But these *pogroms* triggered a relocation as profound as the first Diaspora nearly two thousand years before. In the resulting migration, over two million people voyaged to the United States and Palestine. The Holocaust eliminated most of those who didn't immigrate. Without the migration, Hitler may have succeeded in destroying Judaism.

The last big wave of migration began soon after the Kishinev *pogrom* in 1902 and culminated shortly after the October 1905 *pogroms* when all hope of a decent life in Russia was lost. Those who left probably constituted a third of the Jewish population under Russian rule. Most came to the United States. But several thousand Zionists escaped to Palestine and fueled the struggle that culminated in the formation of the state of Israel in 1948.

By the time Hitler and the Holocaust were finished, there were few Jews left in Europe. Depending on who's counting and how they're counting, there are about fifteen million Jews in the world today. That this number is so small surprises many people. Probably forty percent of them reside in the United States and another forty percent in Israel. These havens are now the dual centers of Jewish life and culture.

When I visited the Ukraine in 2005, the poverty and depression of the people were evident. I couldn't help but think how different that country might be today had they embraced their Jewish brethren a hundred years before, instead of driving all that talent to America. And how different America might be if it did not have the benefit of its Jews: Robert Oppenheimer, Albert Einstein, Edward Teller, General Mark Clark, Admiral Hyman Rickover, General Robert Magnus, Dianne Feinstein, Milton Friedman, Joseph Stiglitz, Michael Schwerner and Andrew Goodman, Felix Frankfurter, Ruth Bader Ginsberg, Harvey Milk, Carl Sagan, Paul Berg, Albert Sabin, Jonas Salk, Sergei Brin, Steve Ballmer, Mark Zuckerberg, Irving Berlin, Leonard Bernstein, George Gershwin, Bob Dylan, Steven Spielberg, J.D. Salinger, Norman Mailer, Philip Roth, Saul Bellow, Herman Wouk, Ben Bernanke, Lauren Bacall, Kirk Douglas, Scarlett Johansson, Samuel Goldwyn and Louis B. Mayer, the Warner Brothers, Barbara Streisand, Woody Allen, Joseph Heller, E.L. Doctorow, Betty Friedan. Gloria Steinem, Hank Greenberg, Sandy

Koufax, Sid Luckman, Mark Spitz, Peter Max, Richard Avedon, Alfred Eisenstaedt, Annie Leibovitz, Sean Penn, Jon Stewart, Paul Newman, Mel Brooks, Fred Astaire, Jack Benny, Aaron Copland, Oscar Hammerstein, Cecil B. DeMille, Stanley Kubrick, Jerome Robbins, Arthur Miller, Red Auerbach, David Halberstam, Paul Krugman, Larry Ellison, Michael Dell, William S. Paley, Stephen G. Breyer, Arthur Goldberg, Henry Morgenthau, Jr., Jacob Javits, Herbert H. Lehman, Michael Bloomberg, and Bernard Baruch to name but a few.

AUTHOR PROFILE

ALAN FLEISHMAN, in his early years, served as an army officer in a tank battalion with the Third Infantry Division in Germany. In the years prior to becoming an author, he was a well-regarded medical marketing consultant, working with over 100 companies in the USA, Canada, Europe, Latin America, Asia and Israel. Before that, Fleishman spent seventeen years in corporate marketing and sales with Fortune 500 companies, ultimately as Executive Vice President. He was an adjunct faculty member at the University of California, Berkeley, and has served on the Board of Directors of five corporations. He was a board member of the non-profit Abilities United, and the first recipient of the Glaucoma Research Foundation's annual President's Award for meritorious volunteer service. Fleishman hales from Pennsylvania where he graduated from Berwick High School and Dickinson College with honors. The father of a daughter and two sons, the grandfather of two girls and four boys, he lives with his wife Ann high on a hill overlooking San Francisco and the bay.

www.alanfleishman.com

4682504R0

Made in the USA
Charleston, SC
01 March 2010